COVERT IN CAIRO

A FIONA FIGG & KITTY LANE MYSTERY: BOOK #2

KELLY OLIVER

Boldwood

First published in Great Britain in 2023 by Boldwood Books Ltd.

Copyright © Kelly Oliver, 2023

Cover Design by bnpdesignstudio

Cover Photography: bnpdesignstudio

The moral right of Kelly Oliver to be identified as the author of this work has been asserted in accordance with the Copyright, Designs and Patents Act 1988.

A CIP catalogue record for this book is available from the British Library.

Paperback ISBN 978-1-80483-170-0

Large Print ISBN 978-1-80483-171-7

Hardback ISBN 978-1-80483-169-4

Ebook ISBN 978-1-80483-172-4

Kindle ISBN 978-1-80483-173-1

Audio CD ISBN 978-1-80483-164-9

MP3 CD ISBN 978-1-80483-165-6

Digital audio download ISBN 978-1-80483-167-0

Boldwood Books Ltd
23 Bowerdean Street
London SW6 3TN
www.boldwoodbooks.com

For Mischief, Mayhem, and Mr. Flan, my furry muses and writing companions. What they lack in editorial advice, they make up for in snuggles.

1

THE STRANGER

This bloody war had taught me nothing was black and white... except perhaps a strong cup of tea with milk, when you could get it.

My mouth was parched, and my bottom bounced on the hard wooden bench I shared with Captain Clifford Douglas, my glorified chaperone. I glanced over at our carriage companions, Miss Kitty Lane—whom I'd known until a week ago as Eliza Baker—and a stranger who leaned against the wooden armrest, reading.

If only they served tea on this railway. I could use a nice cuppa.

The Egyptian railway carriages were white wooden trollies. Nothing like the black iron horses back home.

Deuced hot, too. The soot flooding in through the window was the same, though. British or Egyptian. It didn't matter. We all choked on the same smoke.

As the carriage clacked along the tracks through the desert from Alexandria to Cairo, I distracted myself with Annie Pirie's *The Pyramids of Giza*. Book in one hand, I held a lavender-scented handkerchief to my nose with the other. If only I'd worn my goggles. I squinted at the pictures, concentrating on keeping my breakfast down.

More astounding than photographs of massive stone monuments jutting up out of the sand were pictures of a diminutive woman in a plaid shirt and flowery straw bonnet working in the dirt alongside male archeologists. Not because a woman couldn't do anything a man could do—at least anything important —but rather because, out of jealousy, men usually didn't allow it.

Annie Pirie claimed it was under one of these grand pyramids that she'd met her future husband while they were both laid up with food poisoning. Having nursed soldiers suffering from that very same affliction back at Charing Cross Hospital, I didn't find anything romantic about the squalls of salmonella.

Still, there was nothing like the vulnerability of the body to move the soul.

Why not fall in love over a bedpan?

After all, I'd met Archie Somersby when he was convalescing with a shot-up arm. He'd asked me to help him write a letter to his mother. *So sweet. Writing to his mum.*

My cheeks burned. *Oh, Archie.* Would I ever see him again? Did I want to see him again, now that I knew he was a government-sponsored assassin? When I closed my eyes, I could still smell his citrus cologne mixed with the lingering scent of Kenilworth cigarettes.

I dropped *The Pyramids of Giza* on the seat next to me and withdrew a fan from my purse. As I did, my fingers grazed Archie's gold pocket watch. On my last assignment, Fredrick Fredricks, renowned German spy and all-round rotter, had left it for me at my hotel back in New York, along with a cryptic note about the Suez Canal and some rot about us working together to stop the war.

How Fredricks had come by the watch, I didn't know. Had he kidnapped Archie? Or worse? I squeezed my eyes shut and snapped my fan open. Waving it vigorously in front of my face, I pushed the terrible thoughts from my mind.

Even with the windows open, it was beastly hot, and the desert seemed to go on forever. Winter in

Egypt was a far cry from the chilly dampness of London or the snow in New York.

No. I couldn't allow myself to think of Archie. Dead or alive.

Instead, I looked out of the window. Once we'd left Alexandria, with its oasis of palm trees, there was nothing but sand and more sand. Only the sky changed from brilliant blue to hazy brown, and along with it the thickness of the air. Heavy with humidity, now it was also laden with fine particles. I wiped my eyes with my handkerchief.

My head bobbed along with the rhythm of the carriage, nearly lulling me to sleep. A bump in the tracks jolted me awake. I fluttered my fan in front of my face, staring over at my pretty traveling companions.

Just days ago, I'd learned the young woman sitting across from me, whom I knew from my last mission as Captain Hall's niece, Eliza, was really Kitty Lane, petty criminal and reform-school girl who'd studied criminology in France. Or, at least, that was *her* story.

On our last mission, I'd thought I was babysitting her, but as it turned out, she was babysitting me—on Captain Hall's orders, no less. Truth be told, I couldn't be sure of her role in our current mission to protect the Suez Canal from whatever fiendish plot Fredrick Fredricks might be planning.

I wasn't keen on teaming up with a young lady who'd recently tied me to a toilet, but orders were orders.

Oblivious to the carriage's shaking and clattering, with her legs stretched across the bench seat, Kitty had her nose buried in the latest issue of *Vogue* fashion magazine. Wearing dark glasses, a flowing pink chiffon skirt dotted with tiny roses, a white blouse with pearl buttons, and an adorable sailor hat, she looked the part of a fashion model herself.

I, on the other hand, was wearing a plain cotton blouse and a bespoke linen skirt with multiple buttoned pockets for carrying items essential to espionage: miniature magnifying glass, spy lipstick, lockpick set, tracing paper, charcoal pencil—in its own leather carrying case, of course, to prevent it from soiling my clothes. I had the skirt specially made on Regent Street. I'd even purchased a Beacon Army Light on my last mission in New York. Shaped like a cigarette case, the palm-sized metal box was really a torch, a jolly good one too, and a lot smaller than its British counterpart.

And, in a shop in a dark alley in an unsavory part of London, I'd purchased a very official-looking embossed card with my credentials. I couldn't wait to try it out.

A good spy could never be too prepared.

As usual, I wore my practical Oxfords in case I needed to make a quick getaway. My only concession to vanity was deep purple flowers on my straw hat. The bonnet was anchored with pins to what was left of my auburn locks. Sadly, for my first mission at Ravenswick Abbey, I'd shorn my beautiful long hair, which had been my most attractive feature. I pressed the hat to my head. I prayed it didn't blow off, for fear of frightening my companions. Without a wig or a hat, I looked like a ginger porcupine.

Even Kitty's Pekingese pup, Poppy, hadn't recognized me when my quills were exposed. She'd barked like she'd never seen me before. I gazed down at the little creature, and she smiled up at me. Yes. The dog smiled. Her tiny black lips turned upward, and her big round eyes gleamed with delight.

Poppy had a pink ribbon in her topknot that matched her owner's outfit perfectly. The furry nuisance sprawled across Clifford's lap, her outstretched paw touching my knee. Only because the animal had rescued me from imprisonment in a loo on my last mission did I indulge her encroachment on my person.

Clifford was another matter. Indulging him often tried my patience. Captain Clifford Douglas had been sent along by the War Office to chaperone us, despite the fact I'd already completed *four* missions. And Kitty, well, for all I knew, she was an assassin in petticoats.

While engrossed in his hunting magazine and fantasies of killing, at least Clifford was quiet for a change.

"I say!" Clifford looked up from his magazine.

Blast. I knew it was too good to be true.

"Gezira Sporting Club has fox hunts with English hounds." Clifford beamed. "Do you ladies fancy a hunt?"

My eyes met Kitty's and we both laughed.

"Don't laugh, old girls, Cairo has jolly fine sporting clubs." Clifford's blue eyes flashed with indignation. "The Jockey Club is famous for its world-class horse races. How about lawn tennis at—"

"We're not in Arabia for sports," I interrupted him before he listed every sporting club on the African continent.

Clifford grumbled into his magazine. "You know, I once met the Egyptologist Lord Carnarvon at the horse races. He was the nicest chap—"

I stopped him before he could launch into one of his endless stories. "Hunting." I gestured from Clifford to Kitty. "Fashion." *Sigh.* "You'd think we were on holiday instead of..." I glanced over at the stranger in our compartment. "Instead of on business."

"You're a fine one to talk, Aunt Fiona." Kitty smirked at me. "You and your *Baedeker's Guide to Cairo*."

Although I'd only known her for a few weeks, on our last mission, the girl had taken to calling me "Aunt," and she couldn't seem to shake the habit. At twenty-five, I was only seven years her senior and hardly an old maid or spinster aunt.

"Given your pile of guidebooks..." Kitty pointed at my one slim volume.

Actually, my Baedeker's and Murray's guidebooks were packed away in my suitcase.

"You're preparing to play tourist." She pursed her rosebud lips.

"I'm learning my way around, not ogling the newest fashions," I said—perhaps a bit too defensively, judging by the stormy change in Kitty's countenance.

I wasn't just learning about Cairo and its environs, but also committing to memory every page of every guidebook. I never knew when my photographic memory might come in handy to recall a city map and find my way back from recon in some dark alley or abandoned building. Still, I wished the War Office would issue me one of those clever disk cameras to wear under my shirt, the lens peeking out from a buttonhole. Then I would have graduated from file clerk to real spy.

"Poppy, old thing." Clifford gazed down at the dog in his lap. "We're going to have such a grand time. I'll show you all my favorite haunts in Cairo."

If only Poppy knew Clifford was reading a special issue of *The Field* devoted to fox hunting in Egypt. Like me, I was sure she would not approve of blood sports, especially those in which her distant cousins served as prey. As if reading my mind, her tongue lolling, Poppy looked up at me with those big dark irresistible orbs. I patted the little beastie's topknot, and she licked my hand.

"No!" Kitty slapped her magazine shut. "They might eat her."

"Good grief," I scoffed. "Who would want to eat Poppy?" She was all fur, for heaven's sake.

"Everyone." Kitty slid off her seat onto her knees and scooped up the pup. "She's delicious." The girl buried her face in Poppy's fur.

"I'm sure Egyptians don't eat dogs." Truth be told, I wasn't sure. I turned to Clifford. "Do they?"

"Don't be ridiculous." Clifford withdrew his pipe from his breast pocket. "Orthodox Muslims consider dogs impure and unclean."

I scowled at him. I considered his pipe impure and unclean.

He ignored me and lit the foul thing.

"Poppy isn't impure." The girl cuddled the squirming ball of fur. "Even if she isn't always clean."

"Kitty." I gestured toward the seat. "Speaking of unclean, please get up off the floor, dear."

"You're sweet as Christmas pudding," Kitty said to Poppy as she pulled the pup onto her lap and then took her seat. "But don't worry, Pops, no one is going to eat you." She nuzzled her face into the dog's muzzle. *Speaking of unhygienic.*

"But the Christians or Coptics might." Grinning, Clifford jerked away from an imaginary smack on the shoulder.

"That's not funny!" Kitty held the dog in a tight embrace.

"Don't worry, old dear." Clifford patted an imaginary weapon concealed under his jacket. "I'll protect her... and you, too."

As if Kitty Lane needed anyone's protection. I'd learned my lesson on the last mission and vowed not to let the girlish giggles and frilly frocks fool me again.

"What do you think of this ensemble for Lady Enid's fancy-dress ball?" Kitty displayed the *Vogue* cover with an illustration of a woman wearing a gaudy orange hoop skirt and tricornered hat that made her look like an oversized pumpkin.

"Lady who?" I gaped at the girl. "What fancy-dress ball?" This was the first I'd heard of a ball. We'd only just disembarked from the ship from England. We hadn't even arrived in Cairo. How in heaven's name did the girl already have an invitation to a ball?

"Lady Enid Clayton, the wife of Sir Gilbert Clayton." Clifford puffed his pipe and then let out a great cloud of foul smoke. "Director of Military Intelligence in the Arab Bureau."

"Friend of Gertrude the Great." Kitty placed Poppy on the seat, in between herself and the stranger.

"Who?"

"Aunt Fiona, you really must keep up," Kitty teased. "You should trade those musty old books for the society pages."

"Petrie, the Hogarths, Gertrude Bell, T. E. Lawrence, and that lot." Clifford held his pipe in front of his mouth. "Archeologists excavating the ancient tombs, don't you know."

"More importantly, they have exquisite balls beneath the southern stars." Kitty clapped her hands together. "Doesn't it sound dreamy?" When she cooed at Poppy, the creature grinned.

I bared my teeth at the little beastie.

"I can't wait for the Christmas pageant." Kitty squirmed with delight.

If it hadn't been for the stranger sharing our compartment, I would have chastised my companions. While I was busy preparing for our mission by studying guidebooks, they were faffing about with pretty dresses, gruesome blood sports, and fussing over a spoiled little dog.

"I guess you can tell our priorities by our reading material." I held up my book. "Mine is written by a scholar and a lady explorer." I nodded for emphasis. "She—"

"If you want to get to know a people," the stranger interrupted, "study their poetry."

I sat blinking at him. His English was heavily accented, but I didn't recognize the accent. And yet there was something familiar about his voice.

Who was this striking man? He wore a red fez hat, white trousers and jacket, and a wide black belt and tall black boots. Not to be outdone by his bushy eyebrows and full beard, his grand mustache curled up on the ends a good two inches on either side of his upper lip. In fact, his facial hair was *so* impressive, I wondered if it might be fake.

"You must read Hafez Ibrahim, poet of the Nile." The stranger opened both his hands in offering. "Or the Prince of Poetry, Ahmed Shawqi." He clasped his hands together in prayer. "Nations are but ethics. If their morals are gone, thus are they."

Was he quoting the poet? *Nations are but ethics.* What in blazes did that mean?

He pounded his fist into his palm. "Gone, I tell you, gone."

"Do I know you, sir?" Clifford dislodged the pipe from his mouth.

There was something uncanny about the man. I too had the uneasy sense of déjà vu.

"You don't even know yourself," the stranger scoffed. "If you English can't make yourselves welcome with arrogant promises of freedom, you resort to armored tanks and Vickers machine guns." His mustaches quivered.

I had a good many fine mustaches in my collection, but none quite as impressive as his. I touched the edge of my seat. Just thinking about my assortment of crumb catchers in the little case below made me as giddy as if I were sniffing spirit gum. I swore, even now, I could smell its intoxicating pungent odor.

"Well, I say," Clifford huffed. "No need to be rude." He tugged on the bottom of his jacket. Good old reliable Clifford. Quick to defend king and country... and any women within a twenty-mile radius.

"Those hunting hounds were brought here to fulfill your countrymen's desire to turn every place into their homeland." When the stranger waved his arms, the loose sleeve of his jacket danced a frenetic jig. "They died from the heat." His dark eyes flashed. "Let that be a lesson to you."

"You know, it's rude to eavesdrop." I tilted my head and appraised this mysterious fellow with his obvious dislike for me and my countrymen.

"We're in a rattling coffin." The stranger winked at me. "Impossible not to."

Cheeky devil. My fan fluttered so fast in front of my face, my wrist could barely keep up.

"Rather hard not to overhear your conversation." He lowered his voice. "Especially since you English love the sound of your own voices so much you project them at high volume—"

"Look here, whoever you are." Clifford stood up. "This is no way to talk in front of the ladies."

Good heavens. I hoped Clifford didn't do something stupid like challenge this fellow to a duel or punch him in the nose.

The carriage swayed and Clifford fell back onto the seat, nearly landing in my lap.

The stranger was right about one thing. With just two bench seats facing each other, and one small window, the compartment was downright claustrophobic.

"Now, now." I patted Clifford's arm. "The ladies can defend themselves, thank you."

I couldn't take my eyes off the stranger. There was something oddly compelling about him. Perhaps it was the faint scent of rosewood or the resounding strength of his convictions.

"Do you read Arabic?" I pointed at the stranger's book, assuming it was the poetry of which he spoke.

"It's the only way to appreciate the character of the poetry and the people." He shook his head. "Of course, the English think everyone in the world should speak their language."

"I speak French and German," Kitty piped up. "And Spanish, and—"

"I suppose you learned a bushel of languages at that boarding school in Lyon," I cut her off. "Along with who knows what else," I said under my breath. I too was fluent in French, thanks to Mrs. Boucher's French class at North London Collegiate School for Girls. But I wasn't one to brag. My German, on the other hand, was appalling. I had to admit, Kitty could come in handy when spying on Fredrick Fredricks and his German comrades. Clifford's German was pretty good too.

"Mere European languages." The stranger held up his book. "Here, you must learn Arabic if you want to do anything but see yourselves reflected in a mirror of your own hubris." He stood up. "At least you have French, young lady." The stranger bowed slightly to Kitty. "Since Egypt was occupied by the French before the English, you'll get by passably well." He opened the door to the compartment. "And now, if you'll excuse me, I, too, have work in Cairo."

As he crossed the threshold, a folded paper fell out of his book.

I reached down and picked it up. The paper was heavy and thick.

"You dropped something," I said to the closed door.

The stranger had vanished.

"What is it?" Kitty said.

"I say." Clifford snatched it from my hands and snapped it open. "Why, it's a map!"

"Heavens." I gazed down at it. "Not just any map." I grabbed it back.

A map of the Suez Canal. Marked with a big black X.

I touched the spot on the map.

Lake Timsah.

Smack-bang at the mid-point of the canal.

Could it be just a coincidence that back in New York, Fredrick Fredricks had hinted at a plot involving the Suez Canal? Or that the War Office had sent us to stop it? And now a strange man accidently drops a map of the canal?

"We have to go after him!" I held the map in the air and sprang up from my seat.

Always obliging, Clifford jumped up.

When Kitty took to her feet, Poppy barked and wagged her tail, as if cheering us on.

Three trains converging on the same track, we collided trying to get out of the door.

What a wreck.

No doubt the stranger was long gone by now.

2

SHEPHEARD'S HOTEL

Cairo was not just an oasis in the desert. It was a magnificent metropolis to rival London or Paris and yet like nothing I'd ever seen before. Palm trees, stone fountains, and stunning colors, both sundrenched bolds and bleached pastels.

Of course, the major cities of Europe lacked palm trees and pyramids. But it was something more. Something about the light. Sitting in the middle of the desert, the light was more vibrant and alive. The light of painters and poets. A far cry from dreary old London.

While the taxi transported us through the streets of the city, Kitty gawked around, oohing and aahing. Poppy stuck her little nose out of the window. And

Clifford pointed out places he'd been on his previous visits to Cairo. "You'll love Shepheard's." He launched into some longwinded story about the last time he'd been there.

Of course, I'd heard of Shepheard's Hotel. Who hadn't? It was one of the most famous hotels in the world. Back in Room 40 at the War Office in London, our premier codebreaker, Mr. Dilly Knox, liked to show off a pilfered ashtray sporting the red and black logo while telling tales about sultry nights on the terrace at Shepheard's. He made it sound like the most romantic place on earth. I was eager to find out for myself.

The taxi driver pulled up in front of the hotel. I touched up my lipstick and reminded myself that I was not here for romance, but for espionage.

Stepping out of the motorcar, I was hit by the spicy scent of cardamom, cinnamon, and cloves mixed with an undercurrent of rotten vegetables. In front of the hotel, a man with a cart was selling roasted sweet potatoes. They smelled heavenly. But just a few steps away, a puddle of stagnant water gave off a foul odor. Cairo smelled both delicious and repellant. The irony of life writ large.

The ground floor of Shepheard's hosted shops and the first floor sported the famous terrace. Both the walkway in front of the hotel and the terrace were abuzz with a sprinkling of tourists mixed in with soldiers of various stripes. And the entire place was adorned with decorations—holly, mistletoe, wreaths. I'd almost forgotten Christmas was only days away. The Christmas decorations seemed out of place in this desert palace. And yet there was something distinctly charming about palm trees trimmed with tin stars.

I climbed the steps to the hotel entrance and glanced around at the potted palms on either side of the entrance and the gaiety all around. The War Office had made it clear that Cairo was as important to the Great War as the Western Front. Yet the mood among the soldiers was giddy and bright. I squeezed past a jovial group of Tommies and stepped into the grand lobby.

In the center of the lobby stood a giant spruce tree. How in the world did they get that giant Christmas tree to Cairo? With its sparkling globes and gingerbread men, the tree lifted my spirits... and then plunged me into despair. This would be my first Christmas without my exhusband Andrew. Of course, I'd lost him to Nancy even before he died. But that didn't make the pain any less.

It would also be my first Christmas away from England. All those years ago, spending Christmases on my grandfather's farm in Devon, who would have guessed I'd end up globetrotting on a mission for British Intelligence?

Mouth agape, I stood paralyzed by the variety of life buzzing around the lobby: Women covered from head to toe in black robes with their colorful shoes peeking out. Women in gay sundresses and floral hats. Another woman in a skirt and white blouse wearing sturdy boots and a pith helmet. Men in white robes with red fezzes perched on their heads. Men in linen suits and straw hats. Soldiers in khaki. Soldiers in white. Soldiers in green. Soldiers in blue. A sea of soldiers from all corners of the earth.

If I stayed here long enough, I'd surely see the entire world pass by.

Kitty clapped her gloved hands together. "Isn't it marvelous?"

With its ornate pillars, Moorish arches, stained-glass dome, Persian rugs, and chairs sporting embroidered antimacassars, the lobby of Shepheard's was indeed marvelous. A cross between a tearoom and a cathedral, all adorned with festive holiday wreaths and bows.

"Smashing," Clifford answered, tipping his hat to one of our countrymen—or should I say countrywomen. Like a stray dog in search of a master, Clifford had a penchant for befriending pretty women.

Judging by her red cheeks and the strands of fair hair escaping from her chignon, she was a wilting English rose. I touched my own warm cheek. What must I look like to the world passing by? A bedraggled English bramble?

After the long dusty trip from Alexandria, we sent the porters up with our luggage and took tea on the veranda under the shade of a potted palm. Dressed in linen tablecloths and adorned with silk flowers, the outdoor tables were a welcome sight. I dropped into an oversized rattan chair and let out a sigh.

Finally, we'd arrived.

A waiter in flowing white robes wrapped with a wide black belt brought three tall glasses of lemonade. My eyes filled with tears of delight. Back home in London, I hadn't seen a lemon since the war started three years ago. Each glass sat on a paper doily atop a small plate accompanied by two butter biscuits.

I bit into the biscuit. *Delicious.* Hidden within the delicate buttery outside was a fragrant treasure— spiced date paste filling. Absolutely scrummy. Unable to contain my ecstasy, I took another bite and then washed it down with bitter lemonade. I was nearly cooing with delight.

The cool beverage and sweet biscuit were an oasis in the desert of deprivation we'd suffered during this Great War. I'd never enjoyed a drink so much in all my years. To top it off, a pleasant breeze caressed my skin. *Heavenly.*

Even the Christmases of my childhood at my grandfather's farm hadn't filled me with so much gratitude and hope... hope that one day this bloody war would end, and we could all enjoy the simple pleasures of life once again. Lemonade, date-filled biscuits, and a cloudless blue sky.

"What are these?" Kitty stole a biscuit off Clifford's plate. "They're delightful."

"They're called *maamoul*." Clifford gestured his approval. "I remember the first time I tasted them." He smiled. "I was on my way back from hunting tigers in India, and I stopped off here in Cairo." He pushed his plate toward Kitty, and she snatched the last of his biscuits. He was always trying to get the girl to eat, but the only nourishment she found at all tempting was the pudding course. "We'd bagged a beautiful—"

"Must we talk about blood sports while eating?" I interrupted. If I hadn't had my mouth full, I would have stopped him before he got started. Otherwise, there was no end to his nattering.

"Yes, well." He sputtered an apology. "Ramadan,

the Muslim period of fasting and prayer, had just ended." He glanced at me. "I was staying at the Savoy up
the street." He pointed with his thumb. "They served
maamoul to celebrate Eid."

"How much time have you spent in Egypt?" Kitty
said.

"Don't encourage him." I patted her shoulder. "Or
we'll be here all night."

Clifford pursed his lips. He sat pouting like that for
the rest of the afternoon. Poor lad. He really wasn't a
bad sort. But after the long voyage, I wasn't in the
mood for his longwinded hunting stories.

After my second glass of lemonade, I was revived
just enough to feel the full weight of our travels. Completely knackered, I squeezed out enough energy to
rise from the table. When I did, through the ferns of a
potted palm, I saw the mysterious man from the
railway breeze onto the terrace and sit across from a
boyish yet intense-looking chap in a smart Egyptian
military uniform. I dropped back into my chair.

"I thought we were going up." Kitty stood up and
glanced around.

"Don't look now," I whispered. "The gentleman
from the railway carriage." I gestured with my eyes.
Although the potted palm was between us and them,

they were within earshot. If I tilted my head just right, I could see the plotting pair through the ferns.

"Please sit down, dear." I bribed the girl with a half-eaten biscuit.

"I say," Clifford huffed. "Isn't that the insulting bounder? I have half a mind—"

"Now, now. We've just arrived." I patted his arm. "Can't we save fisticuffs for later?" I waved down a waiter and ordered a third lemonade.

Kitty asked for another plate of biscuits. Clifford switched to a whiskey cocktail called an Old Fashioned—a name that suited him.

The mystery man and the boyish Egyptian were in the throes of an animated conversation. I couldn't make out what they were saying, just that they were speaking Arabic—in hushed, but harsh, tones. As the baby-faced Egyptian officer spoke, he pecked at the table with his finger.

Blast. An odd fellow dressed in robes and a head-dress appeared directly in my line of sight. Two others trailed behind him, completely blocking my view.

"Douglas, old man, what are you doing in Egypt?" The fellow had the bluest eyes I'd ever seen, no doubt due to the contrast with his tanned complexion. His long face and prominent nose didn't detract from his overall good looks. Although it was queer to see an Englishman wearing robes and a headdress.

"Lawrence?" Clifford stood up and clapped the fellow on the shoulder. "I say, Lawrence, is it you under that *galabeya*?"

I leaned around this Lawrence chap, trying to keep my eyes trained on the plotting pair. I wished Clifford's blasted pal would get out of the way. I couldn't see what my mystery man and his conspirator were doing.

"Carter, Gertie, this is Captain Clifford Douglas." The chap turned to his two companions and waved dramatically. "Douglas, these are my friends Howard Carter and Gertrude Bell. We all like to dig in the dirt, among other things." His brilliant eyes sparkled.

"Ladies." Clifford turned back to us. "This is Lieutenant Thomas Lawrence, who apparently has gone native on us." He chuckled. "They call him Lawrence of Arabia."

Ladies? He couldn't take the trouble to introduce us properly. Or were all *ladies* interchangeable? *Ladies, my size forty-one foot.*

"It's Major, now." The berobed chap put his hand to his heart. "But, as always, it's just Lawrence."

"Major Lawrence of the Arab Bureau?" Back at the War Office, I'd heard about him being a loose cannon, running around the desert, not following orders, inciting the locals to rebel.

"In the flesh." His white teeth gleamed.

When I held out my hand to him, he bowed and kissed it. Not accustomed to being kissed by strange men, I immediately withdrew it.

"Stop teasing the ladies." The woman I took to be Gertrude Bell punched him in the shoulder.

"Ouch!" He held up a fist. "Watch out for this one. Gertie has a wicked temper and a deadly right hook."

"Why, you're Gertrude Bell." Kitty clapped her hands together. "The famous lady explorer."

A pith helmet atop her head, Gertrude Bell had soulful eyes, and a mouth that would have been sweet if her expression weren't so stern.

With his thumb, Major Lawrence pointed to his companion. "She's not what she seems."

Too bad. Except for the pith helmet, she seemed a proper Englishwoman, rather pretty, too, with a carelessness about her that only intensified her beauty.

An attribute not lost on Clifford. He was positively beaming.

If she so much as got a grain of sand in her eyes, he'd be proposing to her by day's end. Clifford couldn't resist a damsel in distress. He proposed to *me* at least

once a month. Although—as he surely knew by now—
I was hardly a damsel in distress.

"Isn't that right, Carter?" Major Lawrence elbowed
his companion in the ribs. "Gertie here is a curiosity, is
she not?"

Mr. Carter grunted. "A lady archeologist is a curiosity, I suppose." Howard Carter's egg-shaped head
was offset by soft caterpillar eyebrows and a rather
large nose.

"I'm not a curiosity," Gertrude said. "Just curious."
When she removed her pith helmet, a coil of light
brown hair sprang out from underneath. "Anyway,
what's wrong with curiosity? Where would humanity
be without it?"

"She's got you there, Carter." Major Lawrence's
high-pitched tinny laugh was unnerving.

Mr. Carter's countenance hardened. "Good day,
ladies." He touched his hat. "Gentlemen, if you'll excuse me, I have to get back to the dig."

"Carter, lighten up." Major Lawrence laughed. "Always ready for a fight, that one."

"I'm a bit of an amateur archeologist myself." Clifford chuckled.

Clifford, an archeologist? I rolled my mind's eye. Clifford fancied himself a cross between Sherlock Holmes
and Sir Lancelot. Now he thought he was Arthur

Evans, too?

Poppycock.

"You should come out to the dig tomorrow morning." Major Lawrence flashed a toothy smile. "Carter won't mind. He never finds anything but pot shards and shoddy ones at that."

"Brilliant!" Clifford pumped the major's hand. "We'd love to visit the site."

"What fun." Kitty squirmed in her chair.

You'd think we were here on holiday, the way my companions carried on. Had they forgotten that tomorrow we were expected at the Arab Bureau for a briefing? Since I didn't know these archeologists—and these days, anyone could be a German agent—I didn't mention our engagement at the bureau.

Instead, I again tried to maneuver into position to see what my mystery man was doing. I wasn't here to sightsee or visit digs. I was here to gather intel on plans to sabotage the Suez Canal. And if I was right, that's what the plotting pair were doing at the next table, making plans. Why else would the stranger have a map with an X marked at the mid-point of the canal? The Suez Canal wasn't exactly a tourist destination.

The Turks had already tried to blow up the canal several times without success. One hundred miles long, the canal was vital to the British war effort.

Without it, ships from India would have to sail all the way around the tip of Africa, which took twice as long. And that was why, as Captain Hall had explained, protecting the canal was a top priority at the War Office.

Finally! The archeologists moved out of the way. Just in time, too. Leaning over the table, the stranger wrote something, handed it to his Egyptian companion, and then got up to leave. It was obvious from their grim faces that they meant business. Once the mystery man was out of sight, the petite Egyptian officer hustled down the steps and out onto the street. Within seconds, both men disappeared into the crowd.

I had to find out what the mystery man had written on that slip of paper. But how?

Glancing around the terrace, I slid out of my chair, popped over to the next table, and sat down. An ashtray encircled with ashes overflowed with stinky cigarette butts. Two demitasse cups sat opposite each other, one empty and one full. The Egyptian officer's side of the tablecloth was stained and dirty from chain-smoking while he'd waited. The mystery man's side, on the other hand, was immaculate.

Quickly, I removed the tracing paper and charcoal pencil case from my skirt pocket. I examined the tablecloth for indentations. *Nothing.* Gently, I ran my hand over the cloth. I opened the leather case and removed the pencil.

"Lady—"

I gasped. It was just the waiter. "You startled me."

"Sorry." He held a towel over his arm. "Permit me to clean the table, lady?"

I pinched the handle of the demitasse between my thumb and forefinger and lifted the cup to my mouth. "I'm not finished yet."

The waiter gave me a queer look as if I'd eaten an insect. "Yes, lady." Shaking his head, he left me.

I withdrew my miniature magnifying glass from the special pocket I'd had made for it in my skirt. I leaned in to reexamine the tablecloth. The Egyptian's side of the tablecloth had several tiny indentations from his finger pecking. He smoked like a chimney and pecked like a rooster. Under the smell of cigarettes lingered the faint scent of jasmine.

"What are you up to, Aunt Fiona?" Kitty stood next to me, staring down at the table. She pointed to a spot near my left hand. "There!"

By heavens, the girl was right. Carefully, I laid the tracing paper over the indentation and gently rubbed the pencil across the paper.

"What does it say?" I could feel Kitty's breath on my ear.

Like magic, the outline of letters and numbers began to form.

K r o k o d i l s e e 1 2–2 2 2 1:0 0

I had the uncanny sensation of déjà vu. Where had I seen that code before? It must have been back in Room 40. But I'd seen hundreds of coded messages working as a file clerk for the codebreakers. What did it mean? Was it a date and time?

21:00. Nine in the evening.

12–22. Could it mean 22 December?

Oh, dear. Only five days from now.

But what is Krokodilsee?

Whatever it was, I had to warn the War Office.

3

THE ARAB BUREAU

The next morning, Clifford and Kitty agreed to postpone our visit to the dig until after we'd checked in at the Arab Bureau.

Anticipating a busy day of espionage, I wore an earth-tone linen skirt with a multitude of bespoke pockets, a light cotton blouse, and, of course, my practical Oxfords. On the way out, I grabbed my brand-new Wolseley pith helmet, sun umbrella, and aviator goggles—and, of course, my handbag for heavier espionage paraphernalia such as Mata Hari's gun. I'd had my beaded evening bag reinforced for just such assignments.

A uniformed Tommy was waiting in front of Shepheard's to transport us by motorcar to the bureau. Clifford hopped into the front, and Kitty and I climbed into the back.

We passed hotels and cafés and one stately but abandoned building. We'd gone only a couple of streets when the motorcar stopped. *Are we picking up someone else?*

"We're here," the Tommy said.

Kitty and I looked at each other.

"This is the Savoy." I pointed toward the hotel's entrance at the embossed letters that spelled Savoy. "Aren't you taking us to the Arab Bureau?"

"The British army has commandeered the entire hotel." He smiled. "The bureau is on the fourth floor in one of the former guest rooms." He hopped out and came around to open the back door of the motorcar.

"The Arab Bureau operates out of a hotel room?" I swung my legs out of the automobile.

"Yep." The Tommy offered his hand. "The whole army does."

"What kind of operation is this?" I muttered to myself as I took his hand.

It wasn't strange to see a hotel packed with men in uniform. Hotels across Europe were the same. But it was odd to see a grand hotel reception desk transformed into a military post. Judging by the layers of sand and dust on carpets and drapes, the British army's cleaning staff at the Savoy wasn't up to the hospitality standards of most luxury hotels.

Upstairs, the cramped suite that housed the Arab Bureau was filled with bric-a-brac, stacks of file folders spilling over onto the floor, dirty coffee cups, mummified insects, and other unidentifiable desiccated matter.

Major Lawrence was playing chess with another man, undisturbed by the office ruins around them. Engrossed in a book, Gertrude Bell sat on a wooden chair near the window.

What were those two doing here? Did they work for the Arab Bureau, too?

The scene was more appropriate to a college campus than a military operation. I couldn't imagine Captain Hall or Major Montgomery tolerating such slovenly behavior in Room 40 of the War Office.

I bit my lip. It was all I could do to stop myself retrieving the file folders and sorting them. If nothing else, the Arab Bureau was desperately in need of a good file clerk. And while Captain Hall might lack confidence in my espionage abilities, my skills as a file clerk were impeccable.

"Welcome to the Intrusive." Major Lawrence looked up from the game.

"Intrusive?" Clifford peered down at the chess-board as if contemplating his next move.

"Unwelcome, uninvited, trespassing..." Lawrence smirked. "The Arab Bureau. They recruit only the best." He waved a rook in front of his face before placing it on a black square.

So, Major Lawrence *did* work for the Arab Bureau. The British army was recruiting archeologists and adventurers now? *Heaven help us.* Then again, what was I but a glorified file clerk?

"We're the last, best hope." Gertrude snapped her book shut.

"We're liars." Lawrence wiped his hands on his robes. "You know as well as I do that Britain has no intention of letting these people—and their lands—alone." He moved his knight and snatched one of his opponent's rooks.

"It's war." His opponent stood up. "What would you have us do?" He looked us up and down.

"Better us than the Germans." Gertrude laid her book on the windowsill and strode over to greet us. "We want to help unite Arabs. The Germans want to divide and conquer."

"We *say* we want to unite the Arabs." Lawrence lit a cigarette. "The proof is in the pudding." He took a puff and blew out a cloud of smoke. "You know the Bedouins almost as well as I do—"

"Don't kid yourself." Gertrude put her hands on her slim hips. "After months in the desert living with them, I know them *better* than you, or any man. Isn't that right, BGG?"

"Gilbert Clayton." The man extended his hand to Clifford. "I'm in charge of this maverick band of oddballs."

"Brigadier-General Gilbert Clayton." Major Lawrence waved his cigarette theatrically. "Excellent commander, horrible chess player."

"Or Bee-Gee-Gee, as we call him." Gertrude straightened the general's tie.

His lips tightened, but like an obedient schoolboy he allowed it.

"Clayton is like water." Major Lawrence leaned back in his chair. "He creeps silently, permeating everything until the whole world is soaked." Dramatically, he took a drag of his cigarette. Everything he did was overdone as if he were performing for an audience.

"Did you come by for a tour of the dig?" Gertrude smiled. "Howard is a grumpy old bear, but thanks to the war, he's the only one digging again. How he managed it, I don't know?"

"What about that pretty Frenchman, Monsieur Lorrain?" The major winked. "Howard may be an old bear, but Jean-Baptiste is a young lion."

"Jean-Baptiste Lorrain is a faker and a flirt." Gertrude waved her hand in front of her face as if shooing away an insect.

"We've come from the War Office." I tugged on the fingers of my glove. "Captain Hall sent us to protect the Suez Canal." I may have exaggerated the importance of our mission just a *teeny* tiny bit. Truth be told, we had strict orders to trail Fredricks, report back, and not interfere.

Major Lawrence laughed. "A gimpy officer, a frilly girl, and a lanky woman." He shook his head. "If this is what it's come to, we'll lose the war for sure."

Lanky woman. What did he mean by that? I glanced down at my legs. At least he didn't call me an ostrich like the boys at primary school had done.

"Aren't we always hearing about how you *single-handedly* led a wild bunch of Arabs across the desert to take Aqaba?" Gertrude rolled her eyes. "And you're nothing but a spoiled public-school boy."

"And you, my dear, are marvelous." Major Lawrence jumped up, grabbed her by the hand, and twirled her around. "If you were the only girl in the world..."

Good grief. He was singing... off key at that.

I felt as if I'd landed in a West End theater performance of the musical comedy *Chu Chin Chow*. Who were these silly people? I slipped my gloves into the pocket of my skirt, removed my pith helmet, and patted at my wig.

"Ah, yes, Blinker sent you." Arms behind his back, General Clayton stood to attention. "To find your missing agent. Bad business, that."

"What missing agent?" My breath caught and my mind flew to Archie, as it always did when I heard about agents in trouble. This missing agent... *it couldn't be him. Could it?* Although I'd only met him a few times, the handsome soldier troubled my thoughts and daydreams.

Instinctively, my hand went to my bag where I kept Archie's gold pocket watch. Had Fredricks delivered it to me as a message or a warning? "Captain Hall didn't mention any missing agents."

Please, God, keep Archie safe.

"The last agent sent by the War Office." General Clayton paced the few steps the messy, cramped room would allow. "He's gone missing. Pity."

"A fine fellow, officer, and gentleman." Major Lawrence gave a mock salute. "Exemplary soldier sacrificed to Old Blighty and all that rot."

What a bounder. Missing agents were no joking matter... and neither were the sacrifices soldiers made for Britain. I'd seen the horrors of war up close when I'd volunteered at Charing Cross Hospital.

"Blown-off limbs and mustard gas burns are far from funny, Major Lawrence." I stared him in the face. "And neither are missing agents. Do you have any idea of the tortures our enemies use?"

"As a matter of fact, I do." A cloud passed over Major Lawrence's ruddy face.

"Good lord." Clifford's face went pale. "I say, you haven't been—"

"The major—and his manhood—barely escaped the Turks." Gertrude slapped the major on the back. "We're lucky to have him back... and intact."

Goodness. What a way to talk. Averting my eyes, I fiddled with the goggles hanging around my neck.

"What is the name of our missing colleague?" Kitty asked.

Occasionally the girl surprised me with common sense.

"Lieutenant Dankworth." The general shrugged. "Bad business."

"Rum do, losing agents." Clifford pulled his pipe from his breast pocket.

"I spotted his pal, Agent Relish, at the theater on Saturday." Gertrude raised her eyebrows.

Relish. A code name, no doubt.

"Maybe he's making a holiday of his stay in Cairo, where days are filled with secrets past and nights with future lies?" She was a poetic sort, this Miss Gertrude Bell.

"Agent Relish is undercover," the general said with a stern look. "I implore you to keep his secret." His countenance brightened. "Speaking of secrets and lies, my wife Enid is inviting everyone to a fancy-dress ball tonight in honor of the families of fallen service men."

"I can't wait." Kitty clapped her hands together. "What fun."

"You'll never guess the theme." The general chuckled. "Ancient Egypt. You really must join us."

"Thank you." What in blazes would I wear to a fancy-dress ball? "Too kind."

"Tell Lady Enid we will be there," Kitty gushed.

Golly. I wished I'd known before I left London. I could have picked up an appropriate costume at Angel's Fancy Dress Shop when I'd purchased my other two disguises. I got goose bumps just thinking about them hanging in the closet back at the hotel. I couldn't wait to try them out.

In the meantime, I'd have to come up with something to wear to Lady Clayton's fancy-dress ball. I had a hunch Fredrick Fredricks would be there. He never passed up a gala ball. And I never missed a chance at Fredricks.

Good thing I'd worn my practical Oxfords. I wiggled my toes. It was going to be a jolly busy day visiting tombs, locating missing agents, and shopping for the fancy-dress ball.

"Let's go tomb robbing, shall we?" Lawrence teased. At least I hoped he was teasing. "Jolly authentic costumes there."

A knock at the door silenced the group. They looked from one to the other with questioning eyes. Finally, General Clayton answered it.

A young man, the spitting image of Napoleon, charged into the room. With his billowing white blouse, long sideburns, and wild dark hair, he looked like a relic of the nineteenth century—a very pretty relic.

"Speak of the devil," Gertrude said under her breath.

"I figured I'd find you reprobates loitering here at the Savoy." His French accent gave his tenor a smoky quality. "I just came to tell you I got a concession to excavate at G-1500." He giggled like a schoolgirl. His soft dark eyes, furry caterpillar brows, and upturned mouth gave him the look of a girl, too.

"In Giza?" Lawrence's mouth fell open. "Borchardt and Gabler's concession?"

The Frenchman smiled. "Now, it's mine!"

"Borchardt?" The name sounded French.

"Ludwig Borchardt. Director, German Archeology Institute. Gabler was his assistant." The general's words were clipped.

"The boarded-up building we passed on the way." Clifford clamped his pipe between his teeth.

That abandoned building. No wonder it looked new, apart from boards over the windows and a heavy chain and padlock on the front doors.

"The German archeologists were thrown out of Egypt along with all the other Germans." The general took a seat behind a desk in the corner of the room, a desk piled high with papers and magazines.

"But not before they made off with a priceless bust of Nefertiti." Major Lawrence picked at a fleck on his robe.

"I thought the war had stopped all excavations," Clifford said.

"A few are starting to open again." The Frenchman smiled. "Howard Carter... and me. Only the best—"

"How much did that cost you?" Gertrude's countenance hardened.

"Mademoiselle Bell, would I resort to bribery?" the Frenchman teased.

"If not bribery then force." She put her hands on her hips as if daring him to contradict her. "Sticks instead of carrots." She threw her head back.

"You overestimate me." Hat in hand, he gave an exaggerated bow. "I'm but a humble scholar like yourselves." He straightened and gazed at me. "*Je suis désolé.* We have not met. I'm—"

"Monsieur Jean-Baptiste Lorrain." I took an educated guess. "Your reputation precedes you."

"*Qui.*" A broad smile brightened his face. "*C'est vrai.* It is true. And you are?"

"Fiona Figg, British Intelligence." I shook his hand.

"I'm Kitty." The girl held out her hand.

With a click of his heels, Monsieur Lorrain bent down and kissed it. "Mademoiselle Kitty." He gazed up into the girl's eyes. "Pretty Kitty. *Enchanté.*" In that moment, he resembled a hungry wolf gazing at a sheep.

She blushed and giggled.

Silly girl.

She said something quickly and quietly in French.

My French was passable but, distracted, I didn't catch it. Was she flirting with him?

Monsieur Lorrain's smile broadened. "I would love to show you mine." He glanced around. "Perhaps the others would like to see too?"

"See *what* exactly?" Clifford took a step in between the girl and the Frenchman. "Captain Clifford Douglas, at your service." He extended his hand.

The Frenchman took his hand. "My new dig, of course." He peeked around Clifford at Kitty.

She was tittering like a chickadee.

"Are you sure you trust us?" Lawrence studied his fingernails. "We might make off with your precious treasures."

"Have you seen my man, Frigo?" He called to someone in the hallway. "Frigo, get in here!"

A man with a square jaw, crooked nose, and chest like an ice box peeked inside. "Boss?"

Major Lawrence whistled. "Is he your good luck charm?"

"The French government wants a piece of this action." Monsieur Lorrain waved his hands. "You British can't take all the spoils."

"Better us than the Germans," Gertrude chimed in with her familiar refrain.

"Thieves are thieves no matter what nationality." Major Lawrence sat up and his chair banged the floor with a thud.

As fascinating as this petite tête-à-tête was, I needed to telephone Captain Hall and report the mysterious man from the railway. I'd been ordered to telephone from army headquarters only to ensure the line was secure. And, apparently, the Savoy was army headquarters in Cairo.

Whatever the stranger was planning, it involved the Suez Canal. The map. The note from the tablecloth. A code I'd seen before.

Captain Hall would likely remind me my mission was to tail Fredrick Fredricks and nothing more. But my instincts told me Fredricks was nearby. It couldn't be a coincidence that on my last mission, Fredricks had taunted me with the Suez Canal. In his farewell note before he'd escaped from jail in New York, the scoundrel had written:

Just as the Suez Canal facilitates commerce between the Red Sea and the Mediterranean, you and I will facilitate peace between your allies and mine, the Central Powers.

Good grief. How the man overestimated his importance... and mine.

And it couldn't be a coincidence that I had found a map with a black X in the middle of the canal, not to mention the date and time I had traced off the table-cloth. No. The Suez Canal was in danger. And Fredricks was involved. I felt it in my bones.

"May we use your telephone to report to Captain Hall?" I patted my wig. Blasted wig was too warm in this climate. But since I looked like a shorn sheep without it, I had no choice. I tucked my pith helmet under my arm.

"What telephone?" The general chuckled. "When you talk to Blinker, ask him to get us a telephone."

"The Arab Bureau has no telephone?" Clifford tilted his head. "What kind of outfit is this?"

"How nineteenth century," I said, wondering the same thing. I slipped my hands into my gloves. "There must be a telephone somewhere."

"In the lobby," Gertrude said.

"No longer the lobby, Gertie," Lawrence corrected her with a smirk. "But army headquarters."

On the way out the door, Clifford and I passed Frigo. The large man was unnerving to say the least. His crooked tobacco-stained teeth were even more un-settling. I picked up my pace and continued down the hall without looking back.

When I reached the lift, I looked back. *Where's Kitty? Sigh.* Annoying girl. "You stay here and call the lift, while I go and fetch Kitty." I marched back to the

Arab Bureau suite and found her flirting with Monsieur Lorrain.

"Kitty dear, we should be going." My teeth were gritted but I used my sweetest tone.

"But Aunt Fiona," the girl whined.

I tightened my lips and escorted her out.

Down in the lobby, after getting the runaround from various army men, we ended up in an office off the reception area. *Yes. Finally.* A telephone sat on a desk manned by a uniformed young woman. *Thank goodness.* Not another arrogant army man.

I approached the desk. "I need to use your telephone."

"I'm sorry, but we don't allow personal calls." The young woman snapped her gum.

"It's a very important business call to the War Office in London."

The woman squinted at me. "And you are?"

"Fiona Figg," I huffed.

"And your title is?" She tilted her head in a most unappealing manner.

Officially, my title was Head File Clerk in Room 40. I didn't think this gum-chewing WAAC would be impressed. But I couldn't very well tell her I was a spy on a dangerous mission.

Clifford stepped up to the desk. "I'm Captain Clifford Douglas." He showed the woman his military identification.

"Apologies." The woman looked up at Clifford. "Why didn't you say so?"

"May we use your telephone to call London?" Clifford was all politeness and charm.

The woman smiled. "Of course, Captain Douglas." She pushed the telephone forward to the edge of the desk.

"In private," I said.

The woman scowled but got up from her desk, yanked on the bottom of her blazer, and then marched out of the room. As a professional woman herself, I'd hoped she'd be more understanding. If I'd been dressed in one of my male disguises, perhaps my Rear Admiral Arbuthnot costume, I'd bet she would have been more accommodating. *Next time.*

The operator connected me to the War Office and Captain Hall's direct line. I glanced at my watch. It had just gone half twelve. Since it was two hours earlier in London, Captain Hall should still be in his office and not off to luncheon yet.

My stomach growled, reminding me I'd had only a cup of tea and half a piece of dry toast for breakfast.

When Captain Hall answered, I clamped the telephone receiver over my ear and, without taking a breath, quickly recounted every detail of my encounters with the mystery man from the railway carriage: his insults, the map, Lake Timsah, the date and time, *12–22 21:00*.

If only I knew Fredricks's role in all of this. Breathless, I sucked in air.

"Good work, Miss Figg."

You could have knocked me over with a feather. Captain Hall's compliments were few and far between. "Thank you, sir." Maybe he was finally taking me seriously as a spy and not just a file clerk.

"We have a man in Cairo undercover as a stagehand." Captain Hall lowered his voice. "I'll arrange for you to meet."

"Yes, sir. Who? Where? When?" Secretly, I hoped it was Archie. How I longed to see him again.

"Patience, Miss Figg." He took an audible breath as if reminding me to do the same. "Agent Relish. At Isis Theater. I'll get word for him to meet you there after tomorrow night's performance."

Could Agent Relish be Archie's code name?

"Black hair and crumb catcher to match." Captain Hall chuckled.

"Yes, sir." I tried to hold my voice steady. If Agent Relish was Archie, he was disguised with black hair and a mustache.

"Brilliant. Unless there's something else, Miss Figg." He paused.

I scanned my memory. "*Krokodilsee.*" In my flurry, I'd forgotten this enigmatic but no doubt important detail. "Whatever that means."

"It's German for Crocodile Lake." I heard Captain Hall shuffling papers on the other end. "Crocodile Lake is another name for Lake Timsah."

"Crocodile Lake," I repeated. *Good heavens.* "The Suez Canal."

"That's right." I heard more papers shuffle. "Listen, don't do anything without Relish."

"Yes, sir." Wasn't he concerned about Crocodile Lake and the canal? "But the canal—"

"We've got it covered." He sounded distracted. "Don't worry. Meet Relish and follow Fredricks, nothing more."

K r o k o d i l s e e 1 2–2 2 2 1:0 0

Yes. I knew it. *Oh, my sainted aunt.* It dawned on me where I'd seen it before. I searched my photographic memory for the details. *Good grief.* A file back in Room 40 *from last year.* The exact same code, the exact same location, the exact same date, except last year, 1916.

Could the Germans be so daft as to try again in the same place at the same time?

"And Miss Figg..." He paused again.

"Sir?"

"No silly getups." He chuckled.

"Getups?" By now, he should have realized how valuable my disguises were to our investigations. No spy worth their salt should go into the field without them.

"I mean it! No disguises." His tone was dead serious. "Act naturally, and don't you dare blow Relish's cover. You hear me?"

"Yes, sir." Instinctively, I stood up straight and saluted, as if he could see me through the telephone line. Thank goodness he couldn't. "Sir, there's something off about that information—"

Captain Hall interrupted me. "Meet Relish. And find Fredricks." More sounds of paper shuffling. "No getups. Understood?"

"But sir. That date is from last—"

"Put Captain Douglas on."

Why in the world did he need to speak to Clifford? What could Clifford possibly have to report?

I glanced around. Through the window, I saw Clifford outside smoking and chatting up the receptionist. "He's not here, sir."

"Kitty Lane?"

Kitty? He wanted to speak with Kitty. That was the last straw. Anyway, I had no idea where Kitty had got to. She was probably flirting with that frothy Frenchman.

"Sir." I was fuming. "Believe me, they have nothing to report."

"Very well."

"Sir, the gen is old. Something is fishy—"

My voice met silence. Captain Hall had already rung off.

I straightened my pith helmet, adjusted my skirt, and snapped my goggles into place.

What I needed now was a strong cup of tea for fortification. And after tea, I'd meet Agent Relish, find Fredrick Fredricks, and stop the plot to blow up the Suez Canal, all on my own, if necessary.

4

THE BALL

After our visit to the Arab Bureau, we took luncheon on the terrace back at our hotel. A lovely breeze and the shade of a palm made for a pleasant temperature despite the blazing sun. The terrace was buzzing. Shepheard's Hotel terrace was *the place* to people watch.

I was curious about the locals, who piqued my interest with their melodious language, flowing robes, and colorful tapestries. Perhaps that explains how Clifford talked me into ordering traditional Egyptian cuisine. After a few minutes, the waiter arrived with plates of stewed legumes like I'd never seen before. Dark leaves were rolled up like cigars. And the bread was round and flat. It looked safe. Watching Clifford take a piece with his hands and put it on his plate, I did the same. The bread was not light but rich and buttery. Compared to the rationed war bread back home, it was heaven sent.

Clifford and Kitty drank beer. I had tea. The Egyptians knew how to make a nice strong cup of tea, which, after the dreck that passed for tea in America, I greatly appreciated.

After eating an entire round of bread and drinking two cups of tea, I ventured a bite of something called *ful*, made up of spiced fava beans. I felt like a fool when my eyes watered, and I struggled to hold back a sneeze. I was quite overcome.

Clifford laughed. "Too spicy for you, old girl?" He tucked into his heaped plate.

I tried. I really did. But my poor palate was not always as adventurous as the rest of me.

Kitty picked at her lunch as usual. "I can't wait to try the puddings." The girl had a wicked sweet tooth. It seemed the only course she ever finished was the pudding.

I was relieved when the waiter brought a beautiful rice pudding. It was fragrant but not spicy. Thank goodness. Kitty and I both made short work of it. The sweet pudding was the perfect complement to my strong tea.

I had a devilish time persuading Kitty that we couldn't prepare our costumes and toilette for Lady Enid's ball *and* visit Monsieur Lorrain at his dig site— especially since we still needed to shop for our fancy-dress costumes.

"After all, you want to look your best when you dance with your handsome Frenchman." I licked my spoon and then tipped the last drop of tea into my mouth. If I was right, and I usually was, Fredrick Fredricks would be at that ball. I wasn't going to miss it for the world. Not when I had a chance to confront the bounder and find out what he was really doing in Cairo and why he'd dragged me across the world to Egypt.

Kitty pursed her lips. "I suppose you're right." Her eyes sparkled. "Dancing is more romantic than trudging around in the dirt." She stood up and twirled her skirt.

I nodded my approval.

Aside from our trip to the Arab Bureau, we hadn't yet ventured outside our own hotel. While Shepheard's was packed with uniformed soldiers, it wasn't until we went in search of costumes for the ball that I noticed just how much the city had been transformed into a gigantic military base. It was as if the British government had commandeered half the hotels and all the hospitals to house and treat Allied troops. Every pore of the city excreted Australian, Canadian, and British soldiers.

Whether they were en route to India, transferring to the Western Front, enjoying leave, or convalescing from war wounds, one way or another, the entire army seemed to pass through Cairo.

A taxi took us across town to the bazaar district and Wikalat Al Balah in particular, a souk famous for clothing and fabrics. "Us" included Clifford, who insisted on chaperoning two "delicate English ladies."

Ha! If he only knew. In fact, I knew very little about Kitty Lane. But I did know she was no delicate English lady. Clifford was oblivious when it came to "English ladies," especially Miss Kitty Lane.

Wikalat Al Balah was a world apart from Shepheard's and the British encampment around Azbakeya gardens. Yes. There were soldiers. But they were outnumbered by men in robes and headdress and women wearing colorful sheath dresses and wraparound gowns.

Cobblestone alleyways between limestone buildings under mudbrick arches were chock full of vendors selling everything from barrels of spices, legumes, and nuts, to silver cigarette cases, knives, and silk scarves. The overlapping of vibrant colors and rich textures put me in mind of a ragged patchwork quilt my grandmother had inherited from her grandmother, an heirloom as precious for the labor of love it represented as for its vulnerability to the ravages of time.

As I made my way through the crowded market, I kept my mission in mind. Concentrate, Fiona. First, find a costume for the fancy-dress ball—one to work its magic on Fredricks. Second, interrogate Fredricks and determine his plan. Third, stop said plan.

With every step came colorful offerings of yet another stall. Stained-glass lamps, engraved gold plates, sticks of incense, dates, nuts, and an assortment of dried roots. The smells alternated between pleasant aromatic spices and perfumes to foul fish and other pungent odors. And the noise volume was just as intense, with the clamor of pots and sales calls from vendors, not to mention the stray dogs and occasional escaped chicken. The market was a veritable circus of delights, with something for everyone and anyone who dared.

Thoroughly enjoying the sights and sounds, I had to remind myself we were here to find costumes for Lady Enid's ball. Obviously, the stalls of raw fabrics wouldn't do. Although they were beautiful. I might have to take some back to London. I wondered if a dressmaker at Harrods could make me a bespoke gown with secret pockets for my spy gear. Right now, we needed premade clothing for tonight.

Most of the tailored clothing was hanging in stalls near the center of the souk. One garment stood out, a purple tunic with an elaborate collar and high waistband of gold, turquoise, and green beads. Seeing my interest, the shopkeeper smiled and nodded her head approvingly. She held up an olive-colored headdress with what looked like a snake. I demurred in favor of a blue and gold headdress with a flower.

Kitty chose a pink wraparound with a yellow beaded waistband and a large collar sporting an interesting geometrical pattern in a bouquet of colors. She was all too happy to accept the snake for her headdress.

I burst out laughing when Clifford tried on a giant headpiece adorned with golden leaves, long fabric flaps, and what looked like a large red gourd protruding out of its crown.

"Perfect." Kitty held up a regal multicolored belt with layers of patterned fabric fanning out from a golden buckle in the shape of a lion.

"I say!" Clifford caressed the fabric. "That's quite a belt."

Kitty handed it to him. He grinned from ear to ear as he wrapped it around his waist. After an intense negotiation with the proprietress in French and his limited Arabic, he was the proud owner of beautiful kingly robes, a colorful band-belt, and a standout headdress.

Our fancy-dress buying was interrupted by a petite young Egyptian woman, who spoke to the proprietress in Arabic. Her arrival was announced by the strong scent of jasmine. The shopkeeper rifled through a pile of European jackets and waistcoats on a table in the back of the stall, and returned with a French military jacket and cap. A man's kit.

I watched out of the corner of my eye as the young woman slipped into the jacket and tucked her long dark hair up into the cap. Transformed from a lovely woman into a young French officer, she seemed familiar. Despite being taught it wasn't good manners, I couldn't help but stare.

Oh, my word! Yes. I recognized her. She was the boyish officer who'd been conspiring with my mystery man back at Shepheard's. *Blimey.* The young finger-pecking rooster was actually a hen.

The proprietress wrapped the uniform in brown paper. The impostor quickly exchanged some coins for the parcel and took off at a good clip, zigzagging through the crowds with ease. In a flash, she was gone.

"Who was that remarkable woman?" I asked the proprietress.

She shrugged.

I tried again in French.

"*Soltanet El-Tarab*," she answered in Arabic. "*La Sultana. Actrice célèbre.*" Luckily for me, she'd switched to French.

"The Sultana," I repeated. "Famous actress."

Famous actress, indeed. She had posed as an Egyptian military officer and conspired with the stranger from the railway. And I'd completely fallen for her disguise. A woman after my own heart.

It was too late to follow La Sultana. She'd already disappeared into the crowd. But if she was *that* famous, she shouldn't be too difficult to find.

* * *

Later that evening, dressed in our newly purchased outfits, Kitty, Clifford, and I attended Lady Enid's fancy-dress ball. Since the party was in our hotel, we didn't have to step outside. Jolly convenient. If I needed to touch up my face or visit the lav, I only had to pop back upstairs.

The ballroom at Shepheard's was world renowned. Even back in Room 40 at the War Office, Mr. Dilly

Knox told stories of grand balls and receptions he'd attended there. He hadn't exaggerated. With its towering ceilings, crystal chandeliers, and decorative Moorish arches, it was grand indeed.

The cavernous ballroom was buzzing with people, mostly soldiers, of course—many not in costume, unless their uniforms counted. There were so many soldiers, I wondered if General Clayton had commanded his troops to attend his wife's party.

An orchestra played loud American music and soldiers swung their partners around the dance floor. The few women in attendance had their pick of the litter, as it were.

Weaving in and out of the crowd, my companions and I made our way to the bar. Even before I'd had a cocktail, the dizzying assortment of shapes, patterns, and colors in Shepheard's ballroom made me lightheaded. Ornate twenty-foot ceilings crowned arched windows which sat atop walls with bands of orange and blue florets, turquoise diamonds, and carved fig leaves. Giant columns stood guard around the circumference of the room. The elaborate Oriental chandeliers hanging from the ceiling looked like lace made from precious metal. Carved mahogany framed stained-glass doors through which rainbow prisms shone.

Once I was clear of the throng, I made a beeline to the first person I recognized, Gertrude Bell. She was standing alone at the other end of the bar. Kitty and Clifford tagged along.

"Quite the shindig, isn't it?" Clifford said.

"Before the war, there were dances every night." Gertrude Bell's voice was wistful.

"Can I bring you a cocktail, Miss Bell?" Dear Clifford. Always accommodating when it came to beautiful women, even when they already had a drink in their hands.

Gertrude lifted her glass. She was the belle of the ball in an Egyptian pale lace tunic and silk slippers. Her face had the healthy glow of someone who lived for the outdoors. Yet she also had a classic, if slightly unkempt, English beauty. "Of course, I never went in for parties." She sipped her champagne and struck a pose.

A middle-aged woman with a plain but open face joined us. Gertrude introduced her as our hostess, Lady Enid Clayton. She was dressed in full WAAC uniform, slouch hat and all. I couldn't tell if she was in costume or merely hadn't changed for the ball.

"Such a brilliant turnout." Lady Enid glanced around the ballroom and then smiled wistfully. "Such a good cause, too. Poor children orphaned by the war."

"Indeed." Gertrude held out her empty glass to Clifford, who happily took it and trotted off for a refill.

The band played a nice waltz. Along with soldiers in their countries' colors, couples dressed as queens, pharaohs, and sheikhs twirled around the dance floor. It was a lively and invigorating scene. I kept my eye out for La Sultana or the mystery man from the railway carriage—not that I had any reason to think they would be here.

Where was Fredricks? He had to be here. Otherwise, why lure me to Cairo? He couldn't resist a grand ball... or being the center of attention. He'd show up. I just had to be patient. Unfortunately, patience was not one of my virtues.

Playing waiter, Clifford returned with an entire tray of champagne and passed glasses all around. When the actual waiter appeared, he scowled as he snatched the empty tray out of Clifford's hands.

I suppressed a giggle when, in full ancient Egyptian regalia and headdress, Clifford escorted Gertrude to the dance floor. Of course, Clifford would pick the prettiest woman in the vicinity—although I very much doubted that Gertrude Bell was anything near a damsel in distress.

Young Monsieur Jean-Baptiste Lorrain appeared out of nowhere and whisked Kitty away to the dance floor. He looked sharp with his dark hair slicked back and wearing full evening kit. Was he too haughty for fancy dress? Or did a nice suit count as a costume for an archeologist? Certainly, when *I* wore one it did.

Monsieur Lorrain wasn't the only one not in costume. Mr. Howard Carter, another archeologist, wasn't wearing fancy dress either—which confirmed my theory about men who dig in the dirt. Shifting from foot to foot in a corner of the room, he looked deuced uncomfortable. I knew the feeling.

Dressed as a pharaoh, General Clayton was a sight. When he came to claim a dance with his wife, I was left quite alone... and not just a little self-conscious about posing as an ancient Egyptian princess. I would have been more comfortable in beard and trousers.

I secreted myself behind a potted fern to better observe the crowd.

An older couple accompanied by a younger woman approached Mr. Carter, who bowed slightly when greeting them. Judging by Mr. Carter's deferential glances at the older man, this just might be his famous benefactor, Lord Carnarvon. The very chap Clifford had gushed on about meeting at the horse races outside London.

The older woman, whom I took to be Lady Carnarvon, glanced around the room as if looking for someone more important than her husband's fore-man. The young woman at her side stared intently at Mr. Carter, who in turn stole glances at her as the older man carried on an animated, if one-sided, con-versation with his foreman.

When the waltz ended, Monsieur Jean-Baptiste Lorrain—with cheerful Kitty on his arm—joined the Carnarvons. Monsieur Lorrain was all smiles. Mr. Carter not so much. In fact, the more Monsieur Lor-rain spoke, the redder Mr. Carter's face became. If only I could read their lips.

Crikey.

Mr. Carter shoved Monsieur Lorrain, who fell back against the wall. Dislodged by the push, Kitty fell back against Monsieur Lorrain. Before the Frenchman could respond, Mr. Carter stomped off, leaving his op-ponent shaking his curly head and laughing. Obvi-ously, there was no love lost between Mr. Carter and Monsieur Lorrain.

Professional jealousy, perhaps? A fight over a con-cession? A love triangle? Something even more tawdry? I couldn't wait to ask Kitty.

No sooner had Monsieur Lorrain dusted himself off than a beautiful young woman dressed as Cleopatra appeared out of the woodwork and began fawning over him. Cleopatra glared at Kitty, who returned the queen's sour look with a sweet smile. Cleopatra snarled something and Kitty slipped away, apparently not a fan of Cleopatra.

Too bad. I had the uncanny sense I'd seen that woman before.

The forward young woman was caressing the Frenchman's cheeks. Even from across the room, I could imagine her cooing into his ear.

He didn't object. In fact, he put his arm around her waist. Was the bounder two-timing Cleopatra by flirting with Kitty? Or vice versa? Monsieur Jean-Baptiste Lorrain was like a magnet, both attractive and repellent. Or perhaps the image of a rotting fruit surrounded by fruit-flies better described the Frenchman's relationship to the young women at the ball.

"There you are, old bean." Clifford joined me behind the fern. "Care to take a turn?" He gestured toward the dance floor. Putting the fears for my sandaled feet aside, I accepted his hand. My past experience dancing with Clifford told me my fears were well-founded.

Luckily Clifford was wearing sandals too. When he stepped on my toes, at least I was grateful that he wasn't wearing boots like the last time I'd danced with him. What Clifford lacked in grace, he made up for in enthusiasm.

Yes! I recognized him from across the room. The broad-shouldered huntsman with the flowing black hair was hard to miss in his slouch hat, tall boots, jodhpurs, and billowing white blouse. Fredrick Fredricks. I knew he'd be here.

He strutted through the dancers and tapped Clifford on the shoulder. Reluctantly, Clifford sputtered and turned me over to Fredricks, who whisked me around the dance floor so fast my feet barely touched the ground.

"About time you showed up." I dug my fingernails into his shoulder.

"Anticipation breeds desire." His broad, white-toothed smile was slightly obscene. "Did you miss me?"

"Don't flatter yourself." I intentionally stepped on his toes.

He pulled me to his chest and flew across the floor.

"Why are we here?" I doubted he would tell me the truth.

"A philosophical question." He grinned. "To live is to suffer, to survive is to find meaning in the suffering."

"Why are we in Cairo?" I dug my nails in deeper.

He winced. "To stop the war, of course."

The man was infuriating. Always talking about

how together we could stop the war. Was he mad? Or just having me on?

On our second lap, we passed Kitty dancing with Monsieur Lorrain. From the sidelines, Cleopatra, arms crossed, stood shooting daggers from her eyes. Had Jean-Baptiste thrown her over for Kitty? Cleopatra looked none too happy. I strained my neck to look back at her slim form. I swear I'd seen her before, *sans* costume. But where?

When the music stopped, Fredricks kissed my hand. "Until soon, ma chérie." He weaved through the crowded dance floor and disappeared.

Distracted by Cleopatra, I hesitated. I started after him but was intercepted by Clifford, with Monsieur Lorrain and Kitty in tow. The gentlemen fetched some drinks, and I took Kitty aside. "Did you see Fredricks? He was just here." I adjusted my wig and headdress, which had shifted from the vigorous dancing.

She shook her head.

Blast. The fiend had alluded me yet again.

"What happened between Mr. Carter and your new friend?"

Kitty gave a sharp glance over my right shoulder. "I'll tell you later."

Laughter behind me caused me to turn around.

When I did, I was face to face with our hosts, Lady Enid and General Clayton.

"Your ball is a smashing success, simply lovely."

Lady Enid smiled, obviously pleased with the compliment.

"Yes, my dear," General Clayton said, tugging on his headdress. "You've pulled it off."

Clifford and Jean-Baptiste returned with champagne cocktails in both hands. Clifford handed one to me, and Jean-Baptiste gave one to Kitty.

"*Mon Dieu.*" Jean-Baptiste laughed. "What are you supposed to be?" He pointed at Lady Enid's khaki skirt and tall boots. "Looking like that, it's a wonder you have any children."

General Clayton stepped closer to the Frenchman. "I'll have you know we have three children." He tugged on his pleated kilt.

"Five," Lady Enid corrected. "Two passed away." She lowered her eyes.

"I'm so sorry." I touched Lady Enid's elbow.

My heart sank. I'd thought not being able to have children was the worst thing possible for a woman. I couldn't imagine having one and then watching it die. I'd seen plenty of men die, too many. It was always heartbreaking, especially the young men who had so much of life ahead of them. But the death of a child, that would be devastating.

"And I don't appreciate you insulting my wife," General Clayton said. The way he balled up his fists, I thought he might punch the Frenchman—who thoroughly deserved it.

"Shall we duel at dawn?" The Frenchman laughed again.

He really was an outrageous fellow. I had half a mind to punch him myself. I sincerely hoped Kitty hadn't formed an attachment to the rascal.

General Clayton's nostrils flared.

"My husband was a champion fencer at the Royal Military Academy." Lady Enid sipped her champagne. "He would make mincemeat of you." She smiled sweetly.

Blimey.

"Pistols or swords, you choose." The general was dead serious.

"*Je suis désolé.*" Jean-Baptiste waved his hands in the air. "I'm a bit tipsy. Just a bit of fun." He slapped General Clayton on the shoulder. "Where's your sense of humor, *mon ami*? You British are always so serious." He turned his lips down into an exaggerated pout. "I'm always telling old Dankworth to lighten up, too."

Dankworth? The missing agent.

"I think it's time you went home." General Clayton grabbed the Frenchman's arm. "Shall I call you a motorcar?" The general practically dragged Jean-Baptiste across the dance floor.

"Come to my dig to watch me break ground," the Frenchman called back to us, slurring his words. "Everyone." He raised his voice. "You're all invited!"

I tried to catch them up to ask about Dankworth, but Lady Enid stopped me. "He's drunk. Don't interfere."

The music stopped and everyone stood waiting for the general to pitch the Frenchman out on his ear.

An oiled strand of hair flopped over Monsieur Lorrain's forehead as he staggered under the general's grip. "Tomorrow morning!" The closer he got to the ground, the louder he became. He stabbed the air with his finger. "The dig!"

The entire room was silent and staring at the scene.

"Good lord." Clifford downed the last of his drink. "Someone ought to tan his hide."

"Don't *you* volunteer to do it." I handed my empty glass to Clifford. "You have more important things to do." I figured if it had worked for Gertrude Bell, then why not me too?

"Like fetch you another drink?" He smiled.

"Precisely." I couldn't help but return his smile.

"Do you want another, my girl?" he asked.

Kitty shook her head.

Obediently, he scampered off to the bar to get me a refill.

"I'm going to make sure Jean-Baptiste gets home all right." Kitty handed me her glass.

"Oh no, dear." I stepped in front of her. "Let General Clayton handle it."

Kitty leaned and whispered in my ear. "You know you're not really my aunt, don't you?"

"Of course, I—"

She took off and disappeared into the crowd.

"Ask him about Dankworth," I called after her.

A young lady leaving with a drunken Frenchman in a foreign city. It was too much even for Kitty Lane.

Astonished, I stood gaping after her.

5

THE DIG

The next morning, anticipating our trip to Giza to visit Jean-Baptiste's archeological dig, Kitty was in high spirits. She was humming Christmas tunes as she pinned her curls behind her ears.

"You really must come along, Aunt Fiona," she said, a hairpin between her teeth.

So, I'm Aunt Fiona again, eh? I tied the laces of my practical Oxfords.

"Jean-Baptiste says pictures don't do it justice." She clamped her little sailor hat onto her head and smiled at her reflection in the looking glass.

I had to admit, I was more than a little curious to see the great pyramids. In the serenity of the desert, wrote Annie Pirie, the solemn majesty of these mighty tombs had looked down upon mankind for generations.

Then again, we weren't here to sightsee. We were here to trail Fredricks and find out his latest plot. Captain Hall told me to wait for Agent Relish. But with the Suez Canal at stake, how could I afford to wait? I hoped to heaven Captain Hall was right and the canal was safe.

If only I knew how to find the mysterious stranger from the railway, or his Egyptian contact, La Sultana. They hadn't been at the party. If I couldn't locate him, I could look for her. How hard could it be to find the most famous actress in Cairo?

A knock at the door signaled Clifford's arrival. Of course, he wouldn't miss the chance to visit a dig, seeing as how he fancied himself an amateur archeologist.

On the way to breakfast, I stopped off at the concierge desk to ask about La Sultana. The concierge told me she performed every Thursday, Saturday, and Sunday night at the Isis Theater. Convenient. The very place I was supposed to meet Agent Relish tonight. Two birds with one stone, as my grandfather used to say. Of course, he meant doves on the farm.

After a lovely breakfast of tea and toast with marmalade, we made our way to the lobby and the offices of Thomas Cook and Sons, where we joined the morning excursion to Giza.

Tonight, at the theater, I'd meet Agent Relish and question La Sultana. Then I'd find the stranger, foil the plot, and make Captain Hall proud. In the meantime, I might as well take the opportunity to see one of the greatest archeological wonders on earth.

According to Kitty, her *friend*, Jean-Baptiste, was sending Frigo to meet us in Giza and then take us to the dig. In the weeks I'd known her, Kitty had made many *friends*, too many if you asked me. But, as she reminded me last night, I was not really her aunt.

"Remember Frigo?"

Of course I remembered Frigo. How could I forget? He was the size of an ice box.

The berobed guide from Thomas Cook led us to the back of the hotel and behind the zoo. Yes, Shepheard's had a zoo with a peacock, a pair of camels, a trio of Arabian horses, and kangaroos and wallabies brought to Egypt as mascots and left behind by Australian soldiers. There was even a panda from China, poor thing.

"Are you preferring donkey or camel?" the guide said with a thick Egyptian accent. He pointed to a group of mangy animals tethered to a rail.

"Good grief." My heart sank. "He doesn't expect us to ride those beasts, does he?"

"I'm afraid so, old thing." Clifford puffed his pipe. "Did I ever tell you about the time I rode a camel across the Sinai?" A smile formed at the edges of his mouth. "Jolly good animal, the camel. Rode all the way to St. Catherine's monastery, the spot where old Moses saw the burning bush. Now that—"

"Clifford, be a dear," I interrupted him before he got carried away with old Moses. "Can you choose the best animals for our journey?"

Clifford was only too happy to oblige. The poor creatures couldn't have known how many of their brethren he'd killed over the years on safaris with his "great pal," the "brilliant South African hunter," Fredrick Fredricks. By now, everyone in the War Office knew Fredricks was a German spy. Everyone except Clifford, who was still in denial.

A few minutes later, Clifford reappeared, leading a string of three camels. Given the choice between falling from a height of six feet and falling from three, I would have chosen the donkeys.

If only I owned a divided skirt or a pair of bloomers like I'd seen in Kitty's *Vogue* magazine. How in the world would I get on the beast, let alone ride it, in my linen frock? I would have to ride side-saddle, like a proper Englishwoman.

Even my practical Oxfords couldn't save me now.

Good news. When Clifford jerked on their leads, the camels knelt, knees to the sand, for easy mounting. Bad news. The belabored beasts grunted and groaned, their cheeks ballooned, and when they turned to view their burden, they spat foul-smelling slime.

Grimacing, I wiped the back of my hand on my dress. I immediately regretted letting go of the wooden frame saddle upon which I sat. For, as soon as I did, the camel raised its hindquarters and I lurched forward, nearly tumbling off into the sand.

I'd just regained my balance when the beast straightened its front legs and tipped me backwards so far that I was sure I would topple over its behind.

"Sway with it and not against it," Clifford said, clearly amused. He and Kitty had both mounted like Bedouins born and raised on the gangly creatures.

After a few minutes of fighting to stay upright, I got the hang of swaying with the camel's gait, which made the journey easier if not less painful. My bottom banged against the wooden saddle with such force, I was sure to have a purple bruise for weeks, a bruise no one would ever see, given its location.

What a sight we were: Englishmen dressed in suits,

waistcoats, cravats, and top hats as if going to the Turf Club. And Englishwomen in corsets under layers of heavy jackets and dresses, wearing our best hats as if we were taking tea instead of a dusty ride to ancient pyramids. Even Kitty sported a fox-fur stole atop her sun frock. No doubt the latest fashion trend. I shook my head. Ridiculous.

The sun was fierce, and my cheeks burned. Luckily, servants walked alongside, holding umbrellas for the ladies. I might have found the scene comical if I weren't concentrating so intently on not falling head over heels.

One long hour later, a grand triangle appeared on the horizon. Within minutes, two more pyramids and the Great Sphinx showed themselves. The photographs in Annie Pirie's *The Pyramids of Giza* didn't capture their magnificence. Their greatness was humbling.

Gobsmacked, I forgot all about my incommodious mode of transportation and reveled in the monuments before me. Miraculous, impossible, stone structures jutting straight up out of the sand. Magnificent.

A commotion just behind me made me twist around in my saddle.

Sitting astride a black stallion, Frigo leaned over and grabbed the rein of Kitty's camel. "I'm taking you to Lorrain's concession." He made a clicking sound with his tongue, and his horse walked toward the pyramids.

Clifford steered his camel after them.

Pulling on the reins, I tried to do the same. The beast wouldn't budge.

"Excuse me." I waved. "Yoo hoo. Mr. Frigo."

Clifford twisted around in his saddle.

"Don't leave me," I shouted.

Clifford tapped his camel with a riding stick, and it ran toward me. "Whoa." Clifford dismounted. "Aren't you coming with us?"

"Blasted beast won't move."

He chuckled as he patted my camel's neck. "I wouldn't leave you."

To whom was he speaking? Me or the camel?

In one graceful movement, he slid my camel's rein through his fingers and mounted his camel again. With a flick of his riding stick, we were off.

Heavens. I had no idea camels could move so fast. I gripped the saddle for dear life.

When we arrived at the dig, Clifford helped me off the animal. I was never so glad to be on my own two feet. Kitty and Frigo were already sitting on chairs positioned near a long table under a tent. I joined them, while Clifford took care of the animals. The shade of the tent was welcome after an hour and a half in the blazing sun. Only my large-brimmed hat stood between me and sunstroke.

Frigo offered me water from a dented metal cup. Undeterred by the greenish tint, I gulped it down as if my life depended on it, which in this dry desert, it probably did. Thankfully, it tasted better than it looked.

A few feet away, two men in robes and headdresses squatted, picking at the earth with trowels. Nearby, a cave-like tomb was barred with a makeshift door and padlock.

To my surprise, the barren sands around the dig were nothing to write home about. Not like the Sphinx or the pyramids. Men digging in the dirt. That was all I saw. The landscape was flat and brown. In fact, the furrows reminded me of my grandfather's farm, only drier. At least on the farm there was an orchard and eventually the brown furrows grew green wheat.

While the earth at my grandfather's farm yielded only fruit and vegetables, the Egyptian desert held unimaginable treasures. My pulse quickened to think of what prizes were hidden inside those nondescript furrows. Even the smallest pot shard could be thousands of years old and might once have graced the palace of a queen.

My *Baedeker's Guide to Cairo* listed so many "must see" pyramids, monuments, mosques, and markets I could stay here for months and still not see all its wonders. Offering both moral probity and practical wisdom, in the name of virtue, Mr. Baedeker warned against unseemly pleasures while informing the adventurous traveler where to find them. I chuckled to myself. *The irony.*

Wiping his brow with a handkerchief, Clifford joined us under the tent. "Is that your entire crew?"

"The war takes all the men away." Frigo shrugged. "European and Egyptian."

"How do the archeologists carry on their work?" Clifford said.

"They don't." Frigo handed the same dented metal cup to Clifford. "Most digs are closed."

Clifford downed the water in one gulp and then dropped into the chair next to me.

Frigo refilled the cup from a waterskin and passed it to Kitty, who sipped and then handed it to me. I wiped the lip with my handkerchief and took a sip.

"Where is Monsieur Lorrain?" I scanned the items on the table: a hand-drawn map of the dig, a large journal, a stack of papers held down by a rock, a dirty coffee cup, along with a half-eaten tin of something, now covered in flies. Monsieur Lorrain did not keep a very tidy dig.

"The boss never arrives before eleven." Frigo lashed the waterskin to his chair.

"He needs his beauty sleep." Kitty giggled behind her hand.

"Is this where Borchardt found the bust of Neferti-ti?" Clifford removed his pipe from his jacket pocket.

Frigo shook his head. "That was in Amarna."

"Bloody Germans pilfering Egypt." Clifford leaned back in his chair and lit the foul thing.

"And what about the French and the British?" I fanned the pipe smoke away from my face.

"I don't speak for the French." Clifford puffed and then emitted a grand cloud of smoke. "But the British are gentlemen and scholars interested in conservation, not theft."

"Conservation at the British Museum in London." I raised my eyebrows. "To the Egyptians, what's the difference? What do they care whether their heritage is on display in London or Berlin?" I was starting to sound like Fredricks. As a South African, he was always complaining about the British "colonizers."

"Good lord, Fiona. How can you say that?" Clifford scowled. "The Kaiser killed your husband with mustard gas."

"Ex-husband." My chest tightened, recalling Andrew's scarred face and last choked-out words about his baby son, the son he'd had with the husband-stealing Nancy. The son my defective body couldn't give him. I took a deep breath and shook the thoughts from my mind. Stiff upper lip, as my father always said.

I glanced at my watch. "It's gone quarter past eleven. When will Monsieur Lorrain arrive?" I couldn't wait all bloody day. I had missing British agents to find and a canal to save, not to mention locating Fredrick Fredricks.

"Can't you give us a tour while we wait?" Kitty batted her long lashes at Frigo.

"No." Frigo crossed his log-sized arms in front of his barrel-sized chest. "We wait." He looked straight ahead, not even glancing over at Kitty. Her pretty smile and long lashes were lost on Mr. Frigo.

A muffled sound came from the boarded tomb. I pricked up my ears.

Was that a human cry? A cold chill ran up my spine. "Is there a mummy in that cave?" I'd heard of a mummy's curse, but of course I didn't believe such nonsense. Still, that horrible sound emanating from the tomb was deuced unnerving.

"We don't know yet." Frigo gave me a strange look. "What have you heard?"

"I heard a voice cry out." I tilted my head. "Listen."

"I don't hear anything." Clifford held his pipe in midair, staring at the mouth of the cave.

"Well, I did." I crossed my arms over my chest.

"Your imagination is playing tricks on you, old girl." Clifford relaxed back into his chair.

"Let's find out." Kitty jumped up from her chair and trotted over to the entrance. "Have you got a key to the lock, Frigo?" she called back.

When Frigo stood up, a set of keys on his belt jangled, giving us the answer. He marched over to where Kitty was fiddling with the padlock.

I dashed across the scree and loose sand.

Kitty had one of her hairpins inserted in the lock.

"What in heaven's name?" I patted my handbag for my lockpick set. Why use a hairpin when I had the real deal?

Thud.

My pulse quickened. "Did you hear that?" I grabbed Kitty's wrist. "There's someone—or something—"

"Move aside," Frigo boomed as he stepped in between me and Kitty.

"Good lord, there's someone in there." Clifford

joined us in front of the tomb entrance.

Frigo selected a key from his bunch and inserted it into the padlock. The lock popped open, and he slid it out of its latch. Slowly, he pushed the door open. "Hello," he said into the darkness.

"We need a torch." I made a mental note to add my new American torch to the handy instruments I carried on my person. Soon I would need a regular tool belt.

Following on Frigo's heels, I stepped into the tomb. Cool damp air made the hairs on my arms stand on end. A dark, dank smell hit my nostrils.

Clifford stepped forward and lit a match. "Good lord."

Just inside the door, the outline of a body came into view.

Blimey. It was lying motionless on the ground.

Kitty gasped, her face a mask of terror in the flickering light of the match.

I knelt by the body and put two fingers on his neck. Pressing harder, I hoped for a pulse. We'd just heard the chap shouting and moving about. He had to be alive.

No. Nothing. But the body was still warm.

I lifted the man's wrist and again felt for a pulse. Nothing. My heart sank. "He's dead."

The noise we'd heard must have been the killer. I shuddered to think. Was the killer still in the tomb with us?

The match went out. The tomb was pitch black. A cold breeze blew across the back of my neck and I shivered. This place gave me the creeps.

A hissing sound and then a flickering light. Clifford had struck another match. He squatted next to the body and held the flame above the face of the dead man.

"Oh, dear." My hand flew to my mouth. "It's Monsieur Lorrain."

The dead eyes of Jean-Baptiste Lorrain stared up at me. Around his head, blood pooled in a tiny puddle.

Carefully, I touched his head. A wet gaping wound met my fingers. I grimaced. "He's been hit on the head."

Why had he been exploring the tomb in his evening suit? Had he fallen and hit his head? The door was locked from the outside. Obviously, he hadn't come to the tomb alone. Someone had locked him inside. And that someone had dealt the fatal blow to his skull.

I glanced around.

There was a murderer on the loose. And perhaps he was still in this tomb.

6

THE CRIME

Frigo sent one of the men back to Cairo to fetch the police. In the meantime, I insisted he get a torch so I could examine the crime scene properly.

Jean-Baptiste *could* have hit his head by accident. But he *couldn't* have locked himself inside the tomb. Someone had intentionally locked him in. And I suspected *that someone* had hit the poor man on the head and then left him for dead.

Frigo held the torch while I assessed the scene.

Jean-Baptiste was wearing the clothes from the night before. So, he must have come here from the ball. The last time we'd seen him at the party, he was drunk as a sailor. In his intoxicated state, did he invite someone out to visit his tomb?

Kitty had seen him home.

"Where did you leave Jean-Baptiste last night?" I asked Kitty.

She may have been the last person to see him alive... apart from the person who locked him in the tomb, of course. *Unless—no, impossible. Kitty wouldn't... would she?*

Trembling, Kitty crouched next to Jean-Baptiste's body, holding his hand. She'd only just met him yesterday, and yet his death profoundly moved her. Poor girl. She brought her face close to his hand as if to kiss it. Could she have fallen for him so quickly? Instead of kissing his hand, she just stared at his fingers.

"I left him at his room in the hotel," Kitty said, finally. She laid his hand over his chest and then stood up. "At Shepheard's."

"Was anyone else with you?" Clifford leaned against the wall of the cave, smoking his pipe.

Frigo must have been in shock to allow smoking inside an ancient tomb full of artifacts. Either that, or he was just Jean-Baptiste's bodyguard. In that case, he'd failed miserably. The big man's eyes shone as he held a lantern above the body of his dead boss.

"No." Kitty wiped dirt from her hands. "I left him very much alone. And very much alive."

"He may have been alive when we got here." I

walked around the body, careful not to step in the pool of blood around his head. "Making those noises." Of course, it wasn't a mummy. I knew that. It was poor Jean-Baptiste calling for help. I glanced around. Unless, of course, the killer was still here, hiding in the tomb. "Clifford, why don't you find another torch and have a look around?" *Just in case...*

"There's another lantern in the tent." Frigo pointed to the tomb entrance.

I bent down to examine Jean-Baptiste's fatal head wound. "Whatever hit him was very heavy and very sharp." The gash was large. "If the blow didn't kill him right away, he must have bled to death." I glanced around. There wasn't as much blood pooled around his head as there should be for such a large gash. Why not?

Carefully, I leaned over the body and patted his pockets.

"What are you doing?" Frigo said.

"Don't worry," I said in a reassuring tone. "I have experience with murder investigations."

"Murder." Frigo's eyes went wide. "Who would want to kill Monsieur Lorrain?"

"Good question." I stood up and brushed a lock of hair from my forehead with the back of my hand. "You would know better than we."

"Me?" Frigo looked like I'd just accused *him* of the bloody crime. "No. Everyone loved the boss."

"Everyone except Mr. Carter, Lady Enid, General Clayton, and Cleopatra." One, two, three, four. I counted on my fingers. "And those are just from last night."

"You are mistaken, lady." Frigo's mustache twitched.

"If you say so." Of course, I was *not* mistaken. Last night, Monsieur Jean-Baptiste Lorrain had insulted Lady Enid and General Clayton. He'd thrown over Cleopatra for Kitty. And he and Mr. Carter had nearly come to blows, over what I didn't know.

I turned to Kitty, who was intent on something she was rolling between her fingers, something quite invisible to me. "What was Mr. Carter discussing with Jean-Baptiste at the ball last night?" I tried to sound nonchalant.

Kitty looked up from whatever was so captivating. "Jean-Baptiste told Mr. Carter he'd never amount to anything because he was a fraud."

"A fraud?" I repeated.

"Mr. Carter is a volatile chap." Clifford had returned with the second lantern. "I read about him years ago. The Saqqara Affair. He told off some French tourists and got fired."

"What affair?" I'd never heard of it. How in the world did Clifford know about such scandals?

"Carter and his men had to rein in some drunken French tourists." He chuckled. "Obviously, not a fan of the frogs."

The question was, did Mr. Carter hate Frenchmen enough to kill one?

"He works for Lord Carnarvon now." I blew at the lock of hair that had fallen back into my face. I really needed a better wig. "Surely Lord Carnarvon wouldn't hire a fraud, or a hothead."

Perhaps there were clues on the body... or in the tomb. "Clifford, search the tomb for the murder weapon, if you please. A bloody rock or other heavy sharp object."

"Yes, ma'am." Lantern in hand and his pipe between his teeth, Clifford was only too happy to oblige.

I knelt beside the corpse to get a better look.

Frigo moved closer, whether to give me more light or to keep an eye on me, I wasn't sure.

I removed Jean-Baptiste's leather wallet from the pocket of his jacket. Inside he had money, a lot of money, in various currencies—French, British, and German. "He wasn't robbed." French and British, alright. But German? Jolly odd. I held up the wad of notes. "So, the motive wasn't money." I continued rifling through the wallet.

"Lady, please have some respect..." Frigo's voice trailed off.

When I looked up at him, there were tears in his eyes.

"Never fear, Mr. Frigo." Wallet in hand, I stood up again. "I will find whoever committed this heinous crime against your boss." I couldn't turn my back on justice. A man had been murdered. And the killer must pay. More to the point, Jean-Baptiste had mentioned Agent Dankworth. Agent Dankworth was missing, and the Frenchman was dead. There must be a connection between the two. I wasn't about to let a British agent go missing in the field. I would find Jean-Baptiste's killer and I would find Agent Dankworth... and, of course, I would find Fredrick Fredricks. That went without saying.

"You?" Frigo sounded incredulous.

"Yes, me." I held up the German notes. "Unless you want the police to discover what your boss was *really* doing here."

In the light of the lantern, Frigo's face took on a ghostly pall.

I continued with my hunch. "He was working with the Germans—"

"No, lady." Frigo shook his head. "Never. He hated the Germans."

It didn't add up. He may not have been working with the Germans. But he was up to something. Frigo's face told me as much.

I stuffed the notes back into the wallet. In addition to the money, the wallet contained a coat-check receipt from Shepheard's and a small photograph of a woman wearing an aviator's jacket and a balaclava... decidedly *not* the woman dressed as Cleopatra who clung to him at the ball. Another jilted lover? A betrayed wife? A long-lost sister?

"Who is she?" I showed the photograph to Frigo. He just shrugged.

If not for money, perhaps a crime of passion. I bent down and slipped the wallet—*sans* photograph—back into the dead man's pocket.

Wait. I felt the corner of something. I teetered on my toes, reached further into his breast pocket, and pulled out a small, slim notebook. When I flipped through the pages, I saw it was a datebook. I held my breath and flipped to the last entry, dated yesterday:

HG at GAI 11.

"HG at GAI 11." I looked up at Frigo. "Do you know what that means?"

He wrinkled his brow and shook his head.

"HG at GAI 11," I repeated. "What do you suppose it means?"

"A code, perhaps?" Kitty held out her hand. "May I see it?"

I handed her the notebook. My leg was cramping, and I had to stand up.

Clifford returned with the lantern. "I couldn't find anything." He gestured toward the back of the cave. "There seems to be another chamber further on, but it's boarded up."

Kitty turned the pages of the notebook. Clifford went to her side and looked over her shoulder as she ran her finger down each page, working backwards.

"I say." Clifford pointed at the book. "Look there." He stabbed the page with his finger.

"What is it?" I joined them and stared down at the page. Dated last week, it had the same notation, "HG at GAI." Instead of 11, it said 10, which made it clear the 11 was indeed a number. But was the number a time or a place?

Kitty continued scanning, page by page.

I took a mental picture of every page as she went.

A rattling from the tomb entrance made me turn

around. At last, Frigo's man had returned with two uniformed policemen. They entered, torches in hand.
Judging by their accents, one was British and the other
was Egyptian. My countryman commanded us to step
aside. Seemed the British constabulary ranked higher
than their Egyptian counterparts.

Kitty slipped the notebook into the pocket of her
sun frock.

I almost scolded her, but then thought better of it.
Yes, we were here to trail Fredrick Fredricks. No, Captain Hall hadn't authorized us to investigate local murders. Still, from my past experience, I knew Fredricks
always managed to have his fingers in every pie, especially the spicy ones. Anyway, there was most certainly
a connection between the dead Frenchman and our
missing agent. That was reason enough to investigate.

I palmed the photograph of the mysterious woman
I'd purloined from the dead man's wallet. Just in time
too. The officers shooed us out of the tomb, but only
after taking down our names and hotel, and warning
us not to leave town.

"I will interview you at your hotel later today." The
British officer gave us a stern look. "Where I expect
you all to stay until I arrive." He tilted his head and
squinted at me. "Have you disturbed the body or surroundings in any way?"

A lump formed in my throat, and I tightened my palm around the photograph.

"No, sir," Frigo answered. "Just guarding the boss, waiting for you."

Obviously, Frigo had his own reasons for lying to the police. I wondered if they had anything to do with the motives for his boss's murder.

"Looks like he fell and hit his head," the Egyptian officer said.

"Yes, sir." Frigo nodded. "Terrible accident."

I was convinced it was murder and not an accident, but I kept my mouth shut. Frigo had covered for me, and I would cover for him... unless, of course, he turned out to be the murderer.

"An accident." The British officer circled the body. "We'll see about that." He glanced up at me. "What are you still doing here? Didn't I tell you to go?" He touched his Billy club.

"Righto." I led the party out of the tomb.

Once outside, I slipped the purloined photograph into my handbag.

The midday sun was blinding. I shielded my eyes with my hand.

Good grief. The camels.

I'd forgotten that our only way back was to ride those mangy beasts.

* * *

When we finally reached the hotel, I had to make the excruciating decision whether to have a refreshing bath or a strong cup of tea. The damp earthy smell of camel clinging to my person gave me no choice but to retreat to my room. I couldn't be seen—or smelled—in public until I'd scrubbed the desert and the camel off my skin.

On the bright side, I'd always found soaking in the bath provided the relaxed state of body I needed to focus my mind. I did some of my best sleuthing in the bath.

As I ran the bath, I reviewed the possible suspects.

First, there was Mr. Carter, no fan of the French, and a particular adversary of Monsieur Lorrain, who had insulted him in public. Next came Lady Enid, also insulted by Jean-Baptiste Lorrain, and of course her husband, General Clayton, who'd threatened a duel at dawn to save his wife's honor. Overly dramatic, if you asked me. And I suspected Lady Enid had her own ways of disposing of an adversary. What about the jealous Cleopatra? She might have killed her lover in a passionate rage. Then there was Frigo, who'd lied to the police and winced at the mention of the Germans.

I stepped into the tub and sank into the warm water. One disadvantage of formulating lists of suspects in the bath was the impossibility of writing them down given the dampness. And, although I had a photographic memory, I first needed to see something to preserve it intact in my mind's eye.

Scrubbing my skin with a cloth and a deliciously lemon-scented soap, I reviewed the clues we'd found in the tomb.

Monsieur Lorrain was hit on the head with a heavy sharp object, which was not found in the tomb. Obviously, the killer had hidden the murder weapon or taken it with him... or her. Unless, of course, Monsieur was killed elsewhere, and his body taken out to the tomb. That also would explain why there was so little blood around the ghastly wound.

The killer must have escaped through some secret passageway. Otherwise, we would have seen him... or her. Either that or the killer was well hidden in the tomb, perhaps in the chamber Clifford found. Although Clifford said it was boarded up. So, scratch that. Then again, if the killer had taken the Frenchman's body to the tomb *after* he'd killed him elsewhere, that would explain why the tomb was locked. It would not explain why we heard someone rumbling around inside.

Jean-Baptiste must have taken this killer to the

tomb, opened the padlock, and entered of his own free will—or at gun point. The killer delivered the fatal blow and then locked his victim into the tomb. How did the attacker know Jean-Baptiste wouldn't be found in time? Perhaps the assailant intended only to wound the Frenchman.

Or if the perpetrator had attacked Jean-Baptiste somewhere else and then carried him out to the tomb, then, with the Frenchman unconscious, how had the killer opened the lock? Lockpick set? Hairpin?

Where there was a will there was a way, as my grandmother used to say.

From what I'd seen of Jean-Baptiste, with his trademark insults, it was just as easy to imagine the Frenchman had started a fight, a fight he couldn't win in his inebriated state. In that case, the police were right. It was an accident. Or self-defense, even.

What of the mysterious clue in the date book? *HG at GAI II*. Once I cracked that code, I'd be closer to solving the crime and perhaps locating Agent Dankworth, too.

A knock on the door interrupted my speculations.

"Aunt Fiona." Kitty's voice was impatient.

I didn't blame her. Although Kitty never complained, she couldn't be happy covered in desert dust and camel muck. On the camel ride back from the tomb, she'd enlightened me about what transpired with Jean-Baptiste when she escorted him to his room. Thankfully, she edited out the whispers and kisses. The most important information was about Agent Dankworth. Apparently, Jean-Baptiste and Agent Dankworth were working together to infiltrate an illegal antiquities ring.

Is that why the Frenchman was killed, and the British agent went missing? Illegal antiquities?

"Yes, dear." I pulled myself up out of the bath and pulled the plug to drain the water. After all, Kitty wouldn't want a dirty bath. "I'll be out momentarily." Fetching a towel, I dried myself, wrapped the towel around my torso, and exited the lav.

Kitty stood staring at me. "I'm always astonished when I see you without your wig."

I touched my head. I must look like a drowned porcupine. I snatched up my wig from the corner of the table and tugged it on. After nearly six months going undercover, I could tug one on in my sleep—that is, if I'd remembered to take it *off* before bed. I straightened my wig. "The lavatory is all yours."

While Kitty bathed, I popped down to the reception desk.

If Jean-Baptiste had gone out again after Kitty left him, someone at the hotel would have seen him.

7

THE FIBER

Sure enough, the receptionist reported the night clerk had mentioned a drunken Frenchman staggering out into the street just before eleven last night. He'd noted the time because his shift started at eleven.

HG at GAI 11. Eleven o'clock. Part of the mystery solved.

If Jean-Baptiste was going to meet someone last night at eleven, who and where?

Who was HG? And where was GAI?

When I got back to the room, Kitty had commandeered the dressing table for another one of her forensic experiments. No doubt something she'd learned at her "boarding school" in France.

She was hunched over a microscope. On the floor

next to her sat a wooden box, presumably the case for the instrument. Poppy was asleep on her lap.

"Look!" She scooted her chair back. Poppy yipped in complaint and jumped down.

"Where in heaven's name did you get that?" The instrument had a brass lens case and a black base. It looked sturdy. A magnifying glass sat below the lens cylinder. Very fancy. Probably French.

"I brought it with me." She stood up. "I got it—"

"Don't tell me." I took her seat. "France."

"Look into it and tell me what you see." She beamed. Poppy sat on the floor next to her, looking up at me expectantly as if she, too, couldn't wait for my reaction.

I leaned my eye into the microscope. I'd never looked into one before. What a strange sensation. The cool eyepiece against my brow. One eye closed. The other looking into another world. I had no idea what I was looking at.

"A scaly orange worm?" Whatever it was, it was creepy.

She laughed. "How about this one?" She removed the slide I'd been looking at and replaced it with another.

I leaned in again. "A blade of grass?" I stared into the microscope. "No. A green straw." When I looked up at her, she was giggling behind her hand. "Alright. Tell me. What am I looking at?"

"Fibers from under Jean-Baptiste's fingernails." She clapped her hands together.

Poppy barked. The girl and her dog were a bundle of excitement. Kitty was more passionate about Jean-Baptiste dead than alive.

"Fingernails." How gruesome.

So, she wasn't just holding his hand and mourning his demise when we found his body in the tomb. She was collecting evidence. Clever girl.

"He had these fibers under his nails from a struggle with his killer." Her eyes danced as she removed several items from her bag and placed them on the table: a small, folded piece of white paper, and a matchstick.

"What kind of fibers?" I leaned closer.

"Your scaly orange worm is actually wool." She replaced the slide again. "See the even, overlapping scales? That's fine wool. Probably from sheep and not camel."

"Orange wool." Had the killer worn an orange jumper? It was a bit hot for jumpers.

"That's right. And the green cylinder is silk." She changed slides again.

I took another look. "So, our killer was wearing silk and wool." Jolly clever.

"Perhaps." She stood behind me, her breath on my neck. "See the tiny white wispy hairlike fibers attached to the bottom of the silk?"

I strained to see through the lens. "I do."

"That's flora, not animal fiber." She used a pencil to point to the strands on the slide.

"A plant? What kind of plant?" My friend and amateur botanist Daisy Nelson would know. Too bad she refused to set foot out of Old Blighty.

"A white one... and fresh too." From her folded paper, she pinched another small bit of green and orange fiber, struck a match, and burned it. "A flower of some sort."

"Now what are you doing? Witchcraft?" Daisy was a witchy woman. For all I knew, Kitty was one too. The acrid smell of burning hair hit my nostrils.

"Confirming the fibers are silk and wool. Cotton smells like burning paper. Wool and silk smell like burning hair." She withdrew a tiny glass vial from her bag. "One more test to go."

Like a chemist in a laboratory, using tweezers, she dropped another tiny fragment of orange fiber into the vial. "In this acid, plant matter will dissolve within minutes. Silk will dissolve within fifteen minutes. But not wool."

"And what will that tell us?" I waved my hand in front of my nose.

"I want to confirm that it *is* plant matter attached to our wool fibers." She tilted the vial back and forth, stopped it with a rubber stopper, and then leaned it against the microscope.

While we waited, I finished dressing for luncheon.

Kitty brushed Poppy's topknot into a soft ponytail and tied it up with a pink ribbon. After a few minutes, she examined the vial. "Just as I suspected." She poked the air with her finger. "Jean-Baptiste was not killed in that tomb."

"Whatever do you mean?" Sitting on the edge of my bed, I pulled on my practical Oxfords. "We heard him alive."

"That may be, but he was attacked elsewhere." She brought the vial over and sat next to me. "The white fibers are gone. Next the silk will disappear. Watch."

We sat together watching the vial. Sure enough, a few minutes later, the green strand dissolved. Only the orange fiber remained.

"Wool." I tapped the vial. "But how do we know Jean-Baptiste was attacked elsewhere? Couldn't the killer have been wearing a silk shirt and wool trousers?"

"It's possible." She stood up, went back to the dressing table to pack up her instrument and paraphernalia.

Poppy followed close on her heels. The pup jumped up on the dressing chair, and watched with interest.

"More likely, the fibers come from a carpet. An orange and green carpet made from fine silk and wool in the Persian style." Kitty placed the microscope in its case and latched it shut. "Rarely are clothes made of both silk and wool. And these fibers are interwoven."

"And you learned all that from your three tests?" Very clever. If Jean-Baptiste was killed elsewhere, then that explained the lack of blood, the lack of murder weapon, and the lack of murderer at the scene.

"Microscope, fire, and solvents can tell us a lot about fibers." She gathered up her paraphernalia and put it away in a small leather pouch.

The girl was a wonder.

"So, if we find a green and orange Persian rug, we may find our killer, too." I gathered up my handbag from the dressing table before it got mixed in with Kitty's chemicals.

"Exactly." She smiled.

I glanced at my watch. "Heavens. We're late for luncheon with Clifford. Wait until he hears what we've found." Kitty, with her fiber forensics, and I, with my interview of the receptionist, had discovered that before his death, Jean-Baptiste met someone at eleven o'clock at a place with a Persian rug.

But who and where?

Kitty bent down, scooped up Poppy, and kissed the squirming ball of fur on the wet nose. "Be a good girl."

She'd better be a good girl. I didn't want any wee accidents.

Waiting for us on the terrace, with his hair slicked back, receding hairline and all, Clifford looked fresh in his linen suit. Kitty's lacy pink hat and frilly pink frock made her appear even younger than her eighteen years. I'd opted for a plain white blouse and a tan cotton skirt, a skirt with lots of pockets, of course.

The older women on the terrace glanced around and smiled approvingly. Good grief. I hoped they didn't think we were the girl's parents.

Since the hotel was overrun with British visitors, Shepheard's had a wide selection of good old English food—toad-in-the-hole, bangers, suet pudding—so my countrymen didn't have to venture into the local cuisine. Clifford insisted it would be good for me to broaden my horizons to order from the Egyptian menu. Perhaps he was right.

Tomorrow.

Tomorrow, I would try something new. Today, I needed comfort food. Even on a good day, toad-in-the-hole was too much. Buttered toast and tea, on the other hand, were the perfect antidote to murder.

Clifford was all too happy to dine on kofta and kebab. Kitty had discovered an Egyptian dessert made of puff pastry with pistachios and sultanas called *Om Ali*, and now she would eat nothing else. Given I'd taken to ordering toast with marmalade and tea for every meal, I shouldn't criticize. At least Poppy agreed with me. She loved toast as much as I did, especially if it was slathered in butter.

Sigh. Clean clothes, a fresh pot of tea, and a pleasant breeze. Who could ask for more? Between sips and nibbles, I removed a notebook and pencil from my handbag. I would put to paper my mental lists of suspects and clues.

"My money's on that Carter chap." Clifford waved his fork, which was laden with some unidentifiable meat. "He hates the French, has a reputation for violence, and was seen arguing with Lorrain." He popped the bit of meat into his mouth. "He's our man."

"I concur."

Clifford gave me an incredulous smile. It wasn't often I agreed with him.

"At least, he is on the top of my list of suspects." I wrote his name on my pad of paper. "Right up there with the mysterious HG at GAI."

"Speak of the devil," Kitty whispered over the lip of her coffee cup. With her eyes, she indicated the table to our left under the shade of a palm frond.

I glanced over.

Mr. Carter was joining Lord Carnarvon and his daughter Evelyn at their table. Lady Evelyn's face brightened and Mr. Carter's reddened as they exchanged greetings.

I strained my ears to hear their conversation.

"Rum do about that French archeologist chap," Lord Carnarvon said, sipping a beverage from a V-shaped glass.

"Lorrain was a hack and thief." Mr. Carter snapped his napkin open and laid it on his lap.

Crikey. The man didn't mince words. Were they talking about Jean-Baptiste's rudeness at the party? Or had they already heard about the murder?

The rest of their animated luncheon conversation was Mr. Carter explaining a crazy-sounding theory that some twelve-year-old king had moved his entire family—mummies and all—across the desert to Giza.

A twelve-year-old king? Ridiculous. Then again, Mary Queen of Scots ascended to the throne at only six days old.

I was chomping at the bit to interview Mr. Carter and his party. How to approach them? I patted my pocket, eager to try out my credentials. Without credentials, why would they tell me, Fiona Figg, glorified file clerk, anything?

Steeling my nerves to try my scheme, I only half listened to Clifford nattering on about a fox hunt at the Gezira Sporting Club later today.

He had ordered a pudding course called *kunafa* that looked like melted cheese with crispy hairs on top. He insisted I try it. Reluctantly, I took a bite. Oh, my. Absolutely scrummy. I knew what I was having for breakfast tomorrow.

Kitty was sampling every pudding course on the menu. It was a wonder the girl's teeth didn't fall out from so much sugar.

Lord Carnarvon waved to the waiter and asked for the bill.

Horsefeathers. I had to make my move immediately before they left the terrace.

"Excuse me." I laid my napkin on the table and stood up. "I'm just going to pay my respects."

Clifford gaped at me.

Mouth full of sweets, Kitty just nodded.

Nonchalantly, I slipped over to Lord Carnarvon's table. "Good day, my lord."

He glanced up at me with a disconcerted lack of recognition.

"Miss Fiona Figg." I bowed my head slightly. "I was at Lady Enid's fancy-dress ball. I was in costume, so you probably—"

"Miss Figg, of course." He stood to greet me. "Have you met my daughter, Evelyn? And this is my man, Carter, Howard Carter."

I smiled sweetly as I scrutinized Mr. Carter's countenance for any signs of homicidal tendencies.

Mr. Carter stood. But instead of greeting me, or even acknowledging my presence, he threw his napkin on the table. "Excuse me. I've got to get back to the dig."

"Before you go, might I ask—"

He'd already turned to go.

When I touched his arm, he flinched and gave me a queer look like I'd just smeared jam on his finest white shirt.

"Where did you go last night after the ball?" Best get right to the point with this man.

Mr. Carter's brow furrowed. He glanced over at Evelyn. "Why is that any of your business?"

The moment I'd been waiting for. I whipped out an embossed card from my skirt pocket. Last time I was in London, I'd had cards printed, very official-looking cards, with my name and title. *Fiona Figg, British Intelligence.* Alright. Not exactly my title. Still, I hoped it worked. I flashed the card at him. "You and Monsieur Lorrain had a terrible row last night and now—"

"Now he's dead." Mr. Carter jammed his hat onto his head.

"How do you know that?" I put my hands on my hips for emphasis. "Unless, of course, you're the—"

Lord Carnarvon waved me away. "Frigo was moping about the lobby just before we came in." He sighed. "Poor chap."

"What?" Carter exploded. "You think *I* killed him? Are you insane?"

I decided I'd better let him simmer down.

"Lady Evelyn, how about you? Where did you go after the ball?" I paid close attention to subtle changes in Mr. Carter's expression.

"My daughter and I both went straight to bed," Lord Carnarvon answered. "Why are you asking us these questions, Miss, Miss..." He was obviously flustered. *Curious.* Did he have something to hide, too?

Lady Evelyn stared down at her plate.

"Mr. Carter, did you also go straight to bed?" I made sure to stand right in front of him so he couldn't escape without knocking me over.

"If you must know, I had a drink in the hotel bar." He took one step closer. So close, I could feel his breath on my face.

"Alone?"

He glanced at Lady Evelyn again.

What was going on between them? Were they together at the bar?

"With Miss Al-Madie, not that it's any of your business." He pushed me aside. "Now if you'll excuse me, I really must get back to the dig."

"May I be excused, too?" Lady Evelyn said, still not looking up from her plate.

"Well, yes, of course, certainly..." Lord Carnarvon sputtered. "I'll come to your room when I'm finished here." He waved for the waiter again.

If they had separate rooms, how did he know his daughter had gone straight to bed? She was acting awfully strangely for an innocent girl.

Lady Evelyn ran after Mr. Carter. There was definitely something going on between those two. She was only seventeen and he was at least forty. Could it be romance or something even more sinister?

As Lord Carnarvon signed for his lunch, I asked about Miss Al-Madie.

He ignored the question and politely bid me good day.

When I returned to our table, Clifford and Kitty were playing the childish game, "I spy with my little eye."

"The letter R," Clifford said.

"Rattan chair," Kitty said.

"No."

"Red poppies." Kitty pointed at the vase of flowers in the center of the table.

"Jolly good."

"Sorry to interrupt your game, but do either of you know a Miss Al-Madie?" I sat down and then picked up my teacup but thought better of it. Even on a hot day, I couldn't take tepid tea.

"Miss Mori Al-Madie." Kitty pushed a half-eaten cube of pastry around her plate. "Jean-Baptiste's *friend*. You couldn't have missed her at the ball."

Aha! "Cleopatra."

Kitty nodded. "Half-dressed Cleopatra."

"You know, I once read Cleopatra stuck pins in her slave girls for amusement," Clifford said, and then quickly added, "appalling."

"You're lucky Miss Mori Al-Madie didn't stick pins

in you, Kitty, the way you were flirting with Monsieur Lorrain."

"I wasn't flirting." Kitty blushed. "I was investigating."

"Investigating what?" I fiddled with the handle of my teacup, wishing I had a fresh cuppa.

"Our missing agent, Lieutenant Dankworth, of course." She laid her fork on the table, took up her napkin, and dabbed at her mouth.

"Did you happen to learn the whereabouts of Agent Dankworth?" I stared her down.

"No." Her cheeks turned a deeper shade of red. "Jean-Baptiste got tired of talking and wanted to, er, do other things."

Just as I suspected. The girl was using our espionage work as a cover to flirt.

"We need to find this Miss Al-Madie." I pushed my cup into the center of the table. "She may be the key."

"Key to what?" Clifford said.

"Our investigation into Jean-Baptiste's murder, of course. She is Mr. Carter's alibi." I stood up. "Let's ask the concierge." The staff had been helpful before.

"We can find her at the Isis Theater rehearsing for tonight's performance." Kitty laid her napkin on the table.

"How do you know that?" I wound the drawstrings of my bag around my wrist.

"She was bragging about it at the party." Kitty shrugged.

The Isis Theater. It must be the most famous theater in Cairo. La Sultana also performed there. Luckily, we could catch the Thursday show tonight.

Clifford jumped up to pull out the girl's chair. "She's an actress?"

"Perhaps last night's performance at the ball was just an act." I squinted at my friends. "She was playing the part of the jealous lover."

"She was pretty convincing." Kitty laughed. "I thought I might have to take her on in the back alley."

"Really, Kitty." I'd hate to see the poor woman—or man—who tangled with Kitty in a dark alley. For all I knew, she was a trained assassin.

Boarding school in France, poppycock.

8

THE PERFORMANCE

The Isis Theater was only a few streets from our hotel. The stone building had fat columns on either side of an arched entrance shaded by a bright red awning.

Inside, the theater was windowless and dark with heavy curtains across a wooden stage and curved rows of seats ready for this evening's performance. The domed ceiling was painted with a pastoral scene of a garden. The burgundy velvet seats showed signs of wear but were no less stately for it.

On stage, a large posterboard with Miss Al-Madie's picture advertised the play. *Romeo and Juliet, An Opera.* I made my way up the aisle for a closer look. With her dark, brooding eyes, she was beautiful. Below her image were the words *Soltanet El-Tarab*, the Sultana.

My word. Mori Al-Madie was La Sultana. And she was the woman I'd seen at the market buying a French army uniform. Cleopatra. La Sultana. And the Egyptian officer. If I was right, she was all three, which meant she was involved with the Suez Canal plot.

I glanced around the theater. Other than a berobed Egyptian sweeping the floor, the place was deserted.

"Excuse me, sir," I called out to the caretaker, who was just above me on the edge of the stage.

He jumped, clearly startled.

"Apologies, sir." I approached the stage. "Where might we find Miss Mori Al-Madie?"

He gave me a quizzical look.

I repeated my question in French.

He narrowed his brows.

Clifford gave it a try, asking the exact same question I had and in much worse French than mine.

"Miss Al-Madie, the owner?" The caretaker smiled. "The owner?"

The caretaker ignored me. "Rehearsal ended a little while ago, but she might still be in her dressing room." He pointed to a door off to the left of the stage. "Through there, sir."

How annoying. The blooming man answered Clifford, but he wouldn't answer me. I'd learned from experience that mustache and trousers opened many doors closed to corsets and skirts—although sometimes skirts had advantages too. If novelist Robert Hichens was to be believed, the real secrets of Egypt lay behind the closed harem doors, accessible only to women and eunuchs. Hopefully, I had brought the right disguise for any door that might need opening. Then again, after too many nocturnal visits, Hichens's protagonist went insane and smashed his head against the Great Sphinx. *Writers. What crazy imaginations.*

Backstage, the smell of lingering jasmine perfume mixed with a dry sawdust scent. Overhead, a network of cables, ropes, and catwalks supported hanging set-piece walls, and stage lights. I wished I had my new American torch. The dark hallway was like a catacomb, except with chairs stacked on either side instead of bones.

Which dressing room was hers? I scanned the doors as we passed, looking for signs. The third door on the left had a nameplate. Mori Al-Madie. No surprise. She was the star of the show, La Sultana, the owner of the theater. A woman owning a theater—you wouldn't see that in London.

Voices came from behind her dressing room door. Even if I could make out what they were saying, it wouldn't do me any good since they were speaking in

Arabic. Miss Al-Madie raised her voice in a heated conversation with a man.

Before I could ask Clifford to listen too, not that his Arabic was any better than mine, a loud crash sent me knocking at the door. "Miss Al-Madie? Are you alright?"

"Just a minute." Her voice was tense.

Was she moving furniture in there? I knocked again.

Hushed voices came from inside. More furniture moving. Then silence.

A woman on the other side of the door cleared her throat and then the door opened. A lit cigarette in her hand, Mori Al-Madie stood before me wearing a silk robe. Her bronze skin was glowing and her dark eyes reminded me of lush orchid petals. She was even more beautiful without make-up and in person than on the posterboards for the play. "Can I help you?" she said in slightly accented English as she blew out a cloud of smoke.

I tried looking over her shoulder into the room, but she pulled the door in close, narrowing my line of sight. Through the sliver between frame and door, I could see a dressing table with a large mirror. Reflected in the mirror were Miss Al-Madie's backside, my own plain visage, and two other figures huddling next to her behind the door. Although I could only see the reflection of his back, one was a man in flowing robes and red fez with tall black boots, which looked strikingly like the mystery man from the railway. The other figure, another man, wore a gray fedora and long trench coat.

Why were there two men in La Sultana's dressing room? Obviously, she didn't want us to see them.

"I'm Fiona Figg and these are my colleagues, Captain Douglas and Miss Lane." I gestured toward Clifford and Kitty, who were so close behind me that they nearly shoved me across the threshold.

"I'm rather busy now." Miss Al-Madie's reflection in the mirror glanced at the robed man next to her.

Unfortunately, I still could only see the reflection of the berobed man's back. But I would bet it was my mystery man from the railway.

"Just one question, if you please." I put my hand on the door and caught it as she tried to close it. "Did you have a drink with Mr. Carter last night after Lady Enid's ball?" I stood on my tiptoes to get a better view into her dressing room. She closed the door so that only her head was sticking out.

She scowled. "Why do you care?"

"On behalf of the British government, we're investigating the murder of Jean-Baptiste Lorrain." Even as the lie stuck in my throat, I whipped out my credentials. "You're Mr. Carter's alibi for Monsieur Lorrain's... demise."

"What?" Miss Al-Madie's cheeks paled. "Why would Carter kill Jean-Baptiste?" Her lip trembled. "Please go away." Her voice cracked and then she broke down. Between sobs, she managed to spit out a few more words. "He warned me you'd come sniffing around." She slammed the door in my face. "Go away!"

Her jasmine perfume, along with a faint undercurrent of crushed pine, lingered in the hallway.

"What was all that about?" Clifford said, pipe in hand. "The poor thing was hysterical." He was a sucker for tears. I was surprised he didn't fall to one knee and propose on the spot.

"Mori didn't confirm Carter's alibi." Kitty raised her eyebrows.

"Indeed." I studied the layout backstage in preparation for my visit tonight. "And who warned her we'd come sniffing around? Poor Monsieur Lorrain? Or the guiltier-by-the-minute Mr. Carter?" Or my mystery man? Whoever he was. And what of the man in the fedora?

With the actress and the mystery man in cahoots, I was more convinced than ever that the murder of the Frenchman was connected to the plot to blow up the canal, not to mention our missing agent. The three were connected. The missing agent. The dead Frenchman. And my mystery man. I just had to prove it.

If I solved Monsieur Lorrain's murder, then I would discover the identity of the mystery man and find Agent Dankworth. And then, Captain Hall would have to give me a promotion. I smiled to myself.

* * *

Later that night, as instructed by Captain Hall, I returned to the Isis Theater to meet the undercover British agent, Mr. Relish, backstage after the opera. Clifford and Kitty accompanied me to the performance, where, thanks to Clifford's affability and charm, we had front-row seats. He'd somehow cajoled the concierge into finding us the best seats in an already sold-out house.

Clifford could talk a donkey into giving up its tail.

I'd seen the opera with Andrew in the West End shortly after we were married, back when I'd considered him my own sweet Romeo. Turned out to be truer than I could have imagined. Like Juliet's Romeo, he died in my arms.

The theater was packed with soldiers and the few

nurses they could round up as dates. When the lights went down, palpable electricity filled the air.

The curtain opened and a chorus sang about the endless feud between the Montagues and the Capulets. I'd forgotten the opera was French. Lucky for me, I could follow along.

It wasn't until the end of Act One that I realized the women's parts were played by boys and men. Weren't women allowed on stage? What of Mori Al-Madie? I thought she was the star of the show.

The duet in Act Two was enchanting. Only lovers aren't afraid of the dark. Only lovers worship the night and dread the dawn. Only lovers could prefer the nightingale to the lark. Beautiful.

A tear rolled down my cheek.

At intermission, applause shook the floor. Soldiers whistled and cheered. When the lights went up, they hurried from their seats to the bar.

With torrents of men storming past me, I pushed myself as far back in my seat as possible and tucked my legs under to avoid my toes being trampled. After the herd had passed, I opened the program and read about the actors, not that I would know any of them.

Good heavens. The fabulous tenor playing Romeo was none other than Miss Mori Al-Madie. What a delightful surprise. La Sultana was a veritable chameleon. For the rest of the intermission, I read the libretto, which was printed in full in the program.

The lights dimmed and the curtain opened. By the time poor Romeo found his beloved dead in the tomb, the theater was dripping with pathos. La Sultana shone as the tortured lover. My, how I envied her mustache and beard.

Romeo's final aria made me misty again.

"Console yourself, poor soul. The dream was too beautiful."

La Sultana had a heavenly voice, a perfect voice. No wonder she was the star.

Wait. Was I hearing things?

She sang the refrain out of order and then repeated, "Love, heavenly flame." Why was she suddenly mucking it up? Had the poor woman forgotten her lines? Was she tired? Or was she so shaken up by the death of Jean-Baptiste that she couldn't perform? Of course, that had to be it. She was probably thinking of her own tragic Romeo found dead in a crypt.

I thought of her conspiring with the stranger from the railway. There could be another reason she was messing up the scene. She was working with the Germans and her mistakes were intentional signals. The notion seemed a bit far-fetched, even for me. But if my experience as a spy had taught me anything, it was that no one was what they seemed.

I glanced around. The soldiers held the hands of their evening's sweethearts. And those who didn't have dates consoled themselves with beer. No one seemed to notice the tenor was stumbling and repeating herself. It was opera, after all... and in French, no less.

During the standing ovation, I made my way backstage with Clifford and Kitty in tow. A committee meeting backstage was bound to draw attention. I made an executive decision to divert my colleagues while I found Agent Relish.

"Clifford, dear." I patted his arm. "Why don't you do some detective work and ask around to find out more about Miss Al-Madie's relationship with Monsieur Lorrain?"

Clifford beamed. "Not a bad idea, old girl." He couldn't resist playing detective.

"A jolly good idea." I returned his smile.

He got to work immediately. "I say, might you help a chap..." Speaking in decent French, Clifford stopped one of the cast members. His first victim, er, interviewee, was a member of the chorus who'd just come around the corner from the stage. The lad was only too happy to chat with the winning captain. Clifford's talent for talking to anyone about anything came in handy for disarming suspects and loosening lips.

With Clifford out of the way, I skirted a sandbag attached to the curtain ropes. Glancing up, I thought of a task involving the catwalk for Kitty. Her frills and lace never stopped her from derring-do.

I was just about to give Kitty her marching orders, when out of the corner of my eye, I spotted Mori Al-Madie dashing toward the theater's back exit. "Follow her." I pointed at Romeo fleeing the scene. "She's up to something."

"On it." Like a comet, Kitty soared after the starlet.

I was tempted to run after them—I hated to miss the adventure—but I had to meet Agent Relish.

Where in blazes is he? Several stagehands buzzed around backstage, but none of them had black hair and a crumb catcher to match. Bad enough Agent Dankworth was missing. We didn't need another missing agent.

"Miss Fiona Figg?"

My heart leaped and I swung around. Talk about mustaches! You could sweep the floor with Agent Relish's spectacular crumb catcher. The matching hair was hidden under a newsboy cap. "Agent Relish?" I held out my hand.

"Discretion, Miss Figg," he whispered as he glanced over my shoulder.

I nodded and withdrew my hand.

Rather than look at me, he tended to a rope hanging from a wooden beam. "The owner of the Isis is working with the Germans," he said to the beam. "Somehow she's getting information out. We need to find out how."

"Mustard!" I heard the booming voice before I saw the large man to whom it belonged.

Agent Relish's alias is Mustard? Who was Agent Dankworth? Pork pie?

"Stop dawdling and get back to work," the man thundered down the hallway. "We want to get out of here sometime tonight."

"Yes, sir." Agent Relish wound the rope around an anchor attached to the beam. "Meet me in an hour at the entrance to the zoo behind your hotel."

"How do you know Miss Al-Madie is working with the Germans?"

He narrowed his brows. "I'll tell you tonight at the zoo. Now go." Agent Relish flashed a stern look and then climbed a ladder up onto a catwalk.

I'd have to wait to find out any more information. Hard to believe the beautiful and talented Mori Al-Madie was working with the Germans. Why would she do that? Why would she betray the British? We were protecting Egypt, after all.

Now where were my companions? No doubt Clifford was chatting up some poor cast member. I probably wouldn't see him again for hours. I exited through the back door of the theater in the hopes of finding Kitty.

The back alley was dark. The light of the full moon shone on figures struggling behind the theater. I moved closer to get a better look. A couple of uniformed Tommies had a young Egyptian woman pinned against the back wall. They were laughing. One of them had his hand over the woman's mouth while the other tore at her clothes.

"Unhand her at once!" I marched toward them.

One of the Tommies looked over at me. "Why? You want some action too, sweetheart?"

"You should be ashamed of yourselves." I stomped my foot. "Shoo!"

Both Tommies glared at me, but neither took his grubby mitts off the girl.

Obviously calling them to conscience wasn't enough. They needed more persuasion. I tugged Mata Hari's pearl-handled pistol out of my handbag. "If you won't listen to me, you'd better listen to my little friend." I waved the gun at them.

"We were just having a bit of fun."

"Move away from her." Holding the gun in both hands straight out in front of me, I took a step forward. "Now!"

Both jumped away from the girl.

"Get out of here before I report you to your superior." I waved the gun again. "Hop it!"

They took off running, laughing as they went. Scoundrels. I had half a mind to shoot.

Once they were out of sight, I dashed over to the young woman.

Her shoulders shook as she adjusted her blouse and then tucked her hair back under her hijab.

"Are you alright?" I dropped the gun back into my handbag and cinched up its strings.

Her lip trembled. "Please don't tell my father."

"You've done nothing wrong."

She averted my gaze. "Please don't tell anyone."

"As long as you're not hurt." I quickly looked her up and down. Luckily, I'd stopped them before they could... I shuddered to think. *Poor girl.*

I noticed a basket of clothes strewn along the alley. "Are those yours?"

"I'm in charge of the costumes." She glanced back at the theater. "Usually my brother is with me, but he's ill." *Aha. She's the costume girl.* If she weren't so traumatized, I'd try to get some information from her.

I slipped my handbag around my wrist and started to gather up the garments. "Are you sure you're alright?"

Plucking a stray Harlequin jacket, I noticed some words embroidered on its hem. Words in Arabic. Next, I picked up a silk chemise and examined its hem. More Arabic words. Were there codes in the costumes, too?

"Yes, miss." She nodded. "Thank you for saving me from those British."

I shook my head. *Protecting Egypt? Rubbish*. What proper Englishman—and Tommy to boot—behaved like that? Assaulting women? *Disgusting*.

"There you are, Aunt Fiona." Kitty had her arm around Romeo, aka Miss Al-Madie, and was guiding her back to the theater.

When the costume girl turned to face Kitty, I stuffed the chemise down the back of my gown.

"I'm going to get Mori a brandy." Kitty gave me a knowing look as she passed. Had she gotten some information out of the actress? Or had she seen me nick the garment?

The costume girl had taken the opportunity to grab her basket and steal away into the night.

I'd like to teach those rotten Tommies a lesson. They'd not only assaulted a young woman but also made yet another enemy. Like we needed any more.

I didn't get the chance to ask her about the words on the hem of the Harlequin jacket, but I had got the chemise.

Holding onto the back of my gown so the chemise wouldn't slip out, I trailed Kitty back into the theater. She led Miss Al-Madie to her dressing room. Still holding onto my backside, I held the door open for them and then followed them in. I glanced around in awe. I'd never been inside the dressing room of a famous actress.

An assortment of bouquets adorned the dressing table, along with make-up pots and brushes. A rack of costumes took up an entire wall in the small room. Aside from the wooden chair at the dressing table, the only other place to sit was a satin divan, which abutted the far wall.

I dropped onto the divan while Kitty helped Miss Al-Madie out of her costume. I took the opportunity to slip the chemise out of my gown and tuck it in my handbag. Good thing I didn't take the Harlequin jacket.

Judging by the dark smudges on her cheeks and her puffy eyes, La Sultana had been crying. Sitting at her dressing table, the actress had given herself over completely to Kitty's gentle care. Kitty was standing, fussing over Mori. It was as if the girl had put a spell on the actress.

At the risk of further upsetting her, I revisited the painful topic. "We want to find Jean-Baptiste's killer as much as you do."

She blanched as Kitty pulled pins from her hair.

"Why did you leave the theater?" I tried a different tack.

Kitty gave me a stern look. What had I done? I was just trying to ascertain why the starlet fled.

With moist eyes, Miss Al-Madie looked up at Kitty. "You tell Miss Figg what I told you." Her voice cracked. She picked up a silver cigarette case and a gold lighter from her dressing table.

"One of the stagehands, a new man, has been spying on her, peeking into her dressing room, and following her." Kitty took up a brush from the dressing table and ran it through Mori's raven locks. "A creepy fellow with black hair and a huge mustache."

Aha. Agent Relish. Of course he'd been following her. "Yes. I saw him too. You did the right thing, of course."

She'd misinterpreted the nature of his spying. Just as well. If she really was working with the Germans, and she found out Relish was onto her, his life would be in danger.

"Is that why you're meeting Mr. Carter again tonight?" A bit forward. But I needed to find out if his alibi for last night held. "To protect you from the stalker?"

"Howard?" Miss Al-Madie gave me a queer look. "Why in the world would I be meeting Howard Carter?" She tapped out a cigarette, put it to her lips, and lit it.

"Didn't you have a drink with him last night after the ball?"

"Heavens, no." She grabbed the brush out of Kitty's hand. "He's always asking." She ran the brush through her hair with punishing force. "And I'm always refusing." A strangled laugh gurgled up in her throat. "I'm too old for him anyway."

Odd. What did she mean by that? He was a good fifteen years older than she. Was she counting in dog years? Perhaps she meant her soul was too old for him. *Unless* she meant Mr. Carter's relationship with the even younger Lady Evelyn.

"You're referring to his liaison with the young Miss Carnarvon?" I took the opportunity to examine the costumes hanging from the rack. Sliding my hand down the velvety fabric of a gown, I lifted its hem. In

the dim light of the dressing room, I didn't see anything untoward.

The actress laughed. "How rude of me." She
snapped open the cigarette case. "Want a smoke?" She
held the case up for Kitty, who to my dismay took one.
Miss Al-Madie lit Kitty's and then her own. She held
the case out to me.

I shook my head. It was bad enough being in the
room with the foul smoke. I couldn't imagine intentionally inhaling the poison.

"I'm not the one you should be interrogating about
Howard." She took a big drag of her cigarette and then
blew a cloud my way. "Like I said. I'm too old for him."

And just like that, Howard Carter's alibi went up in
smoke.

9

THE MEETING

Pacing back and forth in front of the entrance to Shepheard's Zoo, I glanced at my watch. Agent Relish was late. He'd said to meet him here at midnight. Where was he?

My footfalls illuminated only by moonlight, I had to watch my step. The ground was uneven with patches of soft sand threatening to twist my ankle. In the darkness, the silhouettes of swaying palm trees menaced my thoughts like giant adversaries. A cool breeze sent shivers up my spine.

I checked my watch again. Not that it did much good. I could barely make out the hands. Anyway, only two minutes had passed since the last time I checked.

A cracking sound made me whirl around. The

noise had come from the direction of the back entrance to the hotel, which was several yards away.

While the hotel was brightly lit, the path from the back door to the zoo was dark. So, I couldn't see a thing.

I pricked up my ears and listened. Silence. Staring into the darkness, I hoped Agent Relish would come into view. No one. Nothing. If it wasn't Agent Relish, who was it?

I'd give him ten more minutes and then I was going back to the theater to track him down. I gave up pacing and leaned against the iron gate. Hurry up, man. I can't wait all night... especially with creepy noises emanating from the bushes.

Training my eyes on the path, I waited. Two more minutes and then I was getting out of here.

As my eyes further adjusted to the darkness, I spotted shadows moving along the path from the hotel. Not just one, but two. Finally. Was someone with him? How odd.

I started toward the path. The sound of a girl giggling stopped me.

As the voices drew near, I took cover behind a palm tree.

I recognized the man's voice. Mr. Howard Carter.

Where was he sneaking off to now... and with

whom? I listened. Was it Mori Al-Madie? Had the actress lied to us? Perhaps she was closer to Mr. Carter than she admitted.

I peeked around the tree trunk.

Oh, my word.

A few feet away, Mr. Carter was leading young Lady Evelyn Carnarvon up the path. I'd suspected there was something going on between them. *Disgraceful.* He was old enough to be her father. I had half a mind to jump out from behind the tree and whack him with my handbag.

Holding my breath, I waited until they passed. Then I followed them at a discreet distance. If Howard Carter killed the Frenchman, perhaps he'd done away with Agent Dankworth too.

The moonlit path was narrow. A twig cracked under my shoe. *Crikey.* I cringed and squeezed my eyes shut, hoping the couple up ahead hadn't heard. The loud chorus of insects made it impossible to hear what they were saying. Hopefully, it also made it impossible for them to hear me. All I could make out was Lady Evelyn's nonstop chatter.

Mr. Carter led the girl behind the zoo to the barn. Was he going to take the girl away from the hotel at this time of night? Through the desert in the dark? I shuddered to think.

Mr. Carter opened the creaking barn door. He and Lady Evelyn disappeared inside. Imagine the scandal if anyone found out. Lady Evelyn would be maligned in the society pages of every newspaper from Cairo to Chiswick.

I marched to the barn door. I was determined to find out what was going on. I sincerely hoped Lady Evelyn was not involved in murder or a plot against the British government.

Gasp! A hand on my shoulder made me jump nearly out of my skin. My hand flew to my heart, and I turned to face my accoster.

"Kitty, what are you doing here?" I hissed.

She grabbed my arm and pulled me away from the door.

Squinting, I followed her around the side of the barn. As I did, my shoes filled with sand, which made it deuced difficult to walk.

"What's going on?" I said once we were safely hidden from view.

"Mr. Carter and Miss Evelyn." Kitty's high-pitched voice exploded with excitement. She sounded like a teapot whistling. "They're up to something." Her eyes shone in the moonlight. "He lied about the night Jean-Baptiste was killed. And now he's sneaking off with Evelyn."

"Not cricket, to say the least." I reached down, removed one of my practical Oxfords, and dumped out sand. Wriggling my foot back in proved more challenging. "What on earth are you wearing?" I looked the girl up and down. With her blousy silk pajamas, she looked like she'd come straight out of a harem.

"Bloomers." She smiled and held out the fabric on either side of her poufy trousers.

The barn door creaked and out came Mr. Carter, leading a camel. He clicked his tongue, and with a groan the beast fell to its knees. He helped Lady Evelyn mount and then climbed on behind her. When he flicked a whip, the animal lurched forward and then took off at a walk. Lady Evelyn rode side-saddle in front of him, and Mr. Carter held the girl around the waist.

"Come on, Kitty. We have to follow them."

Without another word, Kitty bounded off around the barn.

I couldn't believe I was about to chase a camel across the desert. I shook my head. In the dark, no less.

A minute later, Kitty appeared, leading two donkeys. She pulled one of the creatures to my side. "Get on."

"Here goes nothing." I was as ready for adventure

as the next girl, but really? A midnight ride on a mangy donkey?

"Get on." She held out the donkey's lead-rope. As soon as I took it, Kitty jumped onto her own donkey's back and rode off into the night like an American cowgirl.

Confound it.

Headfirst, I threw myself over my donkey's back. I hoped to heaven the beast wouldn't take off with me hanging over its midsection.

What a smell! Warm and pungent. When I pulled my right leg up and over its rear end, I heard my bespoke evening gown with pockets rip. Not again. Another dress ruined. Espionage was deuced hard on the wardrobe.

Luckily, the War Office had allowed me to expense a lovely lavender number just before I left London. My last intact gown.

Even with the tear in my gown, I couldn't spread my legs wide enough to ride astride. And side-saddle was not an option as there was no saddle. I reached down, grabbed the fabric of my dress with both hands, and split it right up the middle. At least now I could extend my leg far enough to grip the creature's midsection with my thighs.

Next time I went for a midnight donkey ride, I'd

wear one of my pairs of men's trousers. Either that or get bloomers. Then again, it would take more than trousers or a split gown to make me as agile as Kitty.

I gently tapped the donkey with my heels. Nothing. I tried again. The blasted beast wouldn't budge. With a bit more force, much cajoling, and a considerable amount of braying, we finally took off. Bouncing up and down in the dark, I trusted the animal knew to follow his friend.

My senses were on high alert. Everything was sharper and more intense in the desert. The heat, the cold, the sounds, the smells. The night sky was so black it was blue.

By the time I caught up to Kitty almost an hour later, I could see Jean-Baptiste's excavation site up ahead. Breathless, I waved to her.

She stopped her donkey and waited for me. We continued together toward the dig.

Odd. There was a light coming from the entrance to the tomb. Why would Mr. Carter bring Lady Evelyn here? A horrible thought passed through my mind. Was he planning to dispose of her the same way he'd done with Jean-Baptiste? Or worse? As my mother would say, what of her womanly virtue? *Heaven forbid.*

In the moonlight, I saw the silhouettes of two camels near the tomb entrance. Two camels? Mr.

Carter and Lady Evelyn were on one animal. Were they meeting someone? Why the midnight rendezvous? And why at the scene of the murder?

Kitty slowed her donkey to a walk and mine followed suit. As we approached the tomb, she held her finger to her lips. She didn't have to convince me. My donkey was another story. With every step, the little fellow grunted as if I weighed a ton. I had been overdoing the toast and marmalade lately, but it would take more than extra toast at tea to make up for the wartime deprivation.

Near where the two camels were tied up, Kitty dismounted and gestured for me to do the same. Easier said than done. I held onto the donkey's neck, leaned into its torso, threw my right leg over its behind, and then slid until my feet touched the ground, which seemed to have moved even further away.

Muffled voices pierced the darkness. Men's voices.

I took a few steps toward the entrance to hear what they were saying. The sound carried on the night air, but not the diction. I couldn't even tell what language they were speaking. It didn't sound like English or Arabic.

On tiptoe, I crept up to the tomb. Kitty followed on my heels. Literally.

"Ouch." I stifled a pained gasp and turned around to glare at her. She shrugged an apology.

The voices stopped and were replaced by the sounds of movement. A man cried out. And then silence. Complete and utter silence. The silence of a tomb.

Mouths agape, Kitty and I looked at each other. *Now what?*

The girl took off running. As usual, acting before thinking. She disappeared inside the tomb.

Blasted girl. I had no choice but to follow. I was especially vexed because she was usually right.

The tomb was illuminated by two lanterns. One had tipped over and a tongue of flame flickered across the floor. Among the shadows, Kitty crouched near a large rag sack.

As I picked my way over to her, the dampness of the cave penetrated my clothes. It didn't help that I'd ripped my gown up to my waist. My legs broke out in goose bumps. I hugged myself and quickened my pace.

Good heavens. That was no sack. It was a man crumpled in a pile. *Oh, my word.* And next to him lay another man bleeding from the head. Where was Lady Evelyn? She couldn't have committed such a heinous crime, could she?

I stood behind Kitty and stared down at the two motionless forms.

In the lamplight, a torrent of reds and oranges fought for my attention. The blood soaking into the dirt. The matted black hair on the bashed-in head. The flames from the lantern.

It was him. Agent Relish. Now I knew why he hadn't shown up for our rendezvous. *Poor man.* Someone must have discovered he knew about the German agents at the Isis Theater. What if that someone had seen me talking to him? Was I next?

I bent down and felt his wrist for a pulse.

"He's still alive... barely." I moved to the pile of rags next to him.

Of course, it wasn't a pile of rags but a man face down in the dirt. Dare I turn him over?

"Is he... dead?" Kitty said. She had ripped off a piece of her blouse and was applying pressure to Agent Relish's wound.

I squatted next to the lifeless robe and carefully rolled him over.

Oh, my sainted aunt. It was the stranger from the railway carriage. My mystery man.

I reached for his arm to check his pulse. He grabbed my hand. I struggled out of his grasp, falling over on my bottom in the process. I scooted out of his reach. "He's alive," I gasped as I got to my feet and brushed off what was left of my evening gown.

The stranger groaned. "Help me." He opened his eyes and stared right through me.

"Who did this to you?" Kitty said, still pressing on Agent Relish's head with the ball of white fabric from her blouse... white fabric now soaked in red.

Whoever did it must still be in the tomb. Either that, or there was another entrance. I glanced around.

"Howard Carter," I whispered. *Who else could it be?* But where had he gone? And what about Lady Evelyn?

"Yes." The stranger tried to sit up but couldn't. He writhed and moaned. "Yes."

I had the uncanny sense of déjà vu. Maybe it was the familiar scent of rosewood. Perhaps the lingering smell of the attacker? I tried to memorize it in case I needed to use my nose to sniff out an assailant.

"Lie still." I used a whispered version of the commanding nurse's voice I'd practiced so often at Charing Cross Hospital.

So, it was Howard Carter. He'd attacked these men, rendering them both unconscious. Had Evelyn helped? I spotted a large bloody rock next to Agent Relish. No doubt the weapon. I glanced around. Were they still here? Would Mr. Carter dare attack us too?

Agent Relish groaned.

I didn't have to rely on my experience with triage medicine to know Agent Relish was in much worse shape than the berobed stranger. The British agent needed medical care right away.

I tore off the bottom of my already shredded evening gown and went to assist Kitty. Balling up the fabric, I squatted next to her. "I'll stay here." Grimacing, I applied the wad of cloth to his bloody wound. "You go and get help." After all, I was a volunteer nurse and she rode like a cowgirl.

Kitty nodded. She stood up, dropped her bloody cloth, and pulled something from one of her little boots. "Just in case the attacker comes back." She held out a sheathed knife.

I blinked at her.

Did she always carry a knife in her boot?

She waved the knife at me.

"What am I supposed to do with that?" I opened my handbag and withdrew Mata Hari's gun. "Cut his steak?" I brandished the gun. "I'd rather a bit more distance between me and a killer, thank you very much."

Kitty winked at me and stuffed her knife back into her boot. "I'll do a quick search of the tomb before I go." She disappeared into the tomb. A few minutes later, she was back. "All clear. I'll be back as soon as I can." She sprinted from the tomb.

"Be careful," I called after her as I tucked the gun back into my handbag.

I held the cloth to Agent Relish's wound for what seemed like hours. My knees ached from squatting. With my free hand, I adjusted what was left of my gown and fell back on my bottom. My mother would have turned over in her grave had she witnessed such unladylike behavior. The war had made me a jolly unladylike lady.

The stranger had fallen back into unconsciousness and poor Agent Relish was fading fast. I only hoped Kitty returned with help in time to save him. I knew from my triage experience that the stranger would live, but Agent Relish would not. Not without medical attention and soon.

I pressed harder on his wound. His eyes fluttered open and filled with terror. His mouth moved but no sound came out. Was he trying to tell me something?

I leaned closer.

"Romeo," he gasped. His head lolled to the right at a strange angle. He was unconscious again.

Romeo?

Mori Al-Madie, the theater owner. Agent Relish had warned me the theater was a cover for German spies.

Was she in on it with Carter? Were they a team, after all?

And what of Lady Evelyn?

"Don't die on me, Relish," I commanded, pressing harder on his wound.

10

THE HOSPITAL

Waiting in a dim tomb with a dying man—and possibly many more long-dead ones—was unnerving, to say the least.

My hand was numb from pressing on Agent Relish's head wound. The cave was chilly, and my arms had goose bumps. The dirt-covered ground was deuced cold on my backside. I didn't know which was worse, the desert's brutal noonday sun or its biting night air.

I blew at the fringe of my wig. *Hurry up, Kitty. Hurry.*

A sound made me whip around. Was the attacker still here? I grabbed the gun from my handbag and pricked up my ears.

Silence.

Holding my breath, I waited.

If Mr. Carter had attacked these two poor souls, then either he was still here or there had to be another entrance to the tomb. Otherwise, he would have passed us on the way out. There were only two camels at the entrance, and they obviously belonged to the two injured men. Where was Mr. Carter's camel? The one he rode with Lady Evelyn?

I listened in the darkness. Stillness reassured me I was alone—except, of course, for the injured men.

Mr. Carter must have left his camel at another entrance, a back entrance, snuck into the tomb, and brained the two men. But why? And where was Lady Evelyn while this was going on? That lovely girl couldn't be a cold-blooded murderer, could she?

I thought of Kitty and the knife in her boot.

French boarding school, my cold behind.

I slipped Mata Hari's gun back into my handbag. When I did, I felt the silky chemise. Codes in costumes. Codes in opera. The Isis Theater was a den of spies. If I ever made it out of this tomb, I'd take the chemise to the Arab Bureau. Surely someone there could translate.

"You're a vision of loveliness."

I sucked in air. The voice startled me. "Excuse me?" I glanced over at the stranger, whose dark eyes were trained on me.

Under his thick accent, there was something familiar about his smooth voice. A full mustache and beard covered the lower half of his face. And his head was covered with a headdress, which was remarkably still in place after the attack.

"Have I died and gone to heaven?" He rolled over on his side to face me. "Are you an angel?"

Did Muslims believe in heaven and angels?

"You've been hit on the head." I shifted so I could apply pressure with my left hand to give the right one a break. "Stay still. Help is on its way." At least, I hoped so.

"My guardian angel." The stranger smiled and then closed his eyes again.

Even with his eyes closed, I had the eerie feeling he was watching me. I poked at him with a finger. He didn't move. I pinched him. Nothing. He was unconscious again. I took the opportunity to search his pockets. Who was this mysterious stranger? The man with the map.

In one pocket of his robe, I found a small card embossed with a panther. *Gosh.* Fredrick Fredricks's insignia. I knew it! This man was one of Fredricks's collaborators. I felt the blood drain from my face. I fell back on my heels.

I was right. Fredricks was at the heart of all of it. The Frenchman's murder. The British agent's disappearance. And the Suez Canal plot... *or lack thereof*. I was beginning to suspect the canal plot was just the bait to get me to Cairo. Why, I still didn't know. But I was getting closer to Fredricks. I could feel it.

I searched the stranger's other pocket and found a small photograph. A smiling woman on skis, surrounded by snow. She was wearing a heavy coat and woolen cap and holding ski poles. In the background, there was a lodge and huge mountains. She looked vaguely familiar.

The stranger groaned. Quickly, I stuffed the photograph in my pocket and moved away from him. Had I seen him with Fredricks somewhere? London? Paris? Vienna? New York? Was he Fredricks's secret partner? Or just his contact in Cairo?

The stranger reached up and grabbed at my gown.

I gasped and jerked away.

He fell back, losing consciousness again. Thank goodness.

What would I do if Kitty didn't make it back?

Surely she wouldn't leave me here. Eventually, Clifford would come looking for me. *Wouldn't he?*

A tiny wave of guilt passed through my mind as I prayed neither man would regain consciousness until help arrived. I reached down and felt for a pulse on Agent Relish's neck. He was still alive. *Thank heavens.*

Back at Charing Cross, I'd seen wounded soldiers bleed out before they got treatment. Without medical care, Agent Relish didn't have much longer to live.

Romeo. He'd said Romeo. That was what Relish was trying to tell me. Romeo. The code must be in the songs of La Sultana's Romeo. The words in the hems of the garments. That must be how the Germans communicated the codes to her and then she transmitted them to their operatives during her performance. Clever. Diabolically clever.

Agent Relish had discovered the code and so the Germans tried to dispose of him. The stranger must have got in the way. Or perhaps he knew too much and had to be killed.

Fredricks had lured me from New York to Cairo with enigmatic remarks about the Suez Canal. When I found Fredricks, he had a lot to answer for. And answer he would.

My sticky fingers distracted me from my brooding. Blood had soaked through the last piece of gown I'd torn off. If I ripped any more of my dress, I'd be left in my corset and knickers. The lantern flickered. If it went out, I'd be in the pitch dark, alone with two strange, incapacitated men. Hopefully incapacitated.

Where are you, Kitty? Hurry.

A commotion at the mouth of the tomb made my heart skip a beat.

Finally.

She'd done it! The girl had brought help.

As a bevy of nurses loaded the two men onto stretchers, the stranger reached out to me. "Please. Take my hand."

How could I not oblige an injured man? I held his hand as they carried him from the tomb and into a horse-drawn lorry waiting outside. As they lifted him into the back of the lorry, I withdrew my hand. At least, I tried to withdraw my hand.

The stranger held on tight and wouldn't let me go. I had no choice but to climb into the lorry and sit on a bench next to him. Thank goodness I didn't have to ride back on a donkey. Or worse yet, on a spitting camel.

Kitty had dragged Clifford out of bed. Worried about me, he tried to climb into the lorry. Good old Clifford.

I insisted he go with Kitty. "A girl on her own in the desert."

"Good lord." He ran his hand through his thinning hair. "You're right." Blurry-eyed, he agreed to help her get the donkeys and camels back to the hotel.

I waved to them from the back of the lorry.

Thirty minutes later, we arrived at a huge structure that covered over four solid blocks and looked like a cross between a hotel and a palace.

The Citadel Hospital was another grand Egyptian hotel requisitioned by the British. Inside, high ceilings, grand arches, carved cornices, and ornate wallpaper gave it a palatial air belied by rows of cots, medicine cupboards, and the occasional bedpan.

British nurses dressed in white attended to wounded prisoners from across the Allied world. Australians, Canadians, Americans, Indians, Egyptians, and, of course, our very own Tommies. To think how far these boys had come... and for what? To kill and be killed.

Despite the unfamiliar surroundings, the smells of ether mixed with body odors and the moans and groans of wounded soldiers were all too familiar. So too were the exhausted nurses run off their feet trying to comfort these poor fractured boys so far from their mothers, wives, or girlfriends.

Since the Allies had declared war on the Ottoman Empire, there was fighting all around Cairo and Egypt. But the Suez Canal had been, and continued to be, the enemy's main target. And while I suspected something was amiss about the stranger's map and the information I'd traced off the tablecloth, the canal was still a choice target and every threat had to be taken seriously, which was why I absolutely must find Fredricks.

Where had he disappeared to? It was unlike him not to flaunt his plans and then gloat. Perhaps he'd been wounded and was lying in a hospital somewhere. That was too much to hope.

Given my experience at Charing Cross Hospital, it was only right I lend a well-scrubbed hand. It would be nice to see my efforts rewarded with the easing of pain or a weak smile of appreciation. It was the least I could do to lighten the load of these poor boys. The thrill of travel and spying aside, espionage came with no such overt rewards. Everything we did was covert and in the shadows.

Once the stranger returned my hand to me, I dashed off to find the lavatory and quickly washed away the blood and dirt. If only I could wash away my worry and dread for Agent Relish.

The undercover agent had lost a lot of blood. Too much blood. Still, there was a chance he'd live if he got a blood transfusion. Some hospitals in England had blood deposits. If Citadel Hospital had a blood supply, we might be able to save Agent Relish.

On the far wall of the lavatory hung several nurses' aprons, smocks, and caps. I snagged a smock and apron off a hook, removed what was left of my gown, and wiggled into the smock and then tied the apron over it. I was half-tempted to drop my ragged dress in the dustbin on the way out the door. But then what would I wear to get home?

I stuffed my handbag into an apron pocket and headed for the ward.

Even if blood wasn't in short supply, doctors were. I dashed from room to room looking for a doctor. I passed a tall man in a fedora. "Excuse me, sir," I called after him. "Are you a doctor?"

He ignored me and quickened his pace. If he was a doctor, he was a bloody rude one.

I stopped a young nurse in the hallway.

"I'm looking for a doctor to perform a blood transfusion."

She squinted at me. Her thick kohl and button nose gave her a catlike appearance. With her coiffed hair and face painted, she looked ready for a night out on the town after her shift.

Did she understand English?

I tried French, adding that I worked for the War Office in London.

"Use your judgment." She shrugged.

"What do you mean?" I studied her demeanor. Either this young nurse was unflappable, hardened by too many gruesome encounters, or she was merely distracted by her plans for the evening.

"Our instructions." She stabbed a red fingernail into her palm for emphasis. "When you can't find a doctor, use your own judgment."

"Does it happen often you can't find a doctor?"

She scoffed. "For all intents and purposes, we are the doctors."

"Do you have a blood supply?" I'd seen doctors do transfusions, of course. But I'd never done one myself. I didn't relish the prospect. Around here, it seemed if you wanted it done, you had to do it yourself.

"We've had to ration blood." She started down the hall. "Follow me."

Together we gathered supplies, including a bottle of blood, a vial of morphine, a bottle of chloroform, and various other equipment we would need. We piled everything on a cart, and I wheeled it back to the room where Agent Relish and the stranger were sprawled out on cots.

Agent Relish was pale and barely breathing. I

quickly arranged everything on a table next to his bed: bandages, syringe, chloroform and gauze mask, a vial of morphine, and the bottle of blood. Thankfully, the young nurse agreed to assist me.

She ran to fetch a pole on which to hang the bottle while I went to wash my hands again. When I came back, the young nurse was shaving Agent Relish's head. His black hair fell in bunches onto the floor.

The gash in his head was deep. He needed stitches. Lots of them.

"Romeo." His voice was weak and hoarse. "Last act."

"Yes." I leaned closer to hear him. "What about the last act?" The coded messages must come in the last act.

His eyes went wide, he moaned, and then screamed out in agony. *Poor, poor man.*

I partially filled the syringe with morphine.

"Nurse!" the stranger in the next bed called out.

"In a minute." I knew Agent Relish was in worse shape than the stranger.

"Stop!" the stranger shouted.

I glanced over at him.

"Don't!" He nearly rolled off his cot. The poor man must be delirious.

"Please, sir." I tapped the syringe. "Be patient."

I administered one milligram of morphine to Agent Relish to take the edge off his pain. Then I gingerly cleaned the wound. While the nurse prepared the blood for transfusion, I took up a needle and medical thread to suture his wound. I'd done it before, but it never got any easier, holding a man's life in your hands.

After I'd finished, an otherworldly high-pitched sound emanated from his mouth and his eyes popped open again.

I jumped back.

His body rose and shook in violent convulsions and then he collapsed back onto the cot. Motionless now, his lifeless eyes stared up at the ceiling.

I put two fingers on his wrist searching for a pulse. Nothing.

I felt his neck. Nothing.

Holy Mother of God. No. No. No.

He was dead.

I dropped the needle on the floor. Tears sprang to my eyes.

The young nurse was busy attaching the bottle of blood to the pole.

"We won't be needing that." I wiped my eyes with the backs of my hands. I truly thought we could save him.

"What?" She looked down at the dead man. A cloud passed over her face. "Oh."

"I warned you." A few feet away, the stranger sat up in his cot. "It's not your fault."

I stared at him. Of course it wasn't my fault.

"You aren't to blame." He shook his head.

What did he mean? Of course I wasn't.

The nurse narrowed her brows. "How much morphine did you give him?"

I picked up the syringe. "Only one milligram." I'd purposedly given him the lowest possible dosage.

"Are you sure?" She came to my side and stared down at the glass syringe. "It holds ten times that much. Are you sure you didn't fill it?"

I confirmed that the label read morphine and that I'd given him the correct dosage. "See." I showed her the bottle.

"I tried to stop you," the stranger said.

Blast him. If he hadn't piped up again, the blooming nurse wouldn't be interrogating me. He was becoming a pest. I was half-tempted to refill the syringe and inject him with enough morphine to knock him out.

I picked up the vial of morphine. It was half empty. But hadn't it already been almost half empty? Still, something wasn't right.

I held the morphine vial to my nose and recoiled at the smell. Not the raspberry smell of morphine, but a sweet grassy smell. I glanced around the room. I hoped it was the verdant smell of some doctor's cologne.

I squeezed my eyes shut to quell the nausea.

11

ARCHEOLOGY LESSONS

Of course, I'd seen men die before. I'd even seen them die under my care. But I thought we'd got to him in time. I truly thought we could save Agent Relish.

Nurses bustled about. Volunteers carried supplies and bedpans. Out of the corner of my eye, I even thought I saw a doctor. But everything was happening as if in slow motion, as if I were in the eye of a storm. A great deadly storm.

"Nurse. Nurse. Help me!" The stranger's voice brought me back and time started to flow again.

Agent Relish had discovered something, and I was going to find out what.

The stranger moaned. "Ohhh, my head." He held his head in his hands and writhed.

The young nurse dashed over to him. "We need to remove your headdress, sir." As she unwound the cloth from his head, he batted at her hands. "Please, sir." She glanced over at me with pleading eyes.

Afraid to administer any more morphine, I grabbed the gauze mask, added a drop of chloroform, and headed for the cot.

I was about to clamp the mask on his mouth when the stranger grabbed my wrist.

"No need for that." His grip was firm, too firm for a dying man. And there was that fragrance again. Rosewood.

"Unhand me." I tried to pull out of his grasp.

"Not until you dispose of that gawd-awful mask," he said through his teeth.

I dropped the mask on the floor. He let go of my wrist. I reached down and ripped off the rest of his headdress.

I knew it!

Long black locks fell down around his broad shoulders.

He smiled up at me.

The mysterious stranger was none other than Fredrick Fredricks. He'd been literally right under my nose this whole time. I wanted to strangle him.

"Good to see you again, ma chérie." The scoundrel

was grinning from ear to ear. "I hope I get better treatment than your countryman." He rubbed his head.

"Fredrick Fredricks. I should have known." Without the headdress and the fake accent, I recognized him. How had I not known it was him all along? Was I completely daft?

"Is that a syringe in your hand or are you just happy to see me?" He grinned like a wolf.

If I had one, I would have plunged it into his heart.

No wonder I'd had a queer feeling about him since we met in the railway carriage. Now I knew why. Fredrick Fredricks, infamous South African huntsman turned German spy, who posed as an American journalist... and now was posing as an Egyptian nationalist.

I tightened my lips to prevent emitting a string of curses. *Blast him anyway.* And to think I'd danced with the blackguard at the ball.

"You don't look happy to see me." He pursed his lips in a disingenuous expression of concern.

"What just happened with Agent Relish?" I stomped my foot. "What do you know about the morphine?"

My mind raced as I recounted to myself everything I'd seen the stranger doing—the stranger who was actually Fredrick Fredricks. He'd dropped a map marking the mid-point of the Suez Canal. He'd met with the actress Mori Al-Madie, who had been dressed as an Egyptian army officer at the time. I'd seen him in the mirror in Mori's dressing room. Fredricks and Mori had been plotting together... the time and place I'd traced from the tablecloth. The time and place from a bombing attempt *last year*.

My head was spinning. *Romeo. Last act. The map. The canal.* What did it all mean? "Why did you bring me to Cairo? What is your scheme?" I fought back tears of rage. The bounder had used me most severely.

"I'm surprised you didn't recognize me earlier." Fredricks chuckled.

"Did you kill Jean-Baptiste?" I sharpened my gaze, hoping to cut through his insolence. "Where is Agent Dankworth?" I wasn't going to play coy with him. I was aware that he knew all the British agents in the field. Besides, Dankworth was missing. I wasn't exactly giving away his whereabouts.

"Have you forgotten I was attacked too?" He touched his head.

"Hold still." The young nurse cleaned his wound, which was just a mere scratch under his thick hair.

"Ouch!" He batted at the nurse's hands.

I hoped he was in terrible pain. He deserved it.

The nurse asked for the bandages, and I passed

them to her. Although Fredricks's wound didn't require bandages, let alone hospitalization.

If only someone could bandage my wounded pride. And bring back Agent Relish.

I should have recognized the bounder. It was all so obvious now. Tears stung my eyes.

Good grief. What would I tell Kitty and Clifford? My only consolation was that they hadn't recognized him either. The scoundrel was good, I'd give him that. A veritable master of disguise. If only I were so good.

"Only a matter of luck I wasn't killed." He pouted.

"Bad luck, if you ask me."

"He attacked from behind—"

"Howard Carter?"

He nodded.

"Why would Mr. Carter attack you and Agent Relish?" Fredricks already knew Relish was a British agent. The confounded man always seemed to know everything.

"We discovered stolen antiquities." Fredricks picked at some dirt under one of his fingernails.

Holding onto the handle of Mata Hari's gun through the fabric of my handbag with one hand, I offered him a scalpel in hopes he might cut off a finger.

"Stolen antiquities." I hadn't thought of that. Had Jean-Baptiste learned of Mr. Carter's criminal activities and that's why he was killed? Oh, dear. I should warn Lord Carnarvon about his daughter. Their foreman was a criminal and a murderer. And his daughter was involved in it all.

I had to get rid of this nurse so I could properly question Fredricks. "Would it be possible to bring Mr. Fredricks a glass of water?" I raised my eyebrows in hopes he'd play along.

"Yes, I am parched." He coughed. When he sat up, his robe slipped down around his shoulders, revealing his tanned chest. "But such a lovely young woman shouldn't be reduced to fetching water, unless it's on the stage." His mischievous eyes twinkled as he winked at her. Cheeky cad.

The nurse giggled and scampered off.

I shook my head. Why did women always fall under his spell? I, for one, would never succumb. Never. Not if he were the last man on earth. Exasperating man.

I took the opportunity of the nurse's absence to interrogate Fredricks. "Is Lady Evelyn involved with stolen antiquities?" *What will I tell her father if she is?* It would break his heart to find out his daughter was conspiring—and who knew what else—with his crooked foreman.

"Lady Evelyn?" Fredricks squinted at me.

"Lord Carnarvon's daughter." I lowered my voice. "Is she involved with Mr. Carter?"

"Why, Fiona, I didn't know you were such a gossip." His grin was infuriating.

"Why are you in Cairo?" I fingered Mata Hari's gun through the cloth of my handbag.

"Calm down and I'll tell you everything." His eyes danced. "Ma chérie. You're stunning when angry."

I exhaled. "Start talking."

"Persuasion is my strong suit, as you know." He winked at me. "I'm here to convince the Bedouins to turn against the British." His countenance turned serious. "Captain Lawrence and Miss Bell know as well as I do that your government will not make good on its promises." He looked genuinely pained. "It never does."

Propaganda. That was his strong suit. He was a con man.

"What about the Suez Canal?" I loosened the drawstrings on my handbag in case I needed the gun.

"What about it?" He fingered the bed sheet.

I wished he'd cover himself. His bare chest was bloody distracting.

"You lured me here with suggestive remarks about the canal." I reached down and pulled the sheet up to his chin.

He winked. "Suggestive remarks?"

"Just as the Suez Canal facilitates commerce between the Red Sea and the Mediterranean, you and I will facilitate peace." I quoted his letter by heart.

"We make better friends than enemies." He held out his hand. "Fiona, ma chérie. I know you want this war to end as much as I do."

"Not enough to kill in cold blood." I narrowed my eyes. "I don't go around poisoning countesses and assassinating double agents."

"Not even poor Agent Relish?" His lips turned downward in an exaggerated pout.

I was really starting to hate him. Wordlessly, I glared at him.

"A joke, a very bad joke." He reached for me. "You didn't murder him and neither did I." He wiggled his fingers at me. "Truce?"

"I don't make peace with assassins." I took a step backwards.

"What about your precious Lieutenant Archie Somersby?" He narrowed his brows. "You seem to make an exception for him."

"That's different—"

He cut me off. "How is it any different?" He sat up straighter. "He kills for his country, and I would kill for mine and so would you, if it came to that." His gaze pierced my soul. "So don't take the moral high ground with me."

"Why did you give me Archie's watch?" My voice trailed off. I couldn't stand to think of Archie as a killer. It wasn't true. Archie was nothing like Fredricks.

"Something to remember him by, ma chérie." He shrugged. "I'm sorry about your beloved lieutenant, but it couldn't be helped." He troubled the bed sheet.

"What did you do to him?" I stomped my foot.

"Shhh." He glanced around. "You'll disturb the patients."

The nurse returned with a glass of water.

Fredricks thanked her with the drama of a Shakespearean actor. In return, she fawned over him. *Sickening.* I could hardly watch the touching little scene between patient and nurse. The young nurse tucked the bed sheet around his shoulders and cooed at him.

"Shouldn't you see to the other patients?" Standing arms akimbo, I waited for her to go.

Reluctantly, she left Fredricks's bedside.

"What have you done to Archie?" My cheeks burned.

Fredricks's smile broadened. "Weren't you looking for Lady Evelyn?" He tilted his bandaged head toward the threshold.

I turned around to see what he was looking at.

Crikey.

Wearing a volunteer nurse's outfit and carrying a bedpan, Lady Evelyn Carnarvon entered the room. Her freckled cheeks glowed with good will and cheer. Most ladies wouldn't be caught dead carrying a bedpan. Riding camels in the middle of the night and then volunteering at the hospital at dawn, Lady Evelyn wasn't most ladies... or even most girls.

Screaming. Banging.

A commotion in the next ward sent all the nurses running. "Code red. Code red," one of the nurses yelled as she ran past.

My heart leaped into my throat as I went to the doorway to see what was happening. Another nurse ran past me. More screaming from the next ward. Another soldier wounded or dying. I would have gone to help, but I wasn't about to leave Fredricks. Not now.

I turned back. *Blast it all.*

Too late.

Fredricks was already gone. Obviously, his injury was as false as his heart.

Tears of exhaustion and frustration streamed down my face.

I dropped onto Fredricks's empty cot and put my head in my hands.

"Are you alright?"

A light touch on my shoulder made me look up.

It was Lady Evelyn. "Why, Miss Figg. What are you doing here?"

Choked by emotion, I couldn't answer.

"Let's get you a cup of tea, shall we?" Gently, she helped me up and led me to the break room. She sat me at a table. "Wait here." She went and put the kettle on. After a few minutes, she returned with a steaming cup of tea.

I took a sip.

"Better?"

I nodded.

"You drink your tea and I'll come back and check on you after my shift." She smiled. "Alright?"

I nodded again.

After she left, I followed her. Fredricks had got away from me. I wasn't making the same mistake with Lady Evelyn.

Thankfully, she made her rounds in the other wards of the hospital. I couldn't face watching the orderlies remove Agent Relish's body. So many men had fallen, carrying off corpses was a daily occurrence. Some hospital staff grew accustomed to it—they had to in order to keep going. I would never get used to watching young men die, and for what?

With love and care, Lady Evelyn changed soiled

bandages, fed soldiers their breakfast or helped them write letters home. The diminutive teenager with the bright smile and freckles enlivened even the most pitiful patient. After trailing her for half an hour, I was in awe. She had a calming joyful presence that permeated every room she entered.

By the time Lady Evelyn took a break, I was dead on my feet. After a night without sleep, I felt like an old lady of forty instead of twenty-five. Judging by Lady Evelyn's fresh face and lively spirit, the difference between seventeen and twenty-five was like that between a kitten and a sloth. Whereas she buzzed around tending to wounds—both physical and mental —it was all I could do to change a bandage or fetch a bedpan. Keeping up with her was no easy feat.

Finally, Lady Evelyn fetched her lunch from a locker and sat at a table in the break room. She picked up a magazine and nibbled on her butter sandwich.

My stomach growled, reminding me it had been hours since I'd eaten. I was so discombobulated from lack of sleep and last night's misadventures, I had no idea how much time had passed. I glanced at my watch. Almost noon. *Heavens.* No wonder I was hungry. But now was not the time to think of food. Not when a murderer was on the loose.

The break room was small but neat, with a kitchenette and two small tables. One wall had been converted into a bulletin board where the nurses pinned Christmas cards from home. On a counter beside the gas hob stood a kettle and all the trappings of tea. I filled the kettle with water from the nearby sink and then put it on the hob.

An ensemble of mismatched cups and mugs sat upside down next to the kettle. I turned over two cups that showed no obvious cracks or chips. From a box of Twinings black, I dumped a good amount of tea leaves in the pot. After pouring the boiling water into the pot, I waited a few minutes for the tea to brew, and then poured out two cups.

With cups in hand, I approached the table.

"Care for a cuppa?" I held out one of the teacups on its saucer.

"How delightful." Lady Evelyn took the cup and saucer. "I thought you'd left."

"May I join you?" I sat my cup and saucer on the table across from her.

"Of course." She gestured for me to pull up a chair.

"Before you think me too kind," I sat down, "I have an ulterior motive."

"An ulterior motive." Her green eyes danced, and a smile lit up her face. "Do tell."

"Late last night, I saw you leave the hotel on camelback with Mr. Carter." I took a sip of my tea and watched her reaction from over the rim of the cup.

Her upper lip trembled, and she looked as if she might cry. The change in her countenance was as sudden as an August storm. I'd upset the girl. Espionage was a cruel business.

"I know Mr. Carter lied about his whereabouts..." I softened my tone. "On the night of Jean-Baptiste Lorrain's murder." I didn't take my eyes off the girl.

"Oh, no." She flushed. "Not Carter. He's the best of the best."

The best of the best what? Liars? Murderers? Seducers of young women?

"What were you and Mr. Carter doing riding off into the desert last night?" I kept my voice strong but steady. "Did you stop at Monsieur Lorrain's dig?" I couldn't bring myself to ask if she'd joined Mr. Carter in attacking the two men in the tomb.

"No." She sat up very straight in her chair. "No. No. No."

"No what?" In my sleep-deprived state, the girl was starting to try my patience.

"No, we didn't stop at Monsieur Lorrain's dig." She fingered the magazine, bending one edge of the cover back and forth. "We went to my father's dig." She stared down at the table, still working on the magazine cover. "Carter is teaching me to be an archeologist." The corner fell off the magazine cover. "Please don't tell my father. He doesn't approve. Or I should say my mother doesn't approve and therefore my father won't let me."

"Why ever not?" I took a sip and looked at her over the edge of my cup. If Mr. Carter wasn't at the tomb, then who attacked Agent Relish and Fredricks?

"Proper young ladies don't dig in the dirt," she said in a mocking tone. "Papa wouldn't care if it weren't for Mama."

Ridiculous. Although I was not fond of dirt myself. "Young ladies can do anything young men can do." I tapped the table with my finger. "Anything worth doing."

"I know." She shook her head. "My mother doesn't realize it's the twentieth century."

"Still, a young woman should be careful." Women's equality was one thing. A woman's virtue was another. And riding off in the middle of the night unchaperoned. Really.

She pouted. "Even Papa says I'd make a crack archeologist." When talking about her papa, her countenance changed. The girl was absolutely in awe of him. "Papa says I'm a natural."

"Yes, well. Be that as it may..." As much as I'd have

liked to continue discussing the virtue of women's equality, I had a murder to solve. "Just to clarify, Mr. Carter was with you on the night of Jean-Baptiste's murder. And he was with you last night, too."

"Yes." She nodded. "Every night after Papa goes to bed, Carter takes me out to the dig and gives me a lesson."

"An archeology lesson?"

"Of course. What else?" She suppressed a smile.

I didn't dare say what else a man might teach a girl in the heat of the night. I had been married once, after all.

"Carter and I are friends." She sighed. "He takes me seriously and treats me like a person with a brain instead of just a pretty skirt or a child."

"I see." *What of Mr. Carter's stolen antiquities?* Obviously Lady Evelyn wasn't privy to that side of the man. "Have you ever seen Mr. Carter engage in suspicious behavior? Selling antiquities, perhaps?"

"Goodness, no!" Her cheeks darkened. "Carter is the most honest man I know. He believes the treasures of Egypt belong to the people of Egypt... and to all the world." She sounded smitten. "Carter insists these historical marvels cannot be owned by anyone."

I drained my cup. Should I believe Fredrick Fredricks or Lady Evelyn? I shook my head.

Fiona, don't be an idiot. Of course Fredricks is unreliable. He'd tricked me from beginning to end. Whatever was I thinking even entertaining his nonsense? Anyway, there was something about Lady Evelyn's sincerity and innocence that made me believe her. Her tenderness with the wounded soldiers. Her admiration for her father. The openness of her countenance. Yes. Lady Evelyn was telling the truth. I knew it in my gut.

If Carter had an alibi for Jean-Baptiste's murder and the attack on Agent Relish and Fredricks, then who was the culprit? And why did Fredricks claim it was Carter who hit him? *Come to think of it...* I'd asked Fredricks if his attacker was Howard Carter before he volunteered it. He only repeated what I'd said.

"Carter would never be involved in anything untoward." She pushed her tea away. "It's outrageous that you'd even suggest such a thing."

"What about your midnight trysts?" I raised my eyebrows. After all, any man who took a seventeen-year-old girl out alone after dark couldn't be a saint.

She pulled a diary from her bag. "I told you. He's teaching me archeology." Her indignant tone played up her refined accent. She snatched up the diary, opened it, and started reading. "November 15. Carter taught me how to use a trowel and brushes so as not to damage artifacts. November 18. Carter gave me a lesson on the Rosetta Stone, which is inscribed with three versions of a Memphis decree: ancient Greek, Demotic, and ancient Egyptian hieroglyphs. November 19. Carter brought me to—"

"Alright, alright." I held up my hand. "I get the point."

"If only my parents would allow me... then I wouldn't have to sneak out." She reached her pale hand out to me. "Please, you won't tell my father? Promise me."

"We'll see about that." I patted her hand. "After I corroborate your account with Mr. Carter."

"And if he corroborates, then you won't tell on me?" she pleaded, her eyes welling with tears.

What could I say? I nodded.

"Promise?" Her voice trembled.

Sigh. "Alright. I promise."

After several more reassurances that I wouldn't tell her father, Lady Evelyn went back to her volunteer work.

I was convinced she was telling the truth. Mr. Carter was neither a murderer nor a thief, even if his midnight archeology lessons were inappropriate.

I returned to Fredricks's empty cot. It was already occupied by another injured soldier. Fredricks had flown the coop. At least this time he hadn't tied me up and stolen my clothes like he had in Paris after he'd pretended to be paralyzed from the waist down for months on end, biding his time in a Parisian prison. He was a tricky devil.

I vowed then and there to put him back in prison if it killed me. Fredricks had bested me for the last time.

12

THE GAI

By the time I got back to Shepheard's, it was mid-afternoon. The room I shared with Kitty was empty. Two single beds were neatly made. My side of the room was spartan and tidy. Kitty's bed was a whirlwind of frocks, hats, boots, animal furs, and magazines mixed with Poppy's paraphernalia. They must have left in a hurry.

Who knew what the girl and her dog were getting up to? Maybe they were out gathering chemicals for some new forensic experiment.

I was almost tempted to tidy up her bed. *Almost.*

My stomach grumbled and my head hurt. I hadn't slept or eaten in eighteen hours. In the war between my head and my stomach, the need for sleep won out over the need for food. Resigned to my own limitations, I pulled the heavy satin curtains shut to block out the bright afternoon sun, stripped down to my knickers, and then crawled into bed. I fought back tears of exhaustion.

As my eyes adjusted to the dark, I stared up at a carving in the ceiling. The goddess Hathor with the face of a wise woman and the ears of a cow. I'd learned from my guidebook that Hathor was the goddess of fertility. Too late for me on that front...

* * *

I awoke to the smell of chopped liver. Poppy lay panting next to my pillow. Nothing like dog breath first thing in the morning. Was it morning? I had no idea how long I'd slept.

"Stop it." My attempts to shield my face from her wet tongue failed.

The little beast yipped with excitement when I sat up in bed.

"What is your dog doing on my bed?" It was bad enough having to share a hotel room with the little creature. But sharing my bed? *Outrageous.*

Reading the latest issue of *Vogue*, Kitty lounged fully clothed on her smartly made bed. As if she was preparing for a photography session herself, her frock was neatly arranged around her folded legs with only little pink slippers peeking out from the hem.

"She's making sure you're still alive." Kitty dropped the magazine on her nightstand. "You've been asleep since yesterday." She swung her feet around and sat on the edge of her bed.

I hadn't stayed in bed so long since my divorce from Andrew, when I cried in bed for a week. *What day is it?* Crocodile Lake. The canal.

"Good grief." I rubbed my eyes. "The canal. Is it alright?"

"Yes. it's fine." She came over and snatched Poppy up into her arms. "While you were sleeping, I interviewed Carter."

"Mr. Carter!" I sat up straighter. "What did he say?"

"I cornered him after dinner last night and asked about his late-night outing with Lady Evelyn." She gave me a sly smile. "Do you know what he said?" She stood next to my bed, staring down at me.

"He's training Evelyn to be an archeologist." I stretched and yawned. My stomach growled. I hoped I hadn't missed breakfast.

Kitty's smile faded. "How did you know?" She rubbed Poppy's furry chin.

Now it was my turn to flash a sly smile. "I questioned Lady Evelyn yesterday at the hospital."

Together, we confirmed that their stories matched. Lady Evelyn was telling the truth. And Mr. Carter had an alibi for both Jean-Baptiste's murder and the attack on Fredricks and Agent Relish.

Kitty flopped on her own bed and held Poppy up like a doll. "Do you know who the murderer is, Poppy-poo?"

I crawled out of bed and padded toward the lav. "I'll just have a wash."

"Hop it." Kitty sat up and then snapped her fingers. Poppy jumped down and sat to attention. "Or we'll miss breakfast."

Poppy barked. Obviously "breakfast" was one of the few words in her limited vocabulary.

"Righto." I grabbed a summer dress from the wardrobe. What a relief. The canal hadn't been blown up. Fredricks and his trickery. As I passed the dressing table, I snatched up my handbag and pulled out the purloined chemise, and then disappeared into the lav.

I'd found the lavatory to be a safe haven for the privacy needed to ponder. Except, of course, when certain young ladies tied me to the toilet.

With its ornately carved ceiling and a beautiful Moorish arch around the bathtub, our lav exuded luxury. The checkered tiles on the floor clashed with the mosaic wallpaper and created a disorienting, but not unpleasant, effect. Shepheard's was one of the first hotels in the world to have private lavatories. A fact I appreciated, given the time constraints on my ablutions this morning.

A small table near the sink was overflowing with Kitty's make-up and whatnots. My own necessities were relegated to one corner of the table, and even then were on the verge of being pushed off.

Splashing water on my face, I rehearsed my list of suspects.

If not Mr. Carter, then who?

Lady Enid? General Clayton? Mori Al-Madie? Frigo? Another archeologist?

Fredricks claimed they'd discovered Mr. Carter was dealing in stolen antiquities. Or did he? Come to think of it, I suggested Mr. Carter and he simply agreed.

Of course, he was lying! And yet... what if *someone* was dealing in stolen antiquities and Jean-Baptiste and Agent Relish were on to him? Or her?

For all I knew, Fredricks himself was involved in the illegal antiquities trade. I wouldn't put anything past him. But how would selling treasures help the

Germans? Fredricks's every move was designed to aid our enemies... even his flirting and preening.

Back at Ravenswick Abbey, he'd poisoned the Dowager Countess for turning against Germany and siding with Britain. In Paris, he'd poisoned Countess Pavlova for being a double agent. In Vienna, he'd conspired with Count Czernin to kill poor Elise, the royal nanny. And in New York, he'd connived to assist the suffragettes in hopes they'd win the vote and their pacificism would get America out of the war. Now he was in Cairo to persuade the Bedouins to turn against the British—or so he said.

He wasn't so much in love with Germany as he hated the British for what they'd done to his family during the Boer Wars in South Africa. I didn't blame him on that score. I shuddered to think. The British army had executed his entire family as he—only a boy at the time—watched from a nearby shed. Ghastly.

Of course, no one could prove any of it. Fredricks was always on the margins of these conspiracies, orchestrating from the sidelines, never getting his own hands dirty.

I stared at myself in the looking glass. Crikey, I looked a sight. The dark circles under my eyes and sallowness of my cheeks gave the impression of a ghoulish Harlequin. I needed a long soak in the tub followed by loads of face paint and a darn good wig.

I turned on the tap and then sat on the edge of the bathtub, examining the hem of the chemise.

"Hurry up," Kitty yelled from the other room.

"It's going to take a while to get presentable." I dabbed at my face with a hand towel.

"Vanity won't fill your stomach."

Poppy barked in agreement.

Sigh. I'd have to settle for the darn good wig.

Giving up on the bath, I pulled on my frock, pinched my cheeks, and adjusted my attitude. I'd have to face the day "as is."

Leash in hand, Kitty stood by the door, waiting for me. Poppy wagged and whirled.

"What do you make of this?" I held out the chemise.

Kitty fingered the hem. "Arabic."

I nodded.

"After breakfast, a stop at the Arab Bureau is in order." I stuffed the chemise back into my handbag, and then tugged on my favorite blonde bob.

* * *

Clifford was waiting for us in the breakfast room, which was packed with noisy soldiers and a few tourists. Below the din of the crowd, a quartet played Christmas songs.

Of course. I'd forgotten it was almost Christmas.

The natural light streaming through giant stained-glass windows, along with the music, made for a cheery scene. If only I had the energy to enjoy it.

Anyway, how could I enjoy Christmas when I still had a murder to solve, not to mention the death of a British agent, possibly at my own hand?

Agent Relish's last words came back to me. *Romeo. The last act.* I had to get to the next performance of *Romeo and Juliet.* The key was in the last act.

My stomach growled. The performance wasn't until eight o'clock tonight. I needed sustenance. Nothing like a nice strong cuppa to revive body and soul and fortify one's wits.

Among the diners, the adventurous nibbled on local delicacies and everyone else ate recreations of exactly what they enjoyed back home. A week ago, I would have counted myself among the latter. Now, I wondered if the stranger on the train—aka Fredricks —was right about the British. We try to impose our own image on everything around us, to the detriment of the world and our own imaginations.

"About time you gals showed up." Clifford beamed as the waiter delivered his full English.

I ordered toast with marmalade and tea with a side of *kunafa*. Kitty ordered sweet rice pudding. Pudding for breakfast. My mother would not have approved. But if this bloody war had taught me anything, it was to appreciate the sweetness of the moment.

"Sorry, old thing." Clifford tucked into his baked beans. "Don't want my breakfast to get cold." Scooping up a spoonful of eggs, he smiled. "You know, while you were sleeping it off, I went out to the Gezira Sporting Club. Marvelous place..."

Waiting for my toast, I pulled out my notebook. When I opened it, I was greeted with the notation "HG at GAI II," the abbreviation I'd found in Jean-Baptiste's journal. Decoding this cipher was another key to finding the murderer. So many clues, so few solutions.

Tuning out Clifford's prattle about blood sports at the precious hunting club, I studied the code. "HG at GAI II," I said more to myself than anyone else. *HG at GAI II.*

Who was HG? Who was Jean-Baptiste meeting? What—or where—was GAI? Eleven o'clock would put the meeting time after Jean-Baptiste had left the ball and before he was found dead in the tomb. If HG was someone's initials, then HG most likely was the last person to see him alive, and very possibly the person who had delivered the fatal blow.

The emptiness in my stomach made it hard to concentrate.

Finally, the waiter delivered my breakfast. As slow as black treacle, one by one, he laid out the teacups, the teapot, the toast, the pudding, the silverware, and a tiny pitcher of milk.

Come on, lad. I'm starving.

My mouth watered in anticipation.

In between bites of toast, I told Clifford and Kitty about my run-in with Fredricks at the hospital. "So, the mystery man on the railway was Fredricks all along." I broke off a bit of toast and held it out to Poppy, who gleefully wolfed it down.

"By Jove, I knew I recognized him." Clifford shook his head. "Why in god's name did he wear that ridiculous disguise? We're pals. We hunted together in the Serengeti." He chuckled. "I remember once when Fredricks chased a water buffalo all the way—"

"Yes, dear." I reached over and patted his arm. I had to stop him before he launched into one of his longwinded hunting stories. "Fredricks is not what he seems."

"We've known each other for ages—" Clifford pouted like a scolded child. "He's not such a bad sort."

"*You don't even know yourself,*" I said under my breath. What would it take to persuade Clifford that his pal, Fredrick Fredricks, *was* indeed a bad sort, a German spy, and a scoundrel?

"What about Carter?" Clifford had the good sense to change the subject. "Isn't he our chap? He nearly punched Jean-Baptiste at the ball."

"His alibi holds." I stirred milk into my tea. In my head, I sang along with "What Child is This," one of my favorites and a melody sure to stay with me all day. At least the music was soothing... that and the tea. *Ahhh.* I was feeling better already.

"You'll never believe it." Kitty's eyes danced. "He and Lady Evelyn—"

I reached under the table and pinched her leg.

"Ouch!" She glared at me. I'd promised Lady Evelyn to keep her secret. And once Clifford knew it, the entirety of Cairo, if not all of Egypt and Continental Europe, would know it too.

"Carter and Lady Evelyn?" Clifford rubbed his hands together. "She is a lovely girl."

Seventeen-year-old girl, to be exact. I changed the subject before he could dive headfirst into gossip. "Let's review our list of suspects." I flipped the page in my notebook. "Who shall we interview next?"

"I love a good intrigue as much as the next person,

but aren't we getting distracted from our mission?" Kitty poked at her rice pudding. "We're supposed to locate Fredricks and foil any plans to blow up the Suez Canal, remember?"

A nervous laugh escaped my lips. "Fredricks was having us on." Having me on, more like. "My hunch is that, disguised as the stranger, he purposely dropped the map, and left clues on the tablecloth, to throw us off the scent of his true plan."

"Which is?" Clifford used his knife to corral his last spoonful of beans.

"Uniting the Muslim world against the British." I gritted my teeth. "And turning our territories against us."

"Good lord." Clifford dropped his cutlery and stared at me. "You can't be serious, old bean."

"I believe Agent Relish was attacked because he discovered La Sultana's performances at the Isis Theater are coded messages." I slathered a second piece of toast with thick-cut marmalade. "We have to find out what he knew. We have to get back to the theater and break those codes." Poppy preferred her toast with butter, so I broke off a corner and buttered it.

If I was right, Fredricks had used the Suez Canal plot as a ruse to lure me to Cairo. The business about Crocodile Lake was old intel. I knew that from the file

I'd seen back at the War Office. Captain Hall had assured me the canal was safe. Why did I still have an uneasy feeling?

"We're not in the business of cannons and machine guns. We trade in information." Information that can stop cannons and machine guns. "We need those codes."

"I heard Relish died in hospital when some daft nurse gave him too much morphine." Clifford scraped the last of his scrambled eggs onto his fork.

My cheeks burned. "That daft nurse was me!"

"Blimey." The color drained from his face. "I had no idea, old thing. How did it—"

I sat my cup down a tad too hard and chipped the saucer. "It was an accident." That grassy smell came back to haunt me. I pushed my plate away. "All the more reason we need to get to the bottom of this." Two dead men, one a British agent. A theater full of secret codes, both German and Arabic. And Fredrick Fredricks conniving and scheming to overthrow the British Empire.

Sputtering, Clifford stared at me from across the table.

"What about Fredrick Fredricks?" Although she'd hardly eaten a bite, Kitty pushed her dish away too. "Could he be our man?"

The girl had read my mind. "He was attacked along with Agent Relish. Still, he could have killed Jean-Baptiste." I tossed my napkin onto the table. "But why? Unless the Frenchman was a double agent." I wrote Fredricks's name at the top of my list of suspects.

I might as well write his name at the top of every page of my notebook. Whatever the crime, he was always a suspect. "We need to locate the scoundrel and detain him." I felt sure the murders were connected to the code in La Sultana's performance. "Due diligence requires we interview the other suspects, all of whom are easier to find at the moment than that slippery eel, Fredricks."

I snapped my notebook shut. "Clifford, dear, why don't you interview General Clayton and find out what you can? After all, he did challenge Jean-Baptiste to a duel." I dabbed at my mouth with my napkin. "Kitty and I will pay a visit to Lady Enid. Then we will reconvene to compare notes before the performance tonight."

"Jolly good idea." Clifford threw his napkin onto the table. "I'll head for the Arab Bureau right now."

I could always count on Clifford's willingness to play Sherlock Holmes. While he tackled the gentleman, we could grill the lady.

"While you're at the Arab Bureau." I pulled the

chemise from my handbag. "Can you get Major Lawrence or Miss Bell to translate this script?"

Clifford sputtered and blushed. "Women's lingerie?"

I took out my notebook and pencil and transcribed from memory the other script I'd seen on the Harlequin jacket. Penning the Arabic letters was more like drawing than writing since I was clueless as to their meaning. They were so vivid in my mind's eye, I could trace their shapes perfectly. I ripped the page from my notebook. "This too."

Obviously still not recovered from touching silk lingerie, blank-faced, Clifford accepted the page.

"Surely you've seen women's underwear before?" I grinned.

He was, after all, a grown man well into his late thirties.

"I say, Fiona." His cheeks went as red as burnt ochre.

Suppressing my laughter, I patted his hand. "Off you go, old boy."

* * *

Half an hour later, Kitty and I arrived at Lady Enid's house. Like most British residents, General Clayton and Lady Enid lived near Azbakeya gardens. Their house was not as grand as our hotel, but not modest either.

A maid answered the door.

"British Intelligence." I flashed my credentials.

The maid led us through an arched foyer, and showed us into the parlor, which was decorated with colorful pillows and fabrics in Egyptian style—except for dried fruit and glass Christmas ornaments hanging from a potted palm. A thick Persian rug covered the center of the room. A festive garden scene was woven into the rug's orange background.

Orange and green fibers. I elbowed Kitty and whispered, "The rug."

As soon as the maid left the room, graceful as a swan, Kitty swooped to the carpet and back up again in one nimble movement. She plucked a few fibers from the rug and dropped them into the pocket of her frock.

When the maid returned with a tea tray, Kitty and I were installed in a charming sitting area near a fireplace. The nights were chilly, yes. But a fireplace in Cairo seemed a bit excessive.

The maid poured us each a cup of strong brew and then offered milk and sugar. I took a splash of milk and Kitty took three heaped spoons of sugar. Whether to calm the nerves or invigorate the mind, a nice cuppa was always welcome.

A few minutes later, Lady Enid appeared, wearing a khaki riding jacket, matching skirt, and her jaunty slouch hat. To my surprise, her outfit at the ball wasn't a costume but her normal attire. The entire ensemble hung off her like a flour sack, otherwise she could have been mistaken for a regular in the Royal Horse Artillery.

Unlike other ladies, her leathered face suggested she'd spent considerable time out in the sun without an umbrella.

Lady Enid didn't flinch when I asked her whereabouts after the ball. As if expecting the question, she recounted overseeing the staff cleanup and then going to bed shortly after midnight.

"Do you have any idea who might have killed Jean-Baptiste?" I sipped my tea, which was extraordinarily strong and bitter.

"No clue." She shrugged and smiled. She poured herself a cup of tea as if I'd asked the whereabouts of a missing hairpin.

"Does this mean anything to you?" I pulled out my notebook and showed her Jean-Baptiste's mysterious notation.

She took my notebook and studied it. "HG at GAI

II." She repeated the phrase over and over like a mantra. Her eyes lit up and she slapped the notebook against her knee. "I'll bet it means DAI, *Deutsches Archäologisches Institut*. It's a beautiful facility. Too bad it's still owned by the Germans."

I blinked at her.

"The German Archeology Institute. GAI." She passed the notebook back to me.

Aha! "Where might that be?" I took up my pen.

"You would have driven right past it. It's between your hotel and the Arab Bureau." She waved toward the east. "That handsome but boarded-up building."

Of course. I remembered passing it. I made a note. So, Jean-Baptiste had met someone at the German Archeology Institute the night before he died.

But who?

"Do you know anyone with the initials HG?" Kitty nibbled on a tea biscuit.

I held my breath, waiting for the answer.

Lady Enid thought for a minute and then shook her head. "I'm afraid not. You might ask my husband. He knows everyone."

I'd solved the second half of the code. I only hoped Clifford came back with the first. If anyone could drag it out of the general, it was good old unassuming Clifford.

13

THE HUNT

Back at the hotel, I took a table on the terrace to wait for Clifford while Kitty dashed up to the room to check on Poppy. Or perhaps to run another forensic test she'd learned at "boarding school" in France.

I ordered tea for myself, and for Kitty I ordered something called an *aseer asab*, a local concoction the color of pea soup, which she informed me was sugar cane juice.

A warm breeze carried the smells of the street below wafting up to the terrace. Pungent barnyard smells from passing horses and goats mixed with the aromas of spicy roasted meats and sweet treats from street vendors. The sounds of hawkers, carriages, and chatter reached the terrace too. A cacophony of smells and sounds as invigorating as the city of Cairo itself.

To think, back in London people were bundled up in heavy winter coats or sitting wrapped in shawls in front of their fireplaces. I smiled to myself. Hard to believe it was almost Christmas in the eternal summertime of Egyptian afternoons.

On the walkway below, travelers from the four corners of the earth passed by, enlivening the scene. Cairo was buzzing with life and Shepheard's Hotel was its beating heart, at least as far as my countrymen were concerned.

After several odd looks from waiters and tourists alike, I examined my clothing and adjusted my wig. I wasn't in disguise, so it couldn't be a mustache gone awry or beard dangling off my chin. Deuced unnerving. Was a woman alone such an unusual sight?

I was about to go check myself in a looking glass when Kitty arrived. Her cheeks flushed as she took a seat across from me. She laid her beaded cat bag on the table. Such an adorable bag. I really needed to ask where she got it.

The waiter delivered my tea and Kitty's disgusting green beverage. My floral china cup arrived on a matching saucer with a delicate biscuit accompanying it. The sugar juice came in a tall glass on a saucer with the same small biscuit.

"I'm truly sorry, Aunt Fiona." The girl looked distraught. "But Poppy's had another wee accident."

Wee accident was right. "I trust you cleaned it up before the hotel staff find it and charge the War Office for damages." I closed my eyes. *Sigh.* This must be what it was like to have a daughter.

"I say." Clifford appeared out of nowhere. Beads of perspiration had formed on his ample forehead. "Let me settle up and then you girls come along." He pulled a handkerchief from his breast pocket and wiped his face, which was beet red.

"What's going on?" I hadn't finished my tea—I'd barely started it—and I wasn't about to leave until I had. "Come along where?"

"I went to the Arab Bureau to find General Clayton." He sounded out of breath. "Who do you think I saw there?" He was panting. "Lawrence and Gertrude. They were arguing about some Bedouins they'd misplaced or some such." He sucked in air.

"Why don't you sit down and have a nice cuppa..." I patted the seat next to mine. "Before you burst a blood vessel."

"We don't have time." He sat down anyway.

"Why ever not?" I stared at him.

His usually sleepy blue eyes were on high alert. "That's what I'm trying to tell you—"

"Well, spit it out, man." If I didn't keep him on track, it would be teatime before we found out what he was nattering on about.

"I went to the bureau—"

"Then what?" Kitty smiled encouragingly.

"Gertrude told incredible stories about living in the desert for weeks." He smiled. "Can you imagine a woman alone in the desert?"

"Clifford, dear." I gave him a stern look.

"Right. Well. I asked after General Clayton, you see." He mopped his brow. "And Gertrude said she'd found him the morning after the ball sleeping in his office. Seems he and his wife had a huge row."

"He didn't go home after the ball?" *There goes General Clayton's alibi.*

"What were they fighting about?" Kitty nibbled on her biscuit.

"That's just it." Clifford's blue eyes danced. "Jean-Baptiste. And that's not all..." He flashed a sly smile. "Gertrude said his white shirt was splattered with red stains."

"Blood?" I nearly choked on my biscuit.

Clifford nodded, obviously pleased with himself.

"We'll find the general at the Gezira Sporting Club. But we need to hurry."

Good grief. "That dreadful place with the fox hunts and overheated English hounds?"

"Yes." Clifford's face lit up. "We've got to hop it if we're going to catch the start of the hunt." He glanced at his watch.

"You've got to be joking!"

"We're going on a hunt?" Kitty downed the dregs of her disgusting green drink. "Count me in."

Had the girl lost her mind? "We're going to the club to find the general. Not to engage in nasty blood sports," I huffed.

Before I knew it, talking a mile a minute, Clifford had bustled us out to a taxi. "Gezira Sporting Club, please. And hop it. We don't want to be late for the hunt."

The cab driver looked us over and shook his head. "No ladies allowed."

"You don't transport ladies?" I'd never heard anything so ridiculous in my life.

"The sporting club doesn't allow ladies on the hunt." The driver gave an apologetic shrug. "Ladies can attend tea parties and dances."

"Tea parties and dances." Arms akimbo, I stood on

the curb, wondering what to do next. "Blasted boys' club."

"Sorry, old girl." Clifford opened the back door to the taxi.

"Oh, no, you don't!" I stepped in front of him. "You aren't going without me—"

"What about me?" Kitty said. "I can shoot as well as any man."

I gave her an approving nod. "Without *us*."

"But, but, but..." Stammering, Clifford stepped away from the taxi. "No girls allowed, old thing."

"Don't you worry." I patted his arm. "Give us ten minutes to change and we'll be presentable to your hunting pals, *old thing*."

Slightly more than ten minutes later—and much giggling from Kitty—we had transformed into Rear Admiral Arbuthnot and Harold the helpful bellboy.

It would have been more exciting to try a new disguise but reusing two of my past personae was more economical. Shopping at Angel's Fancy Dress in London was not inexpensive. And the War Office refused to pay for my "getups," as Captain Hall called them.

Kitty's petite frame and fresh face made it difficult for her to pass as a man. But she made a very pretty boy. With some adjustment, Harold the helpful bellboy became Harold Arbuthnot, the rear admiral's younger brother.

Ahh. To think, I first kissed Archie dressed as Harold the helpful bellboy. Ever since, he'd teased me about my mustache. Again, I remembered his gold pocket watch. What had Fredricks done to Archie? Pickpocketed? Kidnapped? Or worse? My hands trembled as I applied my own mustache.

Pull yourself together, Fiona, old thing. You've got a murderer to catch and a German plot to foil.

I straightened my beard and admired my transformation in the looking glass. My strong chin and angular face made for a passable masculine visage. In my sailor whites, polished boots, and cap, I looked rather handsome, if I did say so myself.

Kitty's navy-blue suit with its short jacket and gold buttons looked a bit out of place. But we'd have to devise a believable backstory for her on the way to the club. I gave her a pencil mustache and tucked up her ringlets into a blonde pompadour wig.

Yes, we made a nice couple of chaps.

On the way out, I snagged Kitty's fox-fur stole off her bed and stuffed it into my satchel.

"Why are you taking that old thing?" She tried to grab it from me.

"You'll see, *old thing*."

* * *

The Gezira Sporting Club was only ten minutes from the hotel in an exclusive section of Cairo. During the taxi ride, I pumped Clifford for information about the Arabic text written into the hem of the chemise and Harlequin jacket.

"You did ask, didn't you?"

"Of course I did." His tone was indignant.

He was so wound up and distracted, I feared I'd never get it out of him. As usual, he launched into a longwinded story about Gertrude Bell and Major Lawrence, this time involving a portable bathtub brought into the middle of the Sinai desert.

"Clifford!" I had to get rather cross with him.

Finally, he spilled the beans. "Baron Max Von Oppenheim, rich German banker and amateur archeologist, is working with the Ottoman Empire to stir up anti-British sentiment among Muslims in our territories." He ran his hand through his thinning hair. "Including Egypt, India, and among the local Bedouins."

Fredricks. His mission was to agitate and persuade the Bedouins to turn against the British. Could he be involved with this Baron Max Von Oppenheim?

"What has this baron chap to do with the codes in

the garment hems?" I sincerely hoped this baron business was not another one of his digressions.

"Folks at the Arab Bureau call it the silk conspiracy." He smiled. "Now, thanks to you, they know where
to find the traitors."

Heavens. The costume girl was involved in an in-
ternational conspiracy. Hard to believe. For all I knew,
her brother was a Turkish pasha.

The pieces were falling into place, if somewhat
chaotically.

Now to find out why General Clayton had blood
on his shirt and didn't come home the night the
Frenchman died.

Entering the club was to enter another world. The
browns and tans of desert sand were replaced with
sprawling botanical gardens with fields of green grass,
acacias, jacarandas, and other colorful flowers.

Clifford told the gate attendant we were guests of
General Clayton, which worked as well as any secret
password. We stepped out of the taxi and into a horse-
drawn open carriage driven by an Egyptian, who could
work for the club members but wasn't allowed to be
one himself.

We passed a polo field where mounted cavalry
practiced maneuvers. On the tennis courts, soldiers

lined up for inspection. Even the sporting club had been taken over by the army.

"We have four polo grounds, two racetracks, thirteen tennis courts, cricket and croquet lawns, a golf course, and a tea pavilion." The driver smiled back at us. "And, of course, the hunting grounds."

Of course.

Sitting in the open carriage in the noonday sun wearing men's trousers, jacket, and a full beard was sweltering. How I longed for a light summer frock. Men's clothing might open doors, but the right women's clothing could provide much-needed ventilation. I wondered if bloomers were cooler. I just might have to get some.

Kitty squirmed in the carriage seat. She was sitting on her hands. No doubt to keep from clapping them together in delight. The girl was altogether too excitable, especially when dressed as a boy.

The grounds of the club were so enormous, it took us longer to cross them than it had to reach the club from our hotel. Finally, the driver dropped us off at a hunting lodge.

The lodge, a handsome stone building sporting the Union Flag, sat next to a man-made pond replete with ducks and swans. Men wearing dark woolen jackets, thick breeches, tall boots, and gloves gathered in front of the lodge. Several Egyptians dressed in British red coats led horses from a nearby stable. And a pack of hounds barked and wagged, eager to kill something.

Already mounted on a sleek bay mare, General Clayton was larking around with another member of the field. His black velvet hat bobbed as he laughed.

I nudged Clifford. "He's over there." I gestured with my head.

Clifford held the rein on my horse—a very pretty little black gelding—as I mounted. Thank goodness for trousers. Still, it took me a few tries to get my leg over the horse's rump.

You'd think in those dreamy summers on my grandparents' farm, I might have learned how to ride a horse... or bake a pie. Instead of riding or baking, I always had my nose in a book or the latest issue of *Strand Magazine* for the newest Sherlock Holmes story.

What I lacked in skill, I made up for in determination. I was going to ride in this hunt if it killed me.

Kitty hopped up onto her chestnut mare like a true cowgirl, er, cowboy.

Once mounted, Clifford led his horse over to join General Clayton. Kitty gave her horse a little kick and it followed them over.

"Come on, horse." I tapped lightly on the horse's

sides with my boots. "Go." The horse put its head down and munched on some grass. *Blasted creature.*

Clifford and Kitty had joined the general and were already laughing at his jokes.

My horse still hadn't moved, except one step sideways to get at a better clump of grass. I yanked on the reins, trying to pull its fat head up. And I thought donkeys were stubborn.

The hunt master blew the trumpet, and the hounds were off. After the staff in their red coats had departed on horseback, the members of the field followed.

When all the other horses had taken to the field, mine decided to jerk its head up and take off at a gallop to catch up. I held onto the saddle for dear life.

It was a wonder these single-minded British sportsmen could replicate an English forest in Cairo. The sandy ground, palm trees, and bright sun outside the club grounds seemed to jeer at their attempt. Like the ancient Egyptians whom I'd read about in my guidebooks, the sportsmen had managed to get sycamores and mulberry trees to grow an oasis in the desert.

Fredricks's words from the railway haunted me. "You English see yourselves reflected in a mirror of your own hubris." He had a point. Everywhere you turned in Cairo, the British were trying to turn the city into a replica of home. From toad-in-the-hole to hunting hounds.

To avoid getting whacked in the face with branches, I ducked as my horse raced under a sycamore tree. Up ahead, the hounds ran in a pack and barked an excited chorus.

Without letting go of the saddle, I reached into my satchel and pulled out Kitty's fox-fur stole. I launched it into the trees, hoping to throw the hounds off the scent of the fox they were chasing. *Poor thing.* Imagine getting ripped apart by hounds, even hounds suffering from heat stroke. *Gruesome.*

It wasn't long before the hounds slowed down and their tongues hung out of their mouths from the heat. After an hour of chase, the hunt master blew the horn indicating we were to break. By then, even the hounds were sorely in need of water and my bottom was sorely in need of liberation from this blasted saddle.

Shielding my eyes with my hand, I searched for Clifford, Kitty, and General Clayton. Distracted by the sound of the horn and the anticipation of getting off this blooming horse, I wasn't paying attention when the beast ran under another tree. A large branch swept me off onto the ground.

I heard an uncanny crack as I hit the ground. A

sharp pain shot up my arm. With the wind knocked out of me, I lay there, trying to catch my breath. Now it wasn't just my backside that hurt. My right arm was throbbing. Confound it. I hoped it wasn't broken, the damnable thing.

"Are you alright?" a familiar voice boomed somewhere above me.

The sun prevented me from seeing him, but I recognized him, nonetheless.

I shielded my eyes with my good hand. "Not you again!"

Fredricks dismounted. He let out a thunderous laugh.

"What's so funny?" Jolly inconsiderate to laugh at my misfortune. I held my aching arm.

"Fiona, ma chérie, your beard is hanging from that branch." He pointed and then doubled over laughing.

I touched my chin and immediately regretted it. A jolt of pain shot up my other arm. I cringed.

Good heavens. Sure enough, my beard was blowing in the wind. And my cap was caught between two branches.

"What in blazes are you doing here?" I said through my teeth.

Fredrick Fredricks held out his hand to me. "Looking after you, of course."

Cheeky devil.

"I can look after myself."

"True." He helped me to my feet. "But I enjoy the challenge."

"Worthy adversary and all that rot." I brushed off my trousers. "Ouch!" My arm throbbed. The slightest movement caused a stabbing pain.

"Ma chérie, you're hurt." Fredricks touched my shoulder.

I swatted his hand away. "Ouch!"

"But you're hurt." He moved closer.

"No more nonsense." Taking a step backwards, I leveled my gaze at him. "Tell me why you had that map of the Suez Canal and why you gave the actress the note about Crocodile Lake?" My head was spinning. I reached out for the tree for support. "An attack planned for a year ago."

"We need to get you to hospital." He put his arm around my waist. "You're so pale."

"I'm not going anywhere until you tell me why you're in Cairo and what you're planning for the Suez Canal." Overcome by dizziness, I fell against his chest.

"Ma chérie." He kissed my forehead. "Don't worry about your precious canal. It is safe... for now."

I ignored his soft lips on my forehead and tried to focus. "The map... the note... Crocodile Lake." It was no use. My vision blurred. "Red herrings. Why?" I was quite out of breath.

"Red herrings." He laughed and pulled me closer. "You're very clever."

"Why?" I resisted the urge to faint.

"I suppose you reported my little ruse to the War Office?" His breath was warm against my forehead.

"I tried but Captain Hall wouldn't listen," I gasped, sucking in air. Had he wanted me to report it? To report false information to lead the War Office astray.

"He underestimates you, ma chérie." He sighed. "But the lower the expectations, the greater the esteem when you triumph."

At least someone believed in me. Why did it have to be Fredricks?

"Thank you," I whispered, and then everything went black.

After a trip to hospital—where a nurse bandaged my sprained arm and put it in a sling—I was back in my hotel room, nursing my wounds, lying on my bed, and feeling sorry for myself. Of course, I'd lost Fredricks again. He'd disappeared after delivering me to hospital. At least he'd confirmed that the map, the note, and Crocodile Lake were all red herrings. Or had he?

I turned over on my side. Ouch! My arm ached. But my ego was more bruised than anything else. So much for my disguises. It would be impossible to hide this sling. Thank goodness the bloody thing wasn't broken.

Kitty lounged on her bed reading a magazine, as usual, while Poppy slept snuggled at her side. Clifford sat at the dressing table, smoking his pipe.

Discouraged by the afternoon's events, I didn't even care that he was filling our room with foul smoke.

"It wasn't a total bust," Clifford said, trying to cheer me up. "Even if the hounds doubled back and lost the scent. Seems they took after a stray fox fur some daft woman lost." He puffed. "What in god's name was she doing in the woods?"

I smiled to myself. I may have sacrificed my arm, but I'd saved the fox.

"Tell Aunt Fiona what you found out from General Clayton." Kitty looked up from her magazine. "That will lift her spirits." She grinned from ear to ear.

"Of course. Yes." His countenance brightened and he removed his pipe from his mouth. "You asked me to pump Clayton for information. So, I stuck to him like a hedgehog tick throughout the hunt. At one point, he almost shook me loose when he jumped a fence." He chuckled. "I say, I thought I'd be thrown into a heap. Funny thing—"

"Clifford." I narrowed my brows. "Please do get to the point." My arm ached and I was in no mood for his prattle.

He clamped down on his pipe stem and pouted.

"Sorry." *Sigh.* "Carry on." I nodded my approval.

"Tell her about the stains on his shirt." Kitty was stroking the bridge of Poppy's nearly nonexistent nose. "What was it on his shirt, Pops?" She used her baby voice and then bent down and kissed the pup's topknot.

"The bloodstains?" I struggled to sit up in bed.

"That's just it." Clifford smiled. "It wasn't blood." He poked the air with his pipe. "It was wine."

"Wine?"

"Apparently, at some point during their post-ball row, Lady Enid *spilled* a glass of wine on the general's shirt sleeve." Clifford winked. "He ended up sleeping at the bureau to let her cool off, you see."

"Or so he says." Although, having been married once myself, the story did sound plausible.

"He sounded sincere," Kitty said. "Remorseful even." She threw her legs over the side of her bed and scooped up Poppy. "Tell Aunt Fiona about HG." She straightened the ribbon on the dog's topknot and then glanced over at me, another smug grin on her face.

"HG?" A stabbing pain in my arm reminded me that I was injured. Blast it all. "The HG of HG at GAI II?" I propped myself up on my good arm.

"That's quite a story." Clifford pushed his thumb into the bowl of his pipe and then popped it into his breast pocket. "Once the hounds turned around, in the confusion, the general's horse almost ran—"

"Clifford, dear. Get on with it." *Sigh.* Could the man never just give a straight answer?

"Yes. Well. Sorry." He blushed.

"HG," I reminded him.

"You know how Jean-Baptiste got the Borchardt concession?" Kitty said, stealing Clifford's thunder. "Hermann Gabler was one of the German archeologists working for Borchardt at the German Archeology Institute." Thankfully the girl put me out of my misery and finally answered my question. We would have been there all afternoon waiting for Clifford to get around to it.

"They were all sent packing when the war broke out." Clifford lit his pipe again.

"Hermann Gabler. HG." I swung my legs over the side of the bed and plucked my notebook from the nightstand. "Jean-Baptiste went to meet this Hermann

Gabler chap at the German Archeology Institute the night before he died." I wrote *HG=Hermann Gabler* on my list of suspects.

"That couldn't be a coincidence." Kitty scratched Poppy behind the ears. "No, it couldn't, could it, Poppy-poo?" Poppy licked her face and the girl giggled.

"We've got to find this Hermann Gabler fellow." I circled his name.

"He's supposed to be back in Germany." Clifford blew out a cloud of smoke as he spoke. "If he's in Cairo, he's in hiding."

"Then we have to smoke the rat out of hiding." I snapped my notebook shut.

"How?" Kitty stood Poppy up on her lap and danced her like a toy doll. "Got any ideas?" She used her baby voice again to ask the dog. As if the dog could tell us anything... other than its favorite spot on the hotel's carpet.

"As a matter of fact, I have." Or at least I would, after I cogitated a while. My stomach growled. It was impossible to think on an empty stomach. "Clifford. Be a pet and call down and order us some lunch."

Over a lunch of cheese sandwiches and soda, I formulated a plan. I told my friends about Agent Relish's last words and my suspicions about the coded aria in the last act.

Tonight, we would pay another visit to the Isis Theater to discover what Agent Relish had learned that cost him his life. *Romeo. Last act.*

The plan was to watch the performance, question La Sultana, and then expose the theater as a cover for German spies.

Afterwards, under cover of darkness, I would break into the German Archeology Institute and find this Herr Hermann Gabler chap. If he were hiding out in Cairo, and if Jean-Baptiste had met him at the institute the night before he'd died, then Herr Gabler very well could be secreted at the institute. I planned to find out.

I didn't bother to mention this part of the plan to my friends. A respectable espionage agent should be able to handle some assignments on her own... especially if she hopes to get promoted.

14

THE ISIS THEATER

Later that night, dressed in our finest, we returned to the theater to watch La Sultana perform Romeo, again.

The Isis Theater was even more picturesque than I'd remembered. With the theater lights on, the vibrant greens and yellows glowed iridescent as if they were illuminated from the inside.

We took our seats in the orchestra section near the front of the theater. Again, the audience filled with soldiers and their dates. The crowd hummed in anticipation.

I recognized a few faces. We weren't the only ones taking in the same opera a second time. The last time, I'd come for a rendezvous with Agent Relish.

Now he was dead.

I shuddered just thinking about that horrible sound he emitted and those convulsions. *Poor man.* What had Agent Relish discovered here that had cost him his life?

I considered the sequence of events right before his death. I'd gone to wash my hands. The nurse went to get more supplies. How long had we left the bottles unattended? Long enough for Fredricks to tamper with them? Could he have added more morphine to the syringe when I wasn't looking?

If Fredricks had set me up to kill the man, I'd never forgive him.

The nerve. Showing up to rescue me after my fall at the hunt club. Fredricks appeared and disappeared again like a ghost. A bloody annoying ghost.

"You're flushed, Aunt Fiona." Kitty fanned me with her program. "Are you alright? How's your arm?"

"I'm fine, dear." I patted her hand. She was a good girl, most of the time—except that time she'd tied me to a toilet. With her flair for forensics, she'd almost redeemed herself. *Almost.*

Between the full house and the dark burgundy seats and curtains, a heaviness hung over the audience. The cloud of cigar smoke emanating from the soldiers in the row behind us was suffocating. I didn't understand men's passion for cigars. I wondered what Dr. Freud might have to say about the filthy habit, one he himself shared.

Sometimes a cigar is just a cigar. Ha! I doubt that.

Clifford dabbed his forehead with his handkerchief. Wearing his woolen army uniform, no wonder he was hot.

Even in my lightest bespoke evening gown with pockets, I was sweltering. It didn't help that my blooming arm was throbbing like a bloody bass drum. With my good hand, I took to fanning myself with my program. Kitty continued to fan me from the other side.

At last, the curtain opened, the stage set for another performance of *Romeo and Juliet*. The opera opened with a bang: a choreographed street brawl between the Montagues and the Capulets. It was a big number with lots of singers and dancers on stage.

Later in Act One, Romeo appeared on stage and the audience erupted into applause. La Sultana, dressed as the boy protagonist, took a brief bow before speaking her first lines. When Romeo and Juliet kissed, the soldiers went wild with whistles and shouts.

She doth teach the torches to burn bright.

Juliet may have been the sun, but tonight La Sultana as Romeo illuminated the stage.

After intermission—and no doubt after more wine and spirits—the crowd got louder and rowdier. Scenes between Romeo and Juliet were met with catcalls and vulgar proclamations too obscene to repeat. More than once, I had to avert my gaze from lewd gestures in the front row. I was embarrassed for my countrymen. Here they were in another country behaving like complete cads.

Trying to tune out the rude behavior all around me, I concentrated on the opera.

Rapt, Kitty and Clifford seemed oblivious to the soldiers' bad behavior. Or perhaps they were used to such language and gestures. Clifford, after all, was in the army. Still, I couldn't imagine him ever acting in such an uncouth manner. Kitty, on the other hand...

The last scene found Romeo and Juliet in a tomb. I paid special attention. Agent Relish had said "last act." This was the last act. What did he learn about this act that got him killed? I removed my notebook from my handbag and pricked up my ears.

Just as I suspected. It happened again. La Sultana reversed words, repeated verses, and was mucking up Romeo's final aria. It had to be a secret code.

As she sang, her gaze was fixed on an upper box to stage left.

I followed her gaze, and then slipped my opera glasses from my bag, and peered up into the box.

Oh, my sainted aunt. What's he doing here?

Wearing full evening kit, Fredrick Fredricks sat perched on the edge of his chair, smiling down at the stage. Was he merely enjoying the performance? Or was something more sinister going on? Fredricks stopped smiling and started writing on his program. He was in on it. I knew it. The code.

The code was the key. I'd have to wait to go after Fredricks. Right now, I needed to crack the code.

I put away my opera glasses, took up my pencil and program, and then listened. With my photographic memory, I could easily recall the libretto I'd read in the program from our last visit to the theater. In my notebook, I wrote down any anomalies or places where the actress departed from the written libretto.

Beauty. Love. On. Why. Up.

Like a stutter, she sang the word "up" four times.

Come. All. Nothing. At. Love. Come. Here. Run. I. Soul. Tomb. May. And. Smile. Day.

Again, a stutter on the word "day" four times.

The song ended and Romeo lay dead atop Juliet.

I glanced up at the box, but Fredricks was gone. The fox had escaped yet again.

The mangled song. What did it mean? I had to decode it, and fast. I sensed that the fate of the canal, and possibly the war, depended on it.

While everyone else clapped and whistled, I sat scribbling in my notebook.

"What are you doing, Aunt Fiona?" Kitty peered down at my notes.

Oblivious, Clifford clapped and cheered with the rest of them.

"I don't know yet." I rolled up the program for future reference and tucked it, along with my notebook, into my bag. "Let's go and have a chat with Miss Al-Madie."

After the performance, we waited until the audience had cleared out and then headed backstage. Clifford was eager to congratulate the actress and I was eager to question her.

A queue formed outside her dressing room. Kitty got a lot of dirty looks when she skipped the queue. Clifford followed behind, apologizing all the way.

Still in Romeo's mustache, beard, and heavy brows, La Sultana answered the dressing room door. Instead of Romeo's tan breeches and billowy white shirt, she wore a pale pink silk gown. The juxtaposition of her facial hair and her flowing gown was jarring.

"Congratulations," Clifford said, seemingly unbothered by her beard. "Absolutely smashing performance."

Mori's assistant interrupted to deliver yet another bouquet of flowers. The actress laid them on her dressing table along with several other bouquets. She was popular, and deservedly so. The woman was a stellar actress and ran a profitable theater to boot.

"If we're not disturbing you, may we come in?" I peeked over her shoulder and peered into the dressing room. Was she alone this time? Again, I had the sense that someone was hiding just behind the door. Under the scent of jasmine lingered that crushed pine smell.

"And if you are disturbing me?" She flashed a fake smile.

"Can we cut through your dressing room?" Kitty pressed against the door. "And go out the back way to avoid the crush of this queue?"

Back way? How did Kitty know about a back way?

"I'll allow it for you, Kitty Lane." The actress nodded and opened the door just wide enough to let us pass. Somehow, Kitty had gained her trust. Perhaps because the girl had comforted the grieving actress after Jean-Baptiste's death.

"Superb performance." I glanced around the room looking for clues. "I was wondering, though, I noticed you had some trouble with the last aria... again."

Mori's expression turned to stone. "Whatever do you mean?"

"You kept repeating words and stuttering." I walked the circumference of the small room. I stopped next to the clothes rack and lifted the hem of one of the gowns.

"A speech impediment I've had since childhood." She sat down at her dressing table and tugged at her beard. "It shows up when my voice gets tired. But thanks for noticing." Her tone was sarcastic.

"Apologies. I didn't know..." Was she telling the truth? Of course, she wouldn't admit to singing in code for the Germans.

"No worries." She yanked off her mustache. Her upper lip and chin were pink.

I knew how she felt. Deuced hard on the skin. I examined the gown's hem. Interesting. More words. German words this time. *Türken an Bord*. If I wasn't mistaken, that meant *Turks on board*. On board with what? Blowing up the canal? They'd tried several times before.

"Now, if you don't mind, I need to change." Reflected in the mirror, her gaze was cutting.

"Of course," Clifford said. "Your clothes..."

Kitty took the lead. She parted the clothes on the rack and slipped between a jester costume and an evening gown. Clifford followed her in. Since I wasn't going to get any more information out of the actress, I went in behind him.

Aha! The secret back door. If someone *had* been hiding in her dressing room, they could have made their escape through this door. When we crossed the threshold of the secret door, we were in the alley behind the theater.

As we walked back to the hotel, I tried to shake the uncanny feeling that something was off. If the actress stuttered when her voice got tired, then why wasn't she stuttering just now in her dressing room? What was Fredricks up to in that opera box? La Sultana's fumbles in the last act meant something, something important. Whatever it was, Agent Relish had been killed over it.

For the short walk back, Clifford gushed on and on about Mori's performance. Kitty humored him with encouragement. I needed to concentrate. I tried to shut out the street noises and Clifford's incessant chatter, but it was all too distracting.

When I got back to our hotel room, I locked myself in the lavatory. With nowhere else to sit, I closed the lid to the toilet. I studied the words I'd written in my notebook. I repeated them over and over, but they made no sense.

Agent Relish must have discovered that the Germans were using Mori Al-Madie to deliver coded messages to operatives working undercover in the audience. That's why he was killed. He had been going to tell me the night he didn't show up at the zoo.

I'd watched as uniformed soldiers from Australia, Canada, America, and of course England filed out of the theater. Which of them were actually German spies? Or was Mori Al-Madie's performance meant just for Fredricks? The key was in that code.

My head was spinning with hypotheses. I didn't need more theories, I needed answers.

On the other side of the door, Kitty hummed Christmas songs. She was such a merry girl. Even in the midst of war, she managed to maintain a cheerful disposition. I didn't know if I admired her for it or resented her.

Waiting for the girl to go to bed, my bottom tired of sitting on the hard lid. Stumped for solutions, I paced back and forth in the tight space.

The room was silent. Had Kitty gone to bed? More to the point, how would I sneak out without Poppy alerting her mistress?

Luckily, I'd planned ahead.

I removed a corner of toast from my gown pocket, slowly opened the lavatory door, and tossed the toast into the room.

While Poppy was occupied with her midnight snack, I quickly scooted out of the room.

With my pals now soundly asleep, I could investigate the German Archeology Institute.

15

THE INSTITUTE

The German Archeology Institute was dark and spooky, like a haunted mansion. The midnight hour didn't help calm my frayed nerves.

All the windows and doors were boarded up. But it was obvious from the clean modern stone that the building was new. The Germans must have just finished constructing it before the war, and then were forced to leave.

I stood at the corner of the building, waiting for my eyes to completely adjust to the darkness. The bright moon helped.

As soon as I could see well enough to avoid tripping on my own feet, I picked my way around the institute, looking for an entry point. Around the southern exposure, I descended into a stairwell. *Aha!* The door at the bottom of the well had not been boarded up.

Removing my lockpick set from my handbag with only one hand was challenging. "Horsefeathers!" I tore off the sling and stuffed it in my gown pocket. The damage to my arm had been greatly exaggerated, and mostly by me.

Disguised as a nail care kit, the small leather pouch contained a tension wrench, a pick, and a rake, all neatly tucked into individual sleeves. Just opening the pouch was exhilarating. Picking the lock with one hand would be difficult. If I turned slightly sideways, I could manage using both my hands, as long as I kept the elbow of my damaged wing glued to my body.

A noise on the street made me stop. Ears pricked, I stopped to attention. The last thing I needed was to be hauled off to the nick for breaking and entering. Waiting for my heart to calm down, I took a few deep breaths.

I slid the thin metal tension wrench into the lock, applied pressure, and then skated the metal pick in under the wrench and felt for the pins. I'd learned with lockpicking it wasn't the amount of pressure but the finesse that mattered. I wiggled the pick.

Come on.

Laughter startled me. Holding my breath, I stopped again. Once I'd assured myself it was just lovers finding a dark corner, I went back to the lock.

Again, I adjusted the tension wrench. Again, I applied pressure. Again, I felt for the pins.

Finally. The lock gave. *Bob's your uncle.* I was in. I turned the door handle, slipped inside, and closed the door behind me.

I clicked on my Beacon Army Light. The American torch was lighter than what the British army had on offer, which came in handy for espionage. Smaller was always better for spying.

Now, where was I? The room smelled dry. Dry and uninhabited—at least uninhabited by anything living. Although I could swear there was the faintest scent of crushed pine with a hint of Jasmine as an afterthought.

Jasmine. La Sultana's perfume.

Before taking a step, I scanned the room with my torch. Heavens. The entire room was chock full of antiquities: shelves of pottery and pot shards, carved busts of pharaohs and funerary jars, and other objects that I couldn't identify.

The Germans must have left in a hurry to leave all this treasure behind.

As I shone the light up and down each shelf and onto every corner of the room, I realized what was missing. Dust. Dust and cobwebs.

If the Germans hadn't been here since 1914, there should be three years' worth of dust. Perhaps the institute had a caretaker? Maybe an archeologist from the Allied forces was taking care of the place and that was why one door wasn't boarded up.

Shining the torch in front of me as I went, I made my way across the room and out into a hallway. If only I knew where to look... and what I was looking for.

I reached the front of the building and arrived in a large lobby full of display cases and antiquities exhibited atop pedestals. I tiptoed from case to case and, using my torch, examined the contents. The cases contained painted pots and animal figurines, colorfully painted parchments, and recovered tools. The pedestals sported busts of ancient Egyptians and painted urns.

Odd. Near a window, one table had an assortment of potted plants. I went over to investigate. If the institute had been closed for the last three years, then how were these plants still alive? Asters and dahlias. Even a white chamomile plant. I'd learned on my grandfather's farm about the medicinal purposes of those daisy lookalikes.

Someone was tending to these plants. The question was, who?

As I made my way across the room, I noticed an empty pedestal missing its treasure. I moved closer to examine it. When I shone the torch on the top of the pedestal, I saw a slight outline of whatever had been sitting there. The pedestal was ever so slightly faded around the spot where the article had been.

I pointed the torch at the floor. Perhaps the article had been knocked off in a scuffle. I didn't see any antiquities lying on the floor. Straining my eyes, I looked for pieces of whatever had been sitting atop the pedestal. What was missing and why?

No pot shards. No broken statues. Nothing. The thick carpet was pristine. I bent down to get a closer look. The rug had orange and green diamonds along with blue and gold squares. The pattern suggested something significant in Persian—or was it Turkish?—culture, but I had no idea what.

Wait a minute. Orange and green carpet. Kitty's fiber test. I bent down, plucked a few fibers, and tucked them into the pocket of my gown. Shining my torch as I went, I crawled around the pedestal, examining the carpet.

Good heavens. A bloodstain. A very big bloodstain.

A missing artifact, orange and green carpet, a white plant, a giant bloodstain. This had to be the scene of Jean-Baptiste's attack. The fatal blow had been delivered by whatever heavy object used to sit on that pedestal. And when Jean-Baptiste had hit the floor, he had clutched at the carpet, resulting in the fibers Kitty had found under his fingernails.

Where was the missing artifact—aka the murder weapon?

If I were a murderer, where would I hide a large, solid, and most likely extremely valuable object that I'd used to bludgeon a Frenchman?

As I stood up, a faint scent of citrus took me by surprise.

Pine. Jasmine. Citrus. Maybe there was life in this place after all. Either that or a gin cocktail.

A hand clamped over my mouth from behind. *Ahh-hhhh.* Lack of air choked my scream. My heart leaped into my throat. In a cold sweat, I tried to wriggle out of his grip, but he was too strong. Even if I *could* scream, who would hear me?

I bit his hand as hard as I could.

Now, *he* screamed.

Once he let go, I bolted into the darkness. Con-found it. I'd dropped my torch. The hallway was pitch black, and I ran full tilt into a wall. It knocked the wind out of me. My head was spinning with stars. When I'd caught my breath, I took off again and made it as far as an office near the back of the building. I rattled the door. *Please. Please. Be unlocked.*

I didn't have time to use my lockpick set. My assailant was upon me.

The hand caught me. This time by the arm.

"Unhand me!"

"Fiona?" The familiar tenor sent a shiver up my spine. "What in god's name are you doing here?"

"Archie?" I turned to face him. There was enough light coming through the office door that even in silhouette, I recognized his jaunty fedora and the crazy lock of hair that fell over his forehead. "Why are you here?"

The last time I'd seen Lieutenant Archie Somersby, I'd threatened him with Mata Hari's pearl-handled gun. He'd assassinated a man at Carnegie Hall. I'd had a chance to bring him in but couldn't do it. Instead, I'd let him go. I didn't want to believe Archie was a cold-blooded killer, even if he was just following orders. At gunpoint, he'd said he loved me. Did he mean it? Or was he just trying to save his skin? How would I ever know?

If only Kitty had a fiber test for love.

"I heard you were in Cairo." He chuckled. "I should have known I'd run into you breaking and entering."

"And I heard you were on the run." I tried not to look him in the face. "Or isn't murder a crime in America?" I knew if I looked him in the eyes, I'd lose my resolve.

"Darling, please understand, Schweitzer was going to kill you." Archie took my hand. "I couldn't let that happen."

It was as if an electric current ran up my arm and zapped my heart. Darn him anyway. The scent of his citrus cologne was intoxicating. Even the undercurrent of Kenilworth cigarettes was exhilarating. My knees went weak. My breath caught.

Darn him. He'd killed a man and I didn't care.

I loved him anyway. And I hated myself for it. I stared down at my practical Oxfords.

"Not to mention, I was acting under orders from Captain Hall." He raised my hand to his lips and kissed my palm. "Can you forgive me?"

The kiss radiated heat all the way to my shins. *Forgive him?* I closed my eyes and pushed away thoughts of what I'd *really* like to do to him. I squeezed his hand and leaned closer, luxuriating in the warmth of his body.

"I've missed you." His whisper was low and raspy.

"I've missed you too." I barely got the words out before his lips were pressed on mine. *Oh, Archie.*

Despite the fact I'd met Archie only six months ago, I was completely under his spell. Still, what did I know about him except that he worked for British Intelligence, possibly as an assassin? His clearance level was so much higher than mine, we'd be grandparents before I'd find out what he really did—that is, *if* we married, and *if* I could have children, *which I couldn't.*

A shuffling sound in the hallway made me open my eyes.

Archie let out a grunt and then collapsed at my feet, almost taking me with him.

A hand clamped over my mouth and nose. I struggled to get loose. The sweet clinging smell of chloroform overpowered my senses. My consciousness floated away.

When I came to, my hands and feet were bound. Luckily, whoever did this didn't try to tie my hands behind my back. My arm hurt badly enough without being contorted by ropes.

The room was dark, except for a sliver of light

coming through the window. So, it was still nighttime? My vision was blurry, and I had a dreadful headache. My stomach wasn't too happy either. And along with the lingering odor of chloroform, the faint smell of death assaulted my nostrils, which didn't help my sick stomach.

"Fiona, are you alright?" The voice came out of the darkness.

"Archie?" I blinked hard to force my eyes to see. "Is that you?"

"Are you alright?" His voice was desperate with worry.

"Yes. I'm fine." A little white lie. If only I weren't trussed up like a Christmas goose, I could hold my aching head. "I can't move. My hands and feet are bound."

"Mine too."

A dragging sound came from nearby.

"Is that you?" I held my breath.

"Keep talking and I'll scoot over to you."

I patted the ground next to me. Dirt.

Wait. What's this? My poor mangled handbag. At least the kidnapper had the decency to leave it. Wriggling myself upright, I picked up my bag. It was lighter than usual. *Blast.* The kidnapper must have removed Mata Hari's gun.

I glanced around. What I'd taken for a window was nothing but an opening in the rocks.

"Where are we?" Whoever put us here could be coming back to kill us. Either that or they'd left us here to die. I shuddered at the thought of starving to death in a dark cave.

"Can't you smell the rotting mummies?" Even the exasperation in his voice was reassuring. "We're in a bloody tomb."

"Hopefully not our own." I wished my stomach would calm down. Being alone with Archie didn't help either—at least, I hoped we were alone.

"Indeed." The sounds of Archie's boots scraping across the dirt were getting closer.

"What were you doing in the institute? What are you doing in Cairo?" My questions were rapid fire, but at least they kept me talking. "Are you here to stop the plot—"

"Same as you, I suppose."

Scrape. Scrape.

Soon, I felt his comforting warmth next to me.

He was breathing hard from exertion.

I was breathing hard too. But not from exertion. Come on, Fiona. Get a grip. You're tied up in a tomb, for goodness' sake, not on your honeymoon.

Archie's arm brushed against mine and I suppressed a smile.

Steady on, Fiona. You're a spy on assignment, not a schoolgirl at a dance.

"You first," he said.

"What do you mean?" I hoped he had devised our escape.

"Why are you in Cairo?" He leaned closer. "Why were you at the institute?"

I leaned into him. The scent of citrus and masculinity was reassuring. "Captain Hall sent Kitty and me to Cairo to foil Fredricks's plan to blow up the Suez Canal." That wasn't entirely true. Captain Hall had only authorized us to follow Fredricks and report back. I had strict orders not to do anything else. But with two murders, a missing agent, a theater full of German spies, and a possible threat to the canal, I couldn't just sit on my hands and wait. Unless, of course, I was tied up in the dark.

How long had we been unconscious? What if we were too late to foil the plot? Fredricks had assured me the map and the note were decoys. But decoys for what? Something more sinister than blowing up the Suez Canal?

Surely Kitty would have noticed I was gone. What if she'd been kidnapped too... or worse? I closed my eyes and prayed. *Please, God. If I get out of this, I'll never be cross with the girl again. I promise.*

"There's light coming from the entrance to the tomb, so it must be morning." Archie leaned closer.

Oh, Archie. Why couldn't we just have a normal romantic liaison instead of ropes and caves? Archie's breath warmed my cheek.

Not a window. Not nighttime. The chloroform must have affected me more than I knew. I tugged at the ropes around my wrists. "Ouch." A stabbing pain ran up my arm.

"What's wrong?"

"I hurt my arm fox hunting."

"You fox hunt? Or is it one of your many alter egos?" He chuckled. "I rather miss Harold the bellboy." He pushed against my shoulder. "You make a darn pretty boy."

"You too." My cheeks were hot. Was he flirting with me? Or telling me he preferred Harold? Flustered, I changed the subject back to the pressing matter of the canal plot. "The actress at the Isis Theater is working with the Germans, using code during her performance."

"Code?" His tone became serious.

"She repeats words in a coded sequence." I kicked

my feet to see if I could loosen the ropes. "To German spies in the audience, including Fredrick Fredricks."

"Bloody hell." Archie flinched. "Did you report it to Captain Hall?"

What an idiot I'd been. Going to the institute alone. Not telephoning Captain Hall. "No." What must Archie think of me? "Why are you here?"

"That's classified." He gave me a weak smile.

"Your entire life is classified." I scooted an inch away from him. "I show you my hand, why won't you show yours?"

"I can't." Wrists bound, he reached over and brushed his fingers against my leg.

Oh, my word. He was bleeding. "Your wrist. You're injured."

"Ask anything you like." He inched his way toward me again. "I'll answer yes or no."

He was trying to distract me from all the blood gushing from his wound.

"This is your only chance." He tucked his injured wrist between his legs. "You'd best take advantage of my offer."

I suppressed nightmarish thoughts of Archie bleeding out.

"What do you know about Hermann Gabler?"

"Yes or no, only. I won't say more." Hopefully his playful tone meant his wound was superficial.

"Is Hermann Gabler in Cairo?"

"Yes."

"Is he dealing in illegal antiquities?"

"Yes."

"Is Fredricks in on it?"

"You rang?" Fredricks appeared, holding a torch.

Good grief. What's he doing here? Coming back to make sure we haven't escaped?

"How are you lovebirds getting along?" He shined the light in Archie's face. "Cozy, isn't it?" He flashed the torch at me. "She's a peach, *c'est vrai*? *La crème de la crème*."

"You'll never get away with it, Fredricks." Archie spat out the words.

"Get away with what?" Fredricks laughed. "Wooing the lovely Miss Figg?"

I shot daggers up at him with my eyes. If only looks could kill.

"Sadly, you may be right." Fredricks squatted a few feet in front of us.

Now, I was eye to eye with the fiend.

"The Turks have been trying to sabotage the canal for months," Archie said. "What makes you think you'll succeed when they've failed?"

"The Turks have been hoodwinked by the Germans, just as the Arabs have been by the British." Fredricks slapped his riding stick against the leg of his jodhpurs. "You British promise sovereignty. You promise territory. You promise wealth." He scoffed. "All you deliver are lies and brutality, just as you did in South Africa."

"This isn't the Boer War—"

Fredricks interrupted him. "You colonized South Africa. You colonized Egypt and India. You think you have the rights to the entire world." He shook his fist. "But you're wrong."

"The Germans are not your friends," Archie said.

"They're not my enemies." Fredricks stood up. "And my enemy's enemies are the closest I've got to friends." He raised his riding stick and made to bring it down across Archie's face. He stopped short. "You're a fine one to talk about alliances with the Germans." He scoffed. "Double agent Somersby."

I struggled against my bindings. I wanted to kick the bounder in the shin.

"Fiona, ma chérie, come with me." Fredricks tucked his stick under his arm and held out his hand. "Together, we can stop this bloody war."

Not that again! He was always blathering on about us working together to stop the war. Of course I wanted to stop the bloody war. But there was no way on earth I was going with him, the rotter.

"Together, we can help the Arabs throw off their chains and reclaim their sovereignty." His eyes shone. "Come with me, ma chérie."

"You belong with Fredricks." Archie bumped me with his shoulder.

That was the lowest insult he could have given me. Belong with Fredricks, was he mad?

"Lovers' quarrel, is it?" Fredricks glanced at his watch. "Well, Fiona, what will it be? Me or him? I haven't got all day."

Archie nudged me again. "Follow him."

I looked over at him, and he winked.

Follow him. Archie was right. I *did* belong with Fredricks. My assignment was to follow him, after all. Plus, if I left with the scoundrel now, I could come back for Archie later. *Of course.*

I smiled up at Fredricks. "You," I said with as much conviction as I could muster. "I'll go with you."

"Wonderful." Fredricks's face lit up with surprise. "Let's go, then." He untied my feet. "There's justice to be done." He helped me to my feet.

I held out my bound hands.

"I'm not stupid." Fredricks flashed a sly smile.

"But my arm hurts." My voice was whinier than I intended. It was true, though. My arm did hurt.

"Did my colleague hurt you in transport?" His concern sounded genuine.

His colleague? Hermann Gabler? Mori Al-Madie?

"I'm afraid sacrifices are necessary, ma chérie." He bent down and kissed my hand.

Not so long ago, Archie had done the same—the effect, however, had been completely different. This time, I cringed.

Fredricks put his hand on the small of my back and applied pressure.

I let him lead me out of the tomb.

Just before exiting, I glanced back at Archie.

He mouthed the words, "I love you."

At least, I *thought* that was what he said. Did he think we would never see each other again? Were those his last words? Would he die in this tomb? A chill ran up my spine. My lip trembled. *Oh, Archie.*

And what would stop Fredricks from disposing of me too?

Archie's gold pocket watch! "Do you mind?" With my bound hands, I held out my handbag. "Can you get the gold watch out for me? I want to return it to Archie."

Fredricks shook his head. "You're such a romantic." He obliged and plucked the watch out of my bag.

"Your watch." I held it up as I ran back to Archie's side.

He smiled weakly. "I wondered where that old thing had got to."

I bent down to give it to him.

"You keep it, my darling," he whispered. "Something to remember me by." He said it with the conviction of a doomed man.

My eyes filled with tears. "I'll never forget you."

16

BLACK LIGHTNING

In the early hours of Sunday morning, the Isis Theater was quiet. Not a soul stirring. The dimly lit basement was musty and full of cobwebs.

As I followed Fredricks into the basement, I considered whether I might be attracted to danger. Even my late ex-husband, Andrew, had been a perilous mystery with mercurial moods and a self-destructive streak. My times with Archie were filled with danger. I never knew if, or when, I'd see him again—the status of our relationship always a puzzle. Did he really love me? Did I really love him? Would we ever get enough time to sort it out?

Fredricks led me down a long hallway with a closed door at the end. Where was he taking me? At least he'd unbound my hands. He was unusually quiet as we made our way through the orphaned bric-a-brac littering the hall. Desolate and abandoned, furniture and set pieces were piled willy-nilly all along the hallway walls. A suit of armor lay broken over the top of a dusty headboard. A mouse-eaten wig hung from the arm of a chair, which was missing a leg.

Defective misfits. Pieces that could no longer fulfill their functions.

Not unlike me. Abandoned by Andrew because of my defective womb. If Archie found out, would he abandon me, too?

"Penny for your thoughts, ma chérie?" Fredricks's voice pulled me out of my self-pity.

"You killed Jean-Baptiste and Mr. Relish and you're trying to kill Archie." I stopped in the middle of the hallway. "Are you planning to kill me too?" Unflinching, I looked him in the eyes.

"I'd never do anything to hurt you." His mustache twitched. I never knew when the rotter was being sincere or having me on.

I scoffed.

"I know you're fond of Lieutenant Somersby." He flashed a snide smile. "As a peace offering, I'll make sure someone finds him." He put his hand on my arm.

"Ouch." I flinched. "That hurt."

"Don't feign the fragile female, ma chérie." He took off walking. "It's not becoming."

Bounder. I had a sprained arm, for heaven's sake. I hurried to catch up to him. Was he actually jealous of Archie? Ridiculous man.

He hadn't denied killing Jean-Baptiste or Mr. Relish. And although he'd promised to make sure someone found Archie, he didn't say whether dead or alive.

"Why are we at the theater?" I waited as Fredricks unlocked the door at the end of the hall. "Was it Mori Al-Madie who attacked us?" It had to be her. Why else were we at the theater? She may have dressed as a man on stage, but surely she couldn't have carried me or Archie. Not unless she was a lot stronger than she looked. Or she had help.

"Mori is a friend." Fredricks opened the door and then turned to me. "Just a friend. No need to be jealous, my peach."

Cheeky cad. As if I could have feelings for him... other than hatred. "Why in the world would I be jealous?" I put my hands on my hips. "You have a girl in every port."

"Now, Fiona, don't be like that." He grinned. "You know you're the only girl for me."

A film I'd seen before I left London came to mind.

The Little American. Mary Pickford's character is in love with both a German and a French soldier. The French one dies, and she ends up with the German. *Dear me. Just like Archie and Fredricks.* Except unlike the little American, I didn't plan to end up with my enemy.

If I hadn't sprained my arm, I'd have socked Fredricks right in the kisser. "I know what you're planning." I hung back to see what was inside the room.

"We're planning to stop this terrible war." He took a step closer and gazed down at me with those intense dark eyes. "You're going to help me persuade the Arabs to unite against their colonizers."

The hairs on my arms stood up as if the threshold were suddenly filled with static.

"You and I will stop it. We must stop it. So many lives depend on us." His countenance was fierce. I'd never seen such resolve and determination.

"You're escalating the war, not stopping it." I peeked over his shoulder into the storage room. "Threats on the canal, murdering British agents—"

"That was just a bit of fun." He laughed.

"Fun!" I wanted to kick him. "Blowing up the canal is just a bit of fun?" How dare he!

"Lake Timsah. The map I dropped for you. And the scratching on the tablecloth." He pulled me inside. "I just knew you couldn't resist. Watching you sleuth is delicious, ma chérie." His eyes sparked, and I had to look away.

"And you reported it to the War Office, right on schedule." He grinned.

"You're a sick man." I knew it. He had planted those clues just for me. *Infuriating man.*

"Lovesick, perhaps." He put the back of his hand to his forehead and feigned a swoon. Of course, he looked silly in his billowy white blouse, jodhpurs, and knee-high black boots... with his broad shoulders, muscular build, and long wavy hair.

I suppressed a smirk. The man was mad. But he did have a certain charm.

Fredricks shut the door and turned on the overhead light. "Would you like a cold beverage?" He crossed the room to a large white ice box. He opened it, revealing assorted bottles of champagne, Coca-Cola, and beer but no place for the ice block.

I shook my head. I refused to take anything from the bounder.

The basement room had no windows and was chock full of electronic gadgets of all sizes. "What is this place?"

Ignoring my question, Fredricks removed a bottle of champagne and popped the cork. "We need to celebrate our collaboration."

I licked my lips. The ride back across the desert *had* left me parched. Only to keep up the ruse of going along with his plan, mind you, I accepted a Coca-Cola, the only non-alcoholic beverage on offer. Even on my trip to America, I'd never had a cola.

To my surprise, the bottle was ice cold. "Where is the ice block?"

Fredricks laughed. "It's called a Domelre, a domestic electronic refrigerator."

"An electric ice box? What will they think of next?" I took a sip and nearly spat it out. The fizzy sweetness was overwhelming. Still, it did quench my thirst. Leave it to the Americans to invent a beverage both too sweet and too sharp. They couldn't just settle for one or the other.

In addition to the electric ice box, the large windowless room was furnished with filing cabinets, a giant mahogany wardrobe, a dining table and chairs, a daybed, and a wooden desk equipped with a headset and what looked to be a telegraph machine and another large machine I couldn't identify.

The Isis Theater was more than a medium for coded messages. It was a hidden den of German spies.

"Have a seat." Fredricks gestured to the dining table. He brought a platter from the ice box.

"What do you want with me?" I dropped into a chair.

"In addition to your charming company, I want to calculate how to end this war." He sat across from me and sipped champagne. "For a small island, your countrymen are notorious for violently colonizing the entire world." He lifted a cloth off the platter.

Golly. Strawberries, oranges, and cheese. How did he come by such delicacies? Back home, I was lucky to get war bread and the occasional tomato. In the service of espionage, and out of duty to my country, I picked up a strawberry and bit into it. *Oh, my.* It was heavenly.

For all his faults, Fredricks did offer excellent hospitality. At least he hadn't kidnapped me by force like he did the first time he'd offered me wine and strawberries.

"What about the Germans?" I set aside the wretched bottle of Coca-Cola. "They're violent and underhanded." I'd seen firsthand the results of the German's use of mustard gas. Utterly revolting that any man could do that to another man.

"When push comes to shove, everyone is violent and underhanded." He poured himself another glass of champagne. "Even your beloved Lieutenant Somersby. At least the Germans are honest in their declarations of war, unlike your insidious countrymen who infiltrate even the sewers under the banner of friendship." He sat the bottle down with such force that I felt it on the other side of the table. "And then attack from within like a cancer destroying its host."

"I may not understand the ins and outs of politics, but the English people are honest and hardworking and—"

"Don't be naïve, Fiona." He waved my words away as if they were pesky flies. "The British are as dishonest as they come. They even lie to themselves."

I nearly choked on a bit of strawberry. "I may be naïve, but at least I'm not a killer." I glared at him.

"When push comes to shove," he sneered, "everyone is a killer."

My cheeks burned. "Not me."

He raised his eyebrows. "Agent Relish might disagree."

Overcome by a wave of nausea, I dropped the fruit. "Did you add morphine to that syringe?"

"Moi?" He put his hand to his chest. "Have you forgotten I was attacked too?" He took a strawberry from the tray and popped it into his mouth.

Bang!

There was a loud crash. The door to the room flew open.

I whipped my head around.

"Freeze!" A black-clad figure jumped into the room.

Oh, my word. A flash of black lightning, Kitty was dressed in black from head to toe. Black knee-length bloomers. Black stockings. Black waistcoat over a black silk shirt. She looked like a fencer from a magazine. Instead of a blade, she wielded a revolver.

She bolted into the room, gun drawn and aimed right at Fredricks's head.

"How did you find me?" I dropped a strawberry back onto the tray and stood up. What would the girl think of me, having a tea party with our enemy?

"My little bloodhound." She glanced at the floor where Poppy was turning in circles.

"Poppy to the rescue." I reached down and patted the little creature. "Good girl."

"Put your hands on your head." Kitty's voice was commanding, no longer the giggling girl I knew. "Slowly." She waved the gun at Fredricks.

"Careful," Fredricks said, raising his hands in the air. "That's not a toy, my child." Like a cat about to pounce, he didn't take his eyes off the girl... or her gun.

"I'm taking you in for the murder of Jean-Baptiste Lorrain." Kitty took a few steps closer to her target.

"I didn't kill him," Fredricks scoffed. "Check my alibi. I was at the party until after midnight, and then escorted my friend Miss Al-Madie home."

"You're the second person to give Miss Al-Madie as an alibi," I said. When Kitty wasn't looking, I snatched another strawberry from the tray and popped it into my mouth. After all, this bloody war wasn't over and, even if I survived, I might not get another one for years.

"Stand up, *slowly*." Kitty thrust the gun at Fredricks. "Hands above your head."

"And what about Mr. Relish?" I swallowed the strawberry and went to Kitty's side.

"*Agent* Relish and I were having a friendly chat when someone attacked us." Fredricks stood up. "He died at the hospital, remember."

Technically true. I cringed. If I had killed the man, it was a terrible accident. If Fredricks had somehow sabotaged the morphine bottle to frame me, he was a lowdown good-for-nothing... all while claiming to care for me.

"Move it." Kitty waved the gun. "Keep your hands up."

"Where are you taking him—"

She cut me off. "Whose side are you on?" Kitty shot me a look. "I saw you eating strawberries and drinking champagne with your *dearest* Fredricks."

"I was not drinking champagne."

Fredricks smiled.

"And those stolen glances…" Kitty shook her head. "It would be romantic if it weren't so pathetic."

"Now, see here." Utterly appalled by the suggestion of romance with Fredricks, I was tongue-tied. "That's no way to talk to your… your…"

"My what?" She stepped behind Fredricks and jabbed the gun into his back. "You're not really my aunt."

Bark. Bark. Bark.

Poppy growled and snarled. I'd never seen her so agitated. Her snout was pointed toward the ceiling, and she let out a pitiful howl. What in the world had gotten into her? Perhaps she didn't approve of the way her mistress was behaving. *I must say, neither did I.* Confronting an adversary was no excuse for rudeness —on the part of the dog or the girl.

"Shhhhh. Poppy, behave." I bent down to pet her.

Blimey. That's when I saw them. Black boots approached from the hallway.

When I stood up, I was face to face with a Luger pistol.

"Drop your weapon or I'll kill her." The man standing before me had a pinched face, receding hairline, and the most intimidating expression I'd ever seen. He was holding Poppy hostage.

"Ladies, may I introduce Herr Hermann Gabler?" Fredricks sidestepped Kitty's gun. "Germany's most promising young Egyptologist."

Herr Gabler's brush mustache twitched.

"Not to mention the most corrupt." Fredricks spun around and grabbed the gun out of Kitty's hand.

"Drop it." Gabler dropped Poppy and reached out and caught me around the waist. "Or I'll shoot." He held the Luger to my head.

I closed my eyes and held my breath, waiting for the end.

What did Fredricks care if the German shot me?

17

THE COLLAR

The barrel of the Luger burned cold against my temple. I sucked in air. My palms were sweating, and I was afraid to open my eyes. I waited for the fatal shot.

A clattering nearby startled me, and I opened my eyes.

Fredricks had dropped Kitty's gun on the floor.

Wait. Weren't Fredricks and Gabler on the same side?

The tension between the four of us filled the storage room-cum-spy headquarters. As the walls of the windowless room closed in on me, I gulped air, wondering which one might be my last breath. The strange machine on the desk whirred. I jerked. Herr Gabler tightened his grip on me.

"Kick it over here," Herr Gabler said. The creases in his forehead deepened. The promising *young* Egyptologist obviously looked older than his years. Criminal activity must have aged him prematurely.

Fredricks kicked the gun and it slid across the stone floor.

"Now sit down with your hands in the air." Herr Gabler waved his Luger. "All of you." He gave me a shove. For a small man, he was strong.

I stumbled but managed to sit in the nearest chair.

Fredricks and Kitty followed suit. We all sat around the table with our hands in the air. Poppy cowered under Kitty's chair. *Poor pup.* The strawberries and champagne seemed even more out of place now than they had before.

"Move closer together." Never taking his eyes off us, Herr Gabler bent down and snatched Kitty's gun off the floor. "Move. Now!"

We scooted our chairs closer together until we were all on one side of the table. Kitty was seated between me and Fredricks. The poufy fabric of her bloomers touched my knee. I wished I was wearing trousers. My disguises—Dr. Vogel, Harold the helpful bellboy, Rear Admiral Arbuthnot—were like suits of armor. I always felt more protected wearing men's clothes.

Herr Gabler pointed his Luger at Fredricks. "Put your hands behind your back." He stuffed Kitty's gun into the belt of his trousers.

Fredricks complied, albeit in his usual lackadaisical way. Was he never afraid? I'd never seen him flinch. He could stare down a lion. No wonder Clifford called him the Great African Hunter. Unless this charade with Herr Gabler was yet another one of his tricks.

"Behind the chair." Still pointing the gun, Herr Gabler skated across the floor and came to a stop behind Fredricks's chair. He pulled a length of rope out of his back trouser pocket and handed it to Kitty. "Tie him up." He barked orders like an army sergeant.

Kitty glanced back at me, and then proceeded to tie Fredricks's wrists behind the chair.

"Look, Gabler," Fredricks said. "I know you hate the British as much as I do."

"I hate snitches even more." Gabler held the Luger to Kitty's head. "Tighter. Tie his hands, tighter."

Kitty yanked on one end of the rope.

"That was Dankworth, not me." Fredricks didn't baulk as the rope tightened around his wrists.

Dankworth? The missing British agent? "What does Dankworth have to do with this?" I sized up the distance between me and Herr Gabler. Did I dare make a move on him? I reconsidered. If I did, he might shoot Kitty. Besides, even without a damaged wing, I was no match for the wiry German.

"Nothing... any more." Fredricks shot me a look. "Thanks to Gabler."

"What do you mean?" Had Gabler disposed of Agent Dankworth? Kidnapped him? Or locked him in a tomb?

"Shut up!" Herr Gabler pointed the Luger at me. "All of you." What he lacked in stature, he made up for in gruffness.

Lips tight, I glared at him.

Woosh. The sound of Kitty's foot slicing the air caught me off guard. Again, a black boot flew past me and landed on Herr Gabler's chin.

I gasped.

The girl held onto the edges of her chair and pin-wheeled her feet into the air. Again. She landed a kick to the side of Herr Gabler's head.

Where in the world did the girl learn to do that? "Yes!" I cheered.

The table shook and a champagne glass fell to the floor with a crash.

From under Kitty's chair, Poppy alternated barking and growling.

Herr Gabler grunted as his head swung this way

and that. But instead of dropping his Luger or falling to the floor, the attack just made him angry. He hauled off and struck Kitty with the butt of his gun.

She crumpled into a heap on the floor at my feet.

Oh, no! No. No. No. I jumped up. "What have you done?"

Herr Gabler shoved me back down onto the chair. "Hands behind your back."

"Impossible." I held up my bandaged arm. "My arm is broken." Alright. I exaggerated my injury.

"You're really getting on my nerves." Luger in one hand, Herr Gabler jerked a handkerchief out of his breast pocket with the other. He grabbed me by the hair and stuffed the handkerchief into my mouth.

My wig was wrenched off my head.

"What the hell is this?" He held my wig in his hand like a dirty rag and then threw it across the room. It landed atop the telegraph machine. He wrapped a rope around my torso and tied me to my chair. "Keep it in your mouth or I'll shoot you."

The taste of his dirty handkerchief in my mouth turned my stomach, and the gag made it even more difficult to breathe in the stifling storage room.

"I have an errand to run but I'll be back." He bent down, rolled Kitty over onto her stomach, tied her limp hands behind her back, and then looped the rope around her ankles too. "Nasty girl."

Poor Kitty. I'd been rather impressed with her foot-fighting—which, no doubt, she'd learned at her "boarding school" in France.

"Make any noise and I'll turn around and shoot you." Herr Gabler left and slammed the door.

Thank heavens the heinous man was gone. I managed to spit out the handkerchief. "What's going on here?" If only I could have reached Fredricks, I would have socked him. He'd gotten us into this mess, after all. "Aren't you working with that horrible man?"

"Gabler has a bee in his bonnet." Fredricks tugged at the ropes around his wrists. "He thinks I turned him in for selling antiquities on the black market." He scooted his chair around to face me. "I only wish I had."

"Illegal antiquities." Surely Fredricks wasn't in Cairo to protect antiquities.

"Neither side in this bloody war has the right to pillage Egypt's heritage." His countenance was stern. He was nothing if not an idealist.

"Where is Ag... er, Mr. Dankworth?" I stared down at Kitty to see if she was still breathing.

Throwing my body against the ropes, again I tried to free myself. Struggling with all my might, I strained to break loose. It was no use. For the second time in twenty-four hours, I was bound up like a Christmas goose.

"Keeping lover boy company, I'm afraid." Fredricks cursed as he labored against his ropes. "Did the girl really have to tie me so tight?"

Lover boy? Did he mean... "Archie?"

Had Herr Gabler—or Fredricks—kidnapped Agent Dankworth and deposited him in the tomb with Archie? *Blast it.* I had to liberate myself so I could save Archie and Agent Dankworth. Every time I twisted against the rope, I got a stabbing pain in my arm.

Kitty groaned.

Thank heavens. She was still alive.

I let out a great sigh of relief.

She said something I didn't understand. Heavens. Was she speaking Russian? The whack on the head must have made her delirious.

Tail wagging, Poppy emerged from under the chair.

Kitty lifted her bound hands behind her back and said something else... in Russian. Or was it an Asian language? Chinese maybe?

Poppy put her front paws on Kitty's back and then ducked her furry little head under the rope that connected the girl's hands and feet. What in the world?

The little dog caught the biggest gemstone on her collar on the rope and proceeded to tug and wiggle.

Unbelievable!

The rope began to fray.

"Good girl," Kitty said, encouragingly. She wrenched her head back to glance over her shoulder at Poppy, who was busy using the stone of her collar to saw through the rope.

It must be a real diamond. Otherwise, it couldn't cut through that rope.

Tug. Wag. Yap. Pant. Saw. Snap.

Oh, my word. She did it. With her collar, Poppy had cut through the rope.

Kitty kicked her feet and the rope fell away. Now only her hands were tied.

"Bravo." I would have clapped my hands if I could. "Good doggie."

Kitty flipped over onto her back, sat up, and jumped into a squatting position—all with her hands still tied behind her back. Now, she was squatting on the floor next to the table where Fredricks and I were tied to chairs. She was as agile as a cat.

Like a circus contortionist, she slid her arms around under her legs until her arms were tied in front of her body. She drew her knife from her boot, and then stood up and came behind me.

Suddenly, the rope fell away from my body. How did she do that so fast? Her wrists were bound. Nimble fingers?

Whatever she'd done, I was free.

"My turn," Fredricks said, wiggling his fingers.

I dashed over to him.

"Are you mad?" Kitty said, shaking her head. "Don't untie him."

She had a point. He was our enemy, after all.

"He's tied to a chair, for heaven's sake." I slapped the back of his chair. "Do you plan to take chair and all?" Had she changed her mind about taking him in? We couldn't just leave him here for Herr Gabler.

Poppy growled, alerting us to approaching footsteps.

I froze. "He's coming back!" I stage whispered, glancing around for a hiding place.

"Quick. Get into the wardrobe," Fredricks said. "I'll cover for you."

I didn't trust him. But I had no choice. The footfalls were getting louder.

Kitty scooped up the pup and dashed to the wardrobe. She held Poppy in one hand and opened the wardrobe door for me with the other. "Hurry."

I climbed into the wardrobe and shut the door.

My heart was racing. I was panting as fast as Poppy.

Filled with old costumes, the wardrobe smelled musty. I huddled between a frilly ballgown and a pirate's outfit. It was too dark to see Poppy, but I could hear her panting. Within seconds, the smell of warm dog breath overpowered the costumes' stale odors.

Kitty whispered something. The pup quit panting and was as still as a grave.

Good grief. Why did I have to think of graves? I pushed the thought from my mind.

"Where are they?" The voice boomed on the other side of the wardrobe.

My hand flew to my mouth. Tears filled my eyes. *Not a sound, Fiona. Not a sound.*

"Gone," Fredricks said.

"I can see that." A chair scraped against the floor. More scraping. Fredricks groaned. *What is Herr Gabler doing?*

"They escaped." Fredricks covered for us, just like he said he would. Maybe Clifford was right. His pal wasn't all bad.

"How?" Herr Gabler didn't sound happy.

"The dog untied them." Fredricks chuckled.

I smiled. It was true. Poppy had rescued us.

Scuffling sounds penetrated the wardrobe. Fredricks groaned again.

What the blazes was going on out there? Was Gabler torturing him?

I felt like jumping out of the wardrobe and kicking the villain. If only I'd gone to boarding school in France.

"No need to take it out on me," Fredricks said, his voice strained. "I'm on your side."

"That's why you reported me to the authorities?" Herr Gabler's German accent only made him sound more sinister.

Herr Gabler and Fredricks might be on the same side, but if Fredricks had turned him in, then he wasn't a complete scoundrel. He had some principles. Still, I didn't believe for a second Fredricks was in Egypt to stop the illegal antiquities trade. He was a German spy on a mission to help *his side* win the war.

"The artifacts belong to the Egyptian people," Fredricks said. "Not to the British. Not to the Germans. And especially not to you to sell for personal gain."

Again, it occurred to me that the murders related to the illegal antiquities trade. Maybe the British agents had discovered Herr Gabler selling illegal treasures. How did the codes at the theater fit in?

It just didn't make sense. Why would Herr Gabler,

an Egyptologist, be involved with Fredricks, a German spy? Yes, they were both on the side of Germany. But what did Fredricks have to do with Egyptology? And more to the point, what did Herr Gabler have to do with whatever Fredricks was plotting?

La Sultana and the Isis Theater were the missing link. If only I could break the code. The coded aria was key.

"Don't be such an idealistic fool," Herr Gabler said.

"I may be an idealist, but I'm no fool."

I agreed with Fredricks. He was no fool.

As my eyes adjusted to the darkness of the wardrobe, I could make out Kitty's silhouette and Poppy squirming in her arms. *Hold still, beastie. Please hold still.*

Poppy sneezed.

I held my breath.

Silence.

Kitty pinched me.

Ouch. Why did she do that? I bit my lip.

The wardrobe door flew open.

I gasped.

Kitty exploded out of the wardrobe feet first. Swinging from the clothes bar, she kicked Herr Gabler. Both of her little booted feet landed squarely on his nose.

Herr Gabler yelled something in German and flew backwards, hitting the table with a loud thwack.

I peeked out of the wardrobe.

Like an angry badger, Herr Gabler growled and lifted himself off the table. His nose was bleeding. Kitty must have broken it.

Herr Gabler fumbled for his Luger, which had fallen to the floor.

Oh, no.

"Run!" Kitty shouted as she crossed the room. Poppy led the way, her little toenails tapping against the floor.

I dashed after them, stopping only to retrieve my wig from the desk.

"Watch out," Fredricks shouted. "He's got a gun."

I glanced back in time to see Fredricks stick a foot out and trip the German, who, with a mouth full of curses, landed face first on the floor.

"Don't dillydally, ma chérie." Fredricks struggled against the ropes. "Save yourself... and your beloved lieutenant, if you must." He winked at me. "Unless you're saving yourself for me."

How could he flirt at a time like this?

I tugged on my wig.

"Your toy gun is hidden under the telegraph machine." Fredricks wriggled one hand free and gestured toward the desk.

I dashed back to the desk, snagged Mata Hari's gun, and tucked it into my handbag.

"Go. Save yourself." Fredricks held up the rope. "Don't worry about me."

I stood blinking at him.

"Your concern is touching." He smiled weakly. "Now go!"

Herr Gabler growled and sprang to his feet.

I sprinted down the hallway as fast as my Oxfords would carry me.

I didn't look back again.

18

THE INTERROGATION

Dawn was just breaking when we arrived back at the hotel. We found Clifford pacing the lobby. Had he been up all night? The wrinkles in his suit and the purple bags under his eyes suggested as much.

Somehow the bright colors of the hanging tapestries, the baroque patterns of the wool rugs, and the enormous height of the ceilings seemed even more extravagant after a sleepless night. My head was spinning.

Dodging a porter carrying a big stack of parcels for a well-dressed woman, Clifford rushed up to us. "I say, where have you been?" His tone was sharp. "I've been worried." He removed the pipe from his mouth. "I had visions of you kidnapped, tied up, pistol whipped... or worse."

Ha! The man was clairvoyant.

"Good lord." He pointed his pipe at Kitty. "What happened to you?"

Kitty did look a sight. Strands of blonde hair had escaped her chignon. Her black fencing vest had a tear where Poppy's collar had grazed it. And she had a giant purple goose egg on her forehead where she'd been pistol whipped.

"You'll never believe it." Kitty clapped her hands together in her now familiar act. From the outside, you'd never know she was a petty criminal plucked off the London streets by the War Office. Forensics expert. Master foot-fighter. What other secrets did she have?

Even if Clifford lapped it up like cream, I wasn't falling for the excitable schoolgirl routine.

"You fill him in." I put my good hand on her arm and glancing around the crowded lobby. "I have to rescue Archie."

Poppy jumped up and down and squeaked until Clifford picked her up. He nuzzled her topknot. "You didn't endanger my little princess, did you?"

Figures. He was more concerned about the dog than he was about us.

Out of the corner of my eye, I saw a dark uniform approach. A police officer marched toward us. He didn't take his gaze off me.

"Miss Fiona Figg?" he said, glancing from Kitty to me and back again. His sandy-colored mustache and Cockney accent, in addition to the navy uniform with gold buttons, indicated he was from the British police force.

Now what?

"Yes." I raised my good hand. "I'm Fiona Figg."

"I need you to come to the station and answer some questions." He adjusted his hat.

No. Not now. I had to get back to the blooming tomb and save Archie before he'd lost too much blood.

"I say, what's this about?" Clifford came to my defense.

"We need to take your statement about Mr. Relish's death." The officer fingered his Billy club.

By *we*, did he mean he and his Billy club? I hoped he didn't plan to use the bloody thing.

"It was an accident." My cheeks warmed. "Or rather, sabotage." I really was too tired for this now, not to mention I had more pressing things on my mind, like saving Archie's life and finding Agent Dankworth.

"Just come with me, please, ma'am." He took my elbow.

Poppy growled at him. My little guard dog. If I spoke in Russian, would she grab the copper's trouser leg in her teeth and stop him taking me off to the nick?

"There's no need for manhandling." I wriggled out of his grip. "Might I at least have a bath first?"

"Sorry, ma'am." He shook his head. "I have orders—"

"Oh, alright." *Sigh. What choice did I have?* My shoulders slumped.

What if Archie's wound was serious? What if he'd already bled out? I shook the terrible thoughts from my mind.

"Ma'am." The copper tugged at my arm. "You can freshen up later. Come on."

After a night without sleep, being tied up and gagged, and hiding in a musty wardrobe, I could only imagine what I must look like. Perhaps the disheveled, odiferous state of my person would encourage them to make it quick.

I adjusted my wig and allowed the officer to lead me outside, where a police motorcar was waiting. What a fuss.

I shielded my eyes. Even the sunrise was brighter than usual. It stabbed at my brain like a red-hot poker.

"I'll bail you out." Clifford's voice carried across the lobby.

"Get to Lorrain's dig and rescue Archie," I called over my shoulder. The copper pulled me outside. "He's tied up! And bleeding—" The copper hustled me off before I could get an answer. Had Clifford and Kitty heard me? Would they save Archie? My heart sank.

Don't die on me, dear Archie.

Everyone on the terrace stopped to gawk as the officer helped me into the backseat of the police motorcar. If I hadn't been so exhausted, I would have been mortified.

I might not be a murderer, but I'd kill for some headache powders.

Only a few blocks away, the nick was a squat pink stone building with lovely navy-blue accents adorned with pretty painted gold leaves. It looked more like a fancy boutique or salon. Inside, the rooms were plain and boxy. The officer led me past the reception area, deposited me in a hallway, told me to wait, and then disappeared. I slumped into one of the chairs that were lined up against one wall.

For a police station, the place was quiet. Sitting in the hallway, leaning my head against the wall, I was alone with my thoughts... and the faint smell of cigar smoke. I closed my eyes, which was probably a mistake. Given how little sleep I'd had in the last twenty-four hours, I could have slept standing up.

I fidgeted into the wall, trying to get comfortable. As I drifted in and out of sleep, a queasy feeling left me drained. The only thing worse than lack of sleep was the twilight just before sleep being constantly interrupted. The coppers might as well have been torturing me.

Every time I drifted off, I had nightmares about Archie tied up and bleeding. Only I knew they weren't dreams. They were all too real.

I searched the pockets of my dress for something to keep me awake. A sweetie or a throat lozenge or anything. Where was a stray biscuit when I needed one? Even a dog treat would have been welcome. All I found was my miniature magnifying glass and my spy lipstick. Turning sideways on my chair, I took the opportunity to use it to touch up my lips.

To distract myself from my pounding head, I took stock of everything that had happened since I arrived in Cairo.

The stranger on the train had turned out to be Fredrick Fredricks in disguise—as much as it galled me to have been taken in by him, I did appreciate a good disguise. French archeologist Jean-Baptiste Lorrain had been murdered after Lady Enid's party and after he met HG at GAI, Hermann Gabler at the German Archeology Institute.

I searched my pocket again. *Whew.* It was still there. The bit of fiber I'd plucked from the orange and green carpet at the institute. *Darn.* I should have given it to Kitty to analyze when I had the chance. I wished these blooming coppers would hurry up. I had murders to solve and canals to protect, and potential lovers to save.

Fredricks had claimed the map and the code on the tablecloth were a ruse. Had he made it his mission to humiliate me? Or was he trying to throw me off the scent of his true plans? Then again, he might have told me it was all a lark precisely because blowing up the Suez Canal at Crocodile Lake *was* the true plan. *You should never trust a liar, especially when he tells you he's lying.*

Mori Al-Madie was delivering the true plans in code in the last act. I had to break that blasted code.

Then there was poor Agent Relish, killed in hospital by my own hand. I shuddered. Would the coppers believe me? If only I had proof that Fredricks had tampered with the morphine bottle. Then I could clear my name *and* finally have the goods on the rotter.

In the mirror of my spy lipstick, I saw the young nurse swaying toward me.

"Excuse me." She stopped in front of me. "I see they've got you here too." Again, her face was painted to perfection with dark eye kohl, arched brows, and bright red lips. Instead of her nurse's uniform, she wore a tight red silk dress. Judging by the way the coppers ogled her as they passed down the hall, her ensemble was quite affecting. "I'm Amelia, by the way." She held out a dainty paw complete with red claws. "Amelia Emerson."

I popped my lipstick back into my bag and stood up. With my injured wing, the handshake was awkward. "Fiona Figg." After introducing myself, I glanced up and down the hall and then leaned in closer. "What did you tell them about the morphine bottle?"

"The truth." Her arched brows fell.

"And what's that?" Did she know something I didn't? Or was she in on it with Fredricks? Good grief. I was getting downright paranoid.

She squinted at me as if I'd asked a trick question. "You gave him too much... and... and... he died." She gave me a sheepish half-smile. "I'm sure it was an accident."

I'm sure it wasn't. "Of course it was an accident." I brushed imaginary crumbs off my dress.

The uniformed copper appeared in the hallway and beckoned to me. "Miss Figg, you're next."

"What else did you tell them?" I whispered. I had to know what to expect before entering that interrogation room. I'd spent enough time in jail to know I didn't like it.

"Nothing." Amelia's face contorted as if I'd accused her of something.

"What did they ask you?"

"Miss Figg." The officer raised his voice. "Come along." From down the hall, he wiggled his fingers at me.

"One minute." I held up my good hand.

"They asked a lot of questions about the man who visited Mr. Fredricks." She shrugged.

"A man visited Fredricks in hospital?" *Why didn't I know about this before?*

She nodded.

The officer marched down the hall toward me.

"Who?" My pulsed quickened. Spit it out, pet, before the copper drags me away.

"Just a man." Her eyelashes batted a mile a minute. "A man with a charcoal fedora hat with a red hatband." She shook her head. "I don't know. Some man."

Charcoal fedora with a red band. The rude doctor... who was not a doctor. The man I'd passed in the hallway at the hospital. The man who'd sabotaged the morphine and killed Agent Relish.

The copper's hand clamped around my arm. "Let's go, lady."

I glanced back at Nurse Amelia Emerson, her hips wagging as she strutted down the hall. The word *siren* came to mind.

"No need to drag me." I pulled out of the copper's grip and followed him into the tiny room.

The interrogation room was only big enough for a square table and four chairs. Another plain-clothed policeman sat at the table, writing on a notepad. He didn't look up. Like a schoolboy learning to draw, he had his full concentration on his work.

The overhead light might as well have been a spotlight shining right into my eyes. My headache was becoming a full-blown migraine. The kind that sent me to bed in a dark room.

"Miss Figg." The uniformed officer announced my arrival.

The plain-clothed man only grunted. Wiry, with a shock of jet-black hair atop an otherwise shaved head, along with a pointy beard, he looked like a terrier.

The uniformed officer pointed at a chair.

I took a seat and waited for the other copper to finish with his crayons. The longer I waited, the heavier the weight in the pit of my stomach. My palms were sweating. Discreetly, I wiped them on my dress.

As I did, my hand passed over my miniature magnifying glass, which reminded me again of the carpet fibers. Blast. If only I'd remembered to give them to Kitty.

"The autopsy on Mr. Relish showed a lethal dose of chloroform." Finally, the plain-clothed copper looked up from his notes. "Did you administer that dose?"

Chloroform! I didn't give him chloroform. How did he get a lethal dose of chloroform? My heart sank. *Oh, my word.* The grassy smell. The morphine bottle must have contained chloroform. A sharp stabbing pain like an icepick to the brain made me cringe. I put my head in my hands. I had checked the label. It had said morphine.

Confound it. I was right. Someone had tampered with the bottle. The murderer put chloroform into the morphine bottle—*dear me*—and I injected the poor man with it. Fredricks... either him or the man in the fedora.

Misery loved company. My headache had been joined by roiling nausea.

Waiting for an answer, the copper stared right through me. Bloody unnerving. I wished he'd go back to his notebook. He hadn't even introduced himself. Rude man.

"I did give the shot, but—"

"So, you admit you gave the fatal injection?" He didn't blink.

"Yes, but—"

"Shhh." He held up a finger. "Just a minute." He bent over some papers on the table and started scribbling.

"But I didn't—"

"Shhh!"

Irritating man. Shushing me like an overzealous librarian. I really was in no mood.

He slid a paper across the table. "Would you sign this confession?"

What? "Heavens, no." I crossed my arms. "I didn't kill Mr. Relish... I mean I killed him, but I didn't murder him." I felt like my head might explode.

"You've already admitted you administered the lethal injection." He tapped his pen on the table.

"If you'll ever let me finish a sentence, I'll explain." I waited for the next shush. It never came. *Finally.* He was ready to listen. "I administered a small dose of morphine. But, unbeknownst to me, someone had sabotaged the bottle."

He tilted his head and squinted at me. "You didn't know you were injecting the patient with chloroform."

He scribbled on his notepad. "You thought it was morphine."

"Exactly."

Bent over his notepad, he continued writing. "Someone else put chloroform in the morphine bottle."

"Right." I rubbed my temples.

"Who?" He stared across the table at me.

"I don't know." Either this copper was a bit off, or I didn't understand his interrogation techniques. Didn't he believe me? "Perhaps the man with the fedora." *Or Fredrick Fredricks.*

He perked up. "Tell me more about this man."

What could I say? I didn't know anything. "The nurse told me a man visited just before Mr. Relish died." I took a deep breath to quell the nausea. "I saw the man leaving the ward. I thought he was a doctor."

"You saw him?" He scowled.

"Yes. But at the time, I thought he was a rude doctor." *Should I tell him about Fredricks?*

If Fredricks faked his injury, he could have put chloroform into the morphine bottle when both the nurse and I were out of the room. He'd killed British agents before. And he'd always gotten away with it because he was a slippery fish. "Have you questioned the patient in the next bed? Mr. Fredricks?"

"We haven't been able to locate him." The officer tapped his notepad with his pen.

Find him and you'll find the killer. I kept my mouth shut. Either Fredricks did it or he knew who did. I only hoped I found the scoundrel before the police did. I wanted to give him a piece of my mind. I wanted to see the look on his face when I hauled him in. I wanted the satisfaction of finally beating him at his own game.

The copper held up a finger and then went back to his notepad.

Chloroform. I should have recognized the smell. If only I'd checked the bottle before preparing the injection. How was I to know someone had tampered with it? It wasn't my fault... was it?

Overcome with nausea and pain, I put my head in my hands. My elbows slid and my head almost hit the table. Given the level of my exhaustion, I wished it had knocked me unconscious and put me out of my misery.

I needed a warm bath, a hot cuppa, and a good night's sleep. But most of all, I needed to make sure Archie was safe.

"What happened to your arm?" The copper didn't look up.

"I fell off a horse at the Gezira Sporting Club." Actually, a branch threw me off a horse during a fox hunt, but I didn't want to admit either of those things to this man.

"How very posh." He closed his notebook.

Did he think I was a toff?

Even if I were, that was no reason to be rude.

19

THE MISSING AGENT

By the time I got back to the hotel, I was dead on my feet. Severely sleep deprived, in full migraine mode, my vision was blurry, and my mouth was as dry as the Arabian desert. I hoped Clifford and Kitty had made it to the tomb in time to save Archie. There was no way I could make it back to the tomb on my own, especially if it meant riding another dung-encrusted ass.

Slightly off-balance, I crossed the lobby, which stretched out before me like an endless sea. Unfamiliar faces stared at me with concern. I didn't even want to think of the mess I'd become. I was queasy from pain and lack of sleep, and it took all my effort to drag myself to the lift.

I'd forgotten to pick up my key at the front

desk, so I rapped on the door to our room. Waiting for Kitty to open it, I leaned against the door frame.

Bed. I needed to lie down.

The door burst open, nearly knocking me over. Dressed in a pink cotton frock with bright yellow flowers, and a yellow sailor hat, Kitty stood smiling at me. "Aunt Fiona, are you alright?"

"No." I pushed past her.

Barking, Poppy jumped up and down and then turned in circles like a whirling dervish.

Clifford paced the room. "Good lord. You look like something the cat dragged in."

"You would too if a fiendish panther had been toying with you." I threw myself onto my bed. "Your *brilliant* friend and hunting pal."

Poppy followed close on my heels.

"What happened?" Kitty grabbed the pillow off her bed and brought it to me.

"Thank you, dear." I added her pillow to my own and propped myself up. "Did you find Archie? Is he alright?"

Clifford and Kitty looked at each other.

"What's happened to Lieutenant Somersby?" Clifford said, pulling out his pipe.

I gave him the evil eye. He pouted but put the offending object away. "Didn't you hear me ask you to go to Lorrain's tomb?"

"No." Clifford's shoulders jerked as if from an unwanted slap on the back. "Why?"

I pulled myself to my feet. "I'll fill you in on the gory details later. Right now, we need to save Archie." I glanced at my watch. It had just gone noon. Those cursed coppers had kept me at the nick for hours.

How long had Archie been tied up without food or water? Not yet twenty-four hours, although it felt like it had been a week since I'd seen him. Even an hour bound up in a dank tomb was deuced unpleasant. And he was bleeding. How badly, I didn't know.

I went to the dressing table and peered into the looking glass. *Good heavens. What a mess!* My wig was ratty and askew, my gown was filthy and streaked with dirt and blood. Where did that come from? I examined my person to make sure it wasn't mine. Must be Archie's. My gown also had a large tear to boot. The purple bags under my eyes made me look a hundred years old. I covered my face with my hand.

Kitty joined me at the mirror. "You need to rest."

She led me to my bed and I sat down with a groan. My head felt like it might explode. I rubbed my temples.

"She's ill, poor thing." Clifford came to my bedside.

"Can I get you a glass of water? How about a cup of tea?"

"That would be lovely." I nodded. "And some headache powders."

Poppy jumped up onto my bed and licked my face. I was too tired to stop her.

Clifford opened and closed his mouth like a gasping codfish. "Righto." He took off at a trot and disappeared from the room.

"Kitty, dear." I lifted my head. "Can you get us back out to Monsieur Lorrain's tomb?"

"I could hire some camels." She sat on the edge of my bed. Her own bed was piled high with clothing.

The thought of riding one of those stinky beasts again turned my stomach. "Is there no other way?" Why didn't they have a motorcar or trolley out to the pyramids? It would be so much more convenient.

"Would you prefer donkeys?" She patted my ankle. "They're slower."

"I would prefer something that didn't have a mind of its own." I shut my eyes. "Or a stomach and everything it entails." Oh dear. My head was under attack by Vickers machine guns, and someone had lobbed a grenade at my stomach. "Archie. He's bleeding—"

A rap on the door signaled Clifford's return.

"A glass of water and a cup of tea," Clifford said. "As ordered."

I pried an eye open.

He sat the beverages on the nightstand and then handed me a packet of powders.

I tried to lift myself on my elbows. But with the hurt arm, it was impossible. With an audible groan, I rolled onto my side and with great effort levered myself upright. "Thank you, Clifford, dear." Whatever his faults, he was loyal, in contrast to my ex-husband, Fredricks, and just about every other person I knew.

Clifford handed me the glass of water and a spoon.

I opened the packet, poured in the powder, gave it a stir, and drank it down. *Ugh.* I washed it down with tea.

Unlike the Americans and the French, the Egyptians knew how to make a good cuppa. Strong tea with a splash of milk.

As my grandmother always said, "If tea can't fix it, it must be darned serious." Only she didn't say darned. "And even then, tea helps." Not even a strong cuppa could console me if I didn't save Archie. If only this blasted migraine would subside. With my vision blurred and my head spinning, I doubted I could even stand up at this point, let alone ride a blooming donkey.

It was difficult to drink tea with one hand. I couldn't hold the saucer and drink at the same time. As I tried to replace the cup on the saucer, the whole kit-and-caboodle slid onto the floor. *Drat.* There went my only hope at revival. I stared down at the dark spot on the carpet and wanted to cry from sheer exhaustion.

Poppy jumped off the bed and licked at the spot. I was almost envious of the little beast.

The carpet! Good grief. My fiber sample. I sat upright and then fished in my pocket for the fiber. I held the frayed orange threads between my thumb and forefinger. "A carpet sample from the German Archeology Institute."

Kitty extended her hand, and I dropped the fiber into her palm.

"Orange and green carpet." I scrabbled around in my pocket. Where was the bit of white plant? "This might establish the whereabouts of Jean-Baptiste's attack." I handed her the chamomile flower. "White plant matter."

"Would you like me to test it now?" Kitty went to the dressing table and dropped the fiber into a small envelope. "Or shall we rescue your Lieutenant Somersby first?"

I stood up but got so dizzy, I had to sit back down.

"We'll go to the tomb." Kitty came to my side. "You get some rest, Aunt Fiona."

"Good idea." Clifford joined her at my bedside.

The last few days weighed heavily on me, as if I was being pressed onto my bed like a dried and wilted flower. As I lay back on the pillows, tears rolled across my temples.

"Everything will be alright, old bean." Clifford stood over me. "You'll see." He bent down and patted my hand. "You'll figure it out." He smiled. "You always do."

"Figure out what?" The light hurt my eyes.

"Everything." He beamed down at me. "And don't worry about Lieutenant Somersby. He's a tough lad." Good old Clifford. "Kitty and I will go and fetch him." He brushed a strand of my wig out of my watery eyes. He really was a decent sort.

"Poppy will stay with you." Kitty lifted the pup onto my bed. "Take good care of Aunt Fiona."

I didn't have the heart to object.

* * *

When I woke up, the room was dark. Had I slept through the night? Why didn't Kitty wake me? Groggy,

I sat up in bed. My gown stuck to my skin, and I felt covered in a thin layer of Egypt.

Did they rescue Archie? Was the canal safe? Had Kitty tested the fibers and discovered the location of Jean-Baptiste's murder, and perhaps the identity of the killer too?

I willed my eyes to adjust to the darkness. What had I missed?

Kitty's bed was empty—or at least empty of her person.

Desperate to scrape off the desert, I decided on a bath. My migraine had dulled into a hangover. Perhaps a soak would help revive me. Then I could go looking for Archie and my companions.

Loath to turn on the light for fear my migraine would come back, I picked my way across the room in the dark to the lav. Once inside, I shut the door, careful not to make any noise. Any sound or bright light might trigger the migraine again. I squeezed my eyes shut and then turned on the light. Opening my eyes halfway, I waited for my poor tired brain to process even the smallest amount of light.

As I turned on the tap, I realized something was missing. It was entirely too quiet. I was reminded of Conan Doyle's story "Silver Blaze," wherein Holmes reports the curious incident of the dog in the night, which turns out to be the absence of the dog in the night.

Why wasn't Poppy barking? Or at least tripping me up as I went to the lav? Had Kitty changed her mind and taken the pup with her to the tomb after all? Gracious me. A lump formed in my throat. Weren't they back from the tomb yet? Had something happened to them? Were they too late? Was Archie dead?

I turned off the tap, adjusted my wig and clothing as best as I could, and dashed out into the other room. Flipping on the light confirmed my fears. Poppy was gone. Had they come back while I was sleeping and taken Poppy out for a walk? The little creature couldn't have escaped, could she? I circled the room like a headless chicken.

Calm down, Fiona.

All three of them were probably just next door in Clifford's room... or down on the terrace... or in the restaurant.

I glanced at my watch. It had gone four. I moved the heavy curtain and looked out the window. The sun was low in the sky. It would be dark in an hour. Nights were long in Cairo in December.

I dashed next door to Clifford's room and knocked. Nothing. I knocked again. No answer. *Curses.* Where were they? Lying unconscious in a tomb? Or laughing over cocktails in the bar?

I went back to my room and stuffed my buttoned pockets with spy paraphernalia. I checked my handbag for Mata Hari's gun.

On my way out of the hotel, I peeked into the bar. Nope. Not there. I hurried out to the terrace and scanned the tables. Not there either. My heart was pounding. I didn't know what else to do. I ran back through the hotel and out the back door, racing around the zoo to the stables. I would have to rent a camel and ride out to Lorrain's tomb myself.

If anything had happened to Archie—or the girl— I'd never forgive myself. Of course, Clifford was the one I should worry about. No doubt Archie or Kitty could take on any comers. *Please, let Poppy be alright.*

When I arrived at the stable, the dragoman was just closing the doors. "Sorry, madam, we're closed." The sleeve of his robe waved in the wind as he gripped the door latch.

"But I need a camel." I fished in my bag for my purse. "My friends are in trouble." I pulled out a note. "I'll pay double." I held out the money.

"Too dangerous in the desert at twilight." He shook his head. "Especially for lady."

"Triple." I pulled out another note.

He tilted his head and waited.

Another note. And another. After another minute, I held a wad of cash. "Here," I said, defeated. "This is all I have."

He snatched the bills from my hand. "Don't blame me if you don't come back." He opened the barn door.

"Thank you, sir." I followed him inside. "I'll get your camel back to you."

"I'm not worried about camel." He smiled. "He knows the way home."

* * *

The desert sunset was a magnificent blanket of reds and golds. If I hadn't been in such a hurry, I could have stopped to admire it. As it was, I would be lucky to reach Monsieur Lorrain's tomb before complete darkness.

Riding a camel was difficult under the best of circumstances. Riding with one hand took all my concentration and then some. As much as it hurt, I had to use my bad arm to steady myself, otherwise I'd fall off the stinky beast.

"Come on, you foul thing," I shouted. "Faster."

The creature let out a pitiful groan. But it did

quicken its pace. The animal could move when it wanted to.

All my muscles were taut. My heart was racing faster than the camel. *Please, let them be alright. Please, let them be alright.* This silent prayer echoed through my head endlessly. *Please, let them be alright.*

When the silhouette of the Great Sphinx of Giza came into view, I let out an audible sigh. Almost there. Of course, I wasn't almost there. The blooming Sphinx dominated the horizon for hectares. At least it gave me my bearings.

The moon rising over the Sphinx took my breath away. It also helped illuminate my way.

Finally. Monsieur Lorrain's tomb was in sight. I gritted my teeth for the last few yards of my perilous journey. I passed the ragged tent, its flaps waving in the breeze. No one had touched anything since Jean-Baptiste's death. At least not officially.

A dim light glowed at the tomb's entrance. Two camels were tied to the hitching post. Someone was inside with a torch. Archie? Clifford and Kitty? That bounder Fredricks or the evil Hermann Gabler? I shuddered. Whoever it was, I was about to find out. I took a deep breath and prepared to dismount.

Dismounting was even more difficult than mounting the beast. My efforts landed me on the sand in a solid thud that knocked the air out of me. I rolled clear of the camel's hooves. Once I'd caught my breath, I picked myself up and brushed myself off.

I wrapped the camel's leather rein around the post. "Stay!"

Picking my way across the rocks and sand, I creeped toward the entrance. *Breathe, Fiona. Just breathe.*

Just in case, I pulled Mata Hari's gun from my bag. Clutching it in both hands, I entered the tomb. "Hello?" I took a few more steps. "Anybody here?" Ears pricked, I stopped and listened. A faint hammering reverberated through the cave. Was someone excavating?

That horrible smell was even stronger than before. I put the crook of my arm over my nose and tiptoed inside. Luckily, I had my small American torch in my handbag. But given I had only one working arm, I had to choose between the gun and the torch. What good would the gun do if I couldn't see? I traded the gun for the torch and clicked it on. Staying close to the wall, I made my way to the spot where I'd last seen Archie.

The deeper I got into the tomb, the louder the hammering and the stronger the smell. Did I hear voices too?

"Hello?" I stumbled along next to the wall. "Archie?"

I shone the torch around the tomb. My heart leaped into my throat.

He was gone. I whirled around. This was where I'd left him. I hoped to heaven he was safe.

The hammering was getting louder.

I continued further into the tomb. "Clifford? Kitty?"

Bark. Bark. Bark.

"Poppy!" My heart leaped into my throat.

"We're here, Aunt Fiona." The small voice came from the back of the tomb.

I exhaled an audible sigh. I was never so relieved in my life. Thank goodness. The girl was alive. But what in heaven's name was she doing?

"Are you alright?" I hurried through the dark tunnel toward her voice.

The hammering stopped.

"It's ghastly." It was Clifford. "You'll never believe it."

What's ghastly? Believe what?

I went as fast as the uneven terrain and limited light would allow. "Where are you?"

"We're here!" The smooth tenor was a balm for my soul.

"Archie?"

What in the blazes were they doing? Had they found a mummy?

"We're here!" A chorus of voices echoed through the cave, followed by a refrain of barking.

I rounded the corner and there they were. Archie, Clifford, Kitty, and Poppy. Three of them had handkerchiefs tied over their noses and were clawing at a pile of rocks. Tail wagging, Poppy pawed at the rocks, clearly enjoying the dig.

"What in heaven's name are you doing?" I clicked off my torch.

Lanterns hung from pegs in either side of the rock wall. Surrounded by loose rocks, they'd managed to open a small passageway. But why?

"That vile smell..." Archie raised an eyebrow. "I'm afraid we found the source." With his charcoal fedora cocked to one side and stripped down to his undershirt and trousers, he looked like an American film star. I averted my eyes from his bare shoulders.

No wonder they were all wearing handkerchiefs. "A rotting mummy?" I didn't take my arm away from my nose.

Poppy sniffed and wagged, clearly not bothered by the smell.

"Afraid not." Archie wiped his brow with the back

of his hand. He pointed to a shoe sticking out of the rubble. "It's Robert."

"Robert?" Archie was on first-name terms with the mummy?

"Agent Dankworth." His shoulders slumped when he said the name.

"Oh, no!" Not a mummy. Another dead agent. "How do you know it's him?"

Archie held up a silver watch and then pointed up to a shriveled hand protruding from the rocks. "It's engraved." He read from the back of the watch. "To Robert, with love Gertie."

First Relish and now Dankworth... although judging from the smell, the order of their deaths was reversed. How long had Agent Dankworth been locked in this tomb?

Blimey. Had one or both agents discovered the codes delivered in the arias at the theater? Or stolen antiquities?

I rubbed my temples.

Who had killed them and why?

I was determined to find out.

20

THE CODE

After the harrowing experience of finding Agent Dankworth's remains, we gathered in the bar at Shepheard's to debrief and take some restorative cocktails.

The Long Bar at Shepheard's was a dark mysterious space at the back of the hotel. Supposedly, the bartender, whose name was Gasperini, could procure anything for anyone, provided they could pay. Kingmakers, widow makers, and depressed poets all passed through the Long Bar.

My friends and I took a table in a back corner. Although we'd missed tea, none of us had much of an appetite. Kitty asked for a sweet biscuit and a plate of cream for Poppy—apparently, the little traitor had refused to act as my guard dog, insisting on going with her mistress instead.

Clifford snacked on nuts as we waited for our drinks to arrive. He insisted I have a brandy to help me recover from the shock. Of course, I'd seen dead bodies before, but never in that state of decomposition. I cringed.

Archie had gone to contact the War Office and inform Captain Hall of poor Agent Dankworth's demise. But he promised to see me again before I left Cairo. Meeting in tombs over dead bodies was not my idea of romance. Anyway, I had no idea how much longer I'd be in Cairo. It depended on Fredrick Fredricks and his propaganda plot. If the rotter was telling the truth about lying, then the Suez Canal plot was a ruse… or a decoy. A decoy for what?

I'm sure Archie knew more than I did. He always did. I had to devise more successful means of getting information out of him. I smiled, imagining a few I'd like to try. I closed my eyes and tried *not* to think of Archie's bare shoulders and that bothersome lock of hair that constantly tempted me to touch it. *Fiona, get a grip. You're not in Cairo to romance Archie.*

No. I was in Cairo to catch Fredricks in an act of espionage or murder. I wouldn't be surprised if the bounder had killed them all himself. Now if I could just prove it.

"I tested that carpet fiber," Kitty said, sipping her Brandy Alexander, a sweet creamy concoction that made brandy almost palatable. "It appears to be the same as what I'd collected from under the victim's fingernails." Jean-Baptiste had been demoted from the object of her flirtations to a mere victim.

"That means Jean-Baptiste was attacked at the German Archeology Institute." I stirred my drink to make sure the sweet cream diluted the strong liquor. "And then he was taken out to the tomb."

"So it seems." Kitty nibbled on her biscuit.

"Herr Hermann Gabler, the German archeologist." I waved my spoon. "I saw evidence he is living at the institute and, since it's closed and locked, no one else can even get inside." I slipped my notebook from my handbag, flipped it open, and circled his name. "Herr Gabler is our prime suspect." Along with Fredricks, of course. I would never cross off his name from my list.

"But why?" Clifford pulled the cherry out of his Old Fashioned and offered it to Kitty. "What was his motive?"

"Maybe Jean-Baptiste found out the German was dealing in stolen antiquities." My stomach growled and I stole a biscuit from Kitty's plate. "Or perhaps the

German didn't appreciate a Frenchman taking over his concession."

"And what of Agents Dankworth and Relish?" Clifford asked. "Who did for them? Was that Gabler too? Doesn't add up."

"Maybe he's a German spy." Kitty dipped her biscuit into her drink. "He found out Dankworth and Relish were British agents, so he killed them." She took a soggy bite.

Clifford waved the waiter over. He'd decided to order dinner after all. With promises of sweet puddings, he persuaded Kitty to join him. Poppy wagged and whirled in the girl's lap, obviously in favor of the dinner plan. I, on the other hand, had other plans.

"Agent Relish discovered the code at the Isis Theater." I sipped my cream brandy. The sweet burn of the alcohol made me cough. "He was just about to tell me about it before he was killed." I regained my breath. "He was killed to stop him telling." I planned to get back to the theater and crack that code. It was Sunday, and I didn't plan on missing my chance. Otherwise, I'd have to wait another four whole days until Thursday.

Still, the theater and the code didn't explain Agent Dankworth's death. According to the pathologist I'd overheard at the tomb, he'd been killed over a week ago. So, Jean-Baptiste could have killed him.

As far as I knew, Agent Dankworth was not undercover at the theater. Had Agent Relish told him about
the German spies at the theater? That didn't make
sense. If Agent Relish knew about the code over a
week ago, he would have reported it to the War Office.
For all I knew, he had. Were the murders of Relish and
Dankworth related or not? And what about Jean-Baptiste Lorrain?

My mind was awhirl with questions. Foremost
among them: *Why would Herr Hermann Gabler kill two
British agents and a French archeologist?* What did they
have in common?

Perhaps the killings were related by cause and effect. One led to the next and then to the next. But why
was Agent Dankworth killed? Unless Fredricks was
right, and this was all about the illegal antiquities
trade. It all came down to the Isis Theater.

Bloody frustrating.

So many questions. Too few answers.

As I drained my glass, I suppressed another bothersome question: *When would I see Archie again?*

So far, I'd heard nothing about an explosion at the
canal. Maybe Fredricks had been telling the truth
when he'd said it was all a ruse. *I sincerely hoped so.*
Then again, the whole Crocodile Lake plan could be a
decoy leading us away from the real explosion.

I glanced at my watch. Nearly half past seven. If I wanted to catch another of Mori Al-Madie's performances, I'd have to hop it. The show started at eight.

Fibbing about having a headache and needing to lie down, I left Kitty and Clifford to their supper.

If only I could break La Sultana's secret code, then I'd learn the truth.

* * *

By the time I arrived at the Isis Theater, the opera had already begun. The usher made me wait in the hall until intermission. I paced up and down the hall, hoping I was right and La Sultana delivered coded messages only in the last act.

When the doors opened for intermission, I rushed in, swimming upstream against the soldiers hurrying to the bar for more libations. My seat was in the back of the theater, so at least I didn't have far to go. As everyone else was getting up and stretching, I plopped into my chair, which was in the middle of row Q with only a partial view of the stage.

No matter. If I was right, I only needed to be able to hear the performance.

I scanned the audience, looking for familiar faces, one in particular. If La Sultana was delivering coded messages, then someone in the audience was receiving them. My hunch was that someone was Fredrick Fredricks.

The lights went down, and my heart sped up. I pulled my notebook and pencil from my handbag and waited. Pencil at the ready, I recorded every word La Sultana repeated.

Sure enough, in the last act, she repeated seemingly random words—words I suspected were not so random after all.

Palace. On. Rest. Tomb. Sucking. And. Is. Dark. And. Tomb. Not. O. O. No.

She repeated each of these words only once this time.

When the lights went up, I sat glued to my seat, comparing notes from the last performance.

The last time, she repeated: Beauty. Love. On. Why. Up. Up. Up. Up. Come. All. Nothing. At. Love. Come. Here. Run. I. Soul. Tomb. May. And. Smile. Day. Day. Day. Day.

The words she repeated this time were different from those before.

The type of code used would be limited, given that it was delivered in an aria. It had to be a very simple code, one easily adaptable and easy to decipher. I had an idea.

Quickly, I circled the first letter of every word.

B. L. O. W. U. U. U. U. C. A. N. A. L. C. H. R. I.
S. T. M. A. S. D. D. D. D.

It had to be significant that she repeated "Up" and "Day" four times instead of just once. I bracketed them out for now:

BLOW[up]CANALCHRISTMAS[day]

Oh, my sainted aunt. "Blow up canal Christmas Day."

Why didn't I think of this simple technique earlier? Had I been away from Room 40 so long I was slipping?

Hurriedly, I circled the first letters from tonight's repetitions.

PORTSAIDCHRISTMASATNOON

Port Said, Christmas at noon. I'd done it. Chuffed... and terrified, I slapped my notebook closed. I'd cracked the code.

Fredricks's ruse *had* been a decoy.

I could only assume the British army had stepped up security and moved considerable troops to Crocodile Lake. Now I knew why there was no explosion. The real plan was to blow up the canal at Port Said on Christmas Day at noon. With the British troops elsewhere, Port Said would be nearly defenseless.

Devious. Devious and clever.

Fredricks had been counting on me to deliver false information to Captain Hall. Otherwise, why lure me to Cairo? He couldn't seriously believe I'd help him persuade the Arabs to turn against the British. But I'd fooled him. I'd discovered the true plan. I had to report it to Captain Hall before it was too late.

Christmas Day at noon. *Three days from now.*

I stuffed my papers back into my handbag and jumped up. "Excuse me." I squeezed in front of soldiers and their dates. "Excuse me." I stepped on a few toes, making my escape from the theater.

To avoid the crowd exiting the theater, I descended the stairs, and slipped around the back. I knew my way around from previous misadventures with Agent Relish and Mori Al-Madie.

As I approached the back door, Miss Al-Madie intercepted me. "Miss, what are you doing backstage?"

"Looking for you, of course," I fibbed. Although I was eager to ask her why she was in cahoots with the Germans, I couldn't spare the time.

"Oh, it's you." She didn't sound pleased to see me.

"Brilliant performance." I clapped my hands together in my best imitation of Kitty. "Even with the repetitions in the last act." I raised my eyebrows into what I hoped were the facial equivalent of question marks.

"Thank you." Her mustache twitched. "Now, if you'll excuse me, I have to change." She tugged her wig off and pulled out a few hairpins. Waves of long black hair fell over her shoulders.

"Give my regards to your costume girl." I stepped in front of her. "And her brother." I immediately regretted it. I'd gone too far.

She scoffed. "You British expect everyone to do your bidding."

"We are at war with Germany." I pointed out the obvious. "Egypt is a British protectorate."

"Yes." She smirked. "My countrymen are forced to fight your bloody war while your Prince of Wales hits golf balls off the pyramids." Her cheeks darkened. "You can all go to blazes." She pushed me out of the way and marched off.

Goodness. Miss Mori Al-Madie had quite a temper. And her insulting remarks about my countrymen only further confirmed my suspicions. She was working with the Germans.

I glanced at my watch. London was two hours behind Cairo. So, almost midnight in Cairo was just before ten in London. I hoped Captain Hall didn't go to bed early.

Now to find a telephone... and someone who would let me use it.

Any hour of the night or day, the streets of Cairo were bursting with energy. Tonight, the pulsations of the crowds made me anxious. Although the walk back to the hotel was short, the dark of night unsettled me. I had the uneasy sensation of being watched. I glanced over my shoulder and quickened my pace.

Thank goodness. The entrance to Shepheard's was in sight. I just had to cross the street and I'd be safely back at the hotel. Watching for motorcars and carriages, I stepped into the street. Someone jostled me from behind.

Ouch! A stabbing pain in my right side threw me to the ground. I looked up in time to see Kitty chasing a berobed man across the street. What in the world was the girl doing here?

I held my side and attempted to stand up. Another berobed passerby helped me to my feet.

"Thank you, sir." I was so lightheaded, I had difficulty getting the words out. The pain sharpened.

"*Bien sûr,* ma chérie." I knew that voice.

Oh, no. Not Fredricks, again.

He held my elbow and led me across the street.

My hand was wet. I glanced down. Blood.

Dear me. "I've been stabbed."

"I'll get you to hospital." Fredricks's voice was full of concern.

"No," I gasped. "Just get me to the hotel." I had to make the telephone call, even if it cost me my life. After all, it was not just my life at stake. Given the importance of the canal, the outcome of the war was at stake.

"I really think—"

"The hotel." I raised my voice. "Now."

"As you wish." Fredricks accompanied me into the lobby. "At least let me call for a doctor."

I nodded. Judging from my experience, doctors were hard to find.

Fredricks led me to a chair in the sitting area just off reception. "Stay here until I get back." He took my hand. "I'll take care of you, ma chérie." He kissed my hand, and then, robes flapping, he dashed off.

I waited until he was out of sight and then headed for the reception desk. The man at the desk was accommodating. When I told him it was a matter of life and death, his eyes went wide but he took me to a telephone in the back office. The blood seeping through my evening dress must have been convincing.

While the operator connected me to Captain Hall's private residence in the Admiralty, I watched the red blossom spread across my lavender gown.

Captain Hall's voice was gruff with sleep.

"The Isis Theater is a front for German spies." I sucked in air. "La Sultana is delivering coded messages in Romeo's aria in the last act—"

"La Sultana?" Captain Hall interrupted me. "Slow down, Miss Figg." I could imagine his eyelids blinking a mile a minute.

"Mori Al-Madie, the theater owner and an Egyptian nationalist working with the Germans..." I pressed my hand into my side.

Papers shuffled. "Just writing this down."

"I think Agents Relish and Dankworth discovered the code and that's why they were killed." My hand was wet with blood. "I cracked the code. They're planning to bomb the canal at Port Said on Christmas Day."

"You're sure—"

"Yes, sir."

"Any word about antiquities sales on the black market?" Judging from the timber of his voice, he'd just woken up.

Illegal antiquities? Were the agents investigating

antiquities? A wave of nausea hit me like a tsunami. "Fredricks mentioned illegal antiquities."

"We've learned that the Germans are funding their espionage operations in Cairo by selling antiquities." Captain Hall exhaled. "Follow the antiquities and find out who is running the operation out of the theater."

"Yes, sir." I looked down at my hand. Big mistake. A red stripe ran from my waist to the hem of my gown.

"Well done, Miss Figg."

"Thank you, sir." I smiled to myself.

"Don't let Fredricks out of your sight."

"I won't, sir." The sight of blood—my own blood—made me woozy. *I really must sit down before I fall down.*

"No disguises." Why was he so obsessed with my disguises? "We'll take care of the canal. We may also send another agent to the theater."

"Yes, sir."

"Anything else, Miss Figg?"

I hesitated.

"Are you alright?"

No, I'm blooming bleeding. "Yes, sir."

"Good work."

I glanced down at my gown. My last evening dress ruined, and one of my favorites.

Espionage was indeed hard on the wardrobe.

The line went dead.

21

ANOTHER BLASTED CODE

The next morning when I awoke, my side was sore, but my arm was considerably better. As my grandmother used to say, "One nail takes out the other."

I stretched and yawned. The room was dark, but dawn was breaking through the window. Time to get up. I may have saved the canal, but I hadn't yet solved the murders of Jean Baptiste Lorrain, or Agents Relish and Dankworth.

I glanced over at Kitty's bed. The girl was asleep. Poppy curled up with her furry little head on Kitty's pillow. Thank goodness. The girl and her dog were safe.

I rolled over. I really should get up. But the quiet and darkness helped me think.

Captain Hall said he would send another agent undercover to the Isis Theater. I wondered if it would be Archie. I cringed. What if he met the same fate as Agent Relish? Then again, Archie could charm the—I stopped myself from continuing that thought, especially if the *charmee* was the beautiful actress.

I didn't mention my confrontation with Miss Al-Madie to Captain Hall. I should have. She must have figured out I was on to her. How had I been so stupid? I'd probably blown it for any undercover agents. In fact, for all I knew, she was my assailant. After all, I was stabbed from behind and didn't see my attacker.

Of course, Fredricks had vanished immediately after he'd fetched the doctor. He didn't even wait for the prognosis. Turns out it was just a flesh-wound. My poor dress was damaged more than my person.

Sigh. At least I had managed to call Captain Hall, and hopefully in time to save the Suez Canal. The British army had to move a whole battalion from Crocodile Lake to Port Said by Christmas, the day after tomorrow. I hoped to heaven they could do it.

Kitty stirred. I rolled over. Poppy stared at me, her large eyes shining in the darkness, as if she dared me to wake her mistress.

I really must get up. I threw back the covers. There

was still investigating to do. Murder weapons to find. Murders to solve.

All three victims were found in the same tomb, which was originally Herrs Borchardt and Gabler's concession. And Herr Hermann Gabler was holed up at the institute when he should be back in Berlin. He had to be our murderer. And Fredricks was his accomplice. I knew it. Now, I just had to prove it.

What had been sitting on that empty pedestal? And where was it now? If it was a treasure valuable enough to display in the lobby of the new institute, surely Herr Gabler wouldn't just throw it away, even if it was the murder weapon.

I had to get back there and find it.

I threw my legs over the side of my bed.

"Wherever you're going..." Kitty's voice came out of the darkness. "I'm coming with you."

Poppy yipped in disapproval.

I had to admit, Kitty's foot-fighting would come in handy if Herr Gabler made another surprise visit.

"Well then, get a move on, dear."

Poppy bounded out of the darkness and onto my lap. When the little beast licked my face, I couldn't help but laugh. "I suppose you want to come too." I patted her on the head. Like her mistress, the dog had hidden talents. "After we get a nice hot bath and cuppa."

I wasn't about to go anywhere, not even to investigate a murder or three, with blood encrusted on my person.

My grandmother had taught me that every decision in life should be faced with a clean conscience and a full stomach.

After a warm bath and a breakfast of tea and toast with marmalade, I was ready for espionage.

Of course, Clifford wanted to go with us. But given his tendency to talk nonstop, he wasn't the best companion on a stealthy mission. When conversation was key to the investigation, however, he was brilliant. I suggested he explore the antiquities markets to find out about illegal trade and whether that was motivation for any of the murders.

Captain Hall had ordered me to follow the illegal antiquities trade and link it back to the Germans. If the Germans were funding their spy ring by selling antiquities, Clifford would find out. If anyone could weasel information out of shady antiquities dealers, it was Clifford.

Thrilled to be given an important assignment, he drained his coffee cup and bade us good hunting.

I patted my pockets to make sure I had all my espionage paraphernalia, and then slipped on my gloves.

* * *

Careful not to be noticed, Kitty and I skated around to
the side door where I had entered the institute on my
last clandestine visit. I used my lockpick set again and
had the door opened in no time. The look on Kitty's
face was priceless. She was obviously impressed with
her "Aunt Fiona."

The cluttered storage room was a challenge. Chock
full of artifacts, it would have been easy for the killer
to hide a murder weapon among all the other antiquities. Kitty and I divided the room in half and began
our search.

As I methodically shone my torch on each object
in the north half of the room, Kitty did the same in the
south half. Eventually, we met in the middle, disap-
pointed that neither of us had found any evidence of
foul play. We ventured out into the hallway to explore
the rest of the facility.

Where would I hide an artifact that I'd used to
commit murder?

Kitty searched the gallery, and I made my way to
the back office. Halfway down the hallway, the aroma

of coffee overpowered the dusty smell of artifacts. My heart sped up.

Someone was here.

I held my breath and extinguished my torch. I waited for my eyes to adjust to the dim natural light coming from windows in the galleries. After a few seconds, on tiptoes, I continued along the wall until I reached the office door.

The office was dark. I stopped and listened. Nothing.

Had the coffee drinker left or was he lying in wait?

Slowly, I turned the doorknob. The door creaked open. I gritted my teeth. Stepping into the room, I half expected to be hit on the head. Inhaling, I clicked on my torch. My pulse was racing as I scanned the room. I didn't see anyone—but that didn't mean he wasn't hiding behind a chair or the desk, waiting to jump out at me.

The office was big with windows that faced the back alley. Along with the usual office furniture, there was a mattress on the floor in one corner and a wooden table. Atop the table sat a cooking pot, a portable gas stove, and a tin kettle. There was even a small ice box.

Someone was indeed living in here. It had to be Herr Gabler. That was how he avoided being deported back to Berlin when the war broke out. He'd hidden here at the boarded-up institute.

Curious, I opened the ice box. A bottle of beer, a couple of potatoes, and a package of dates. Did I expect to find the murder weapon in the ice box? *Come on, Fiona. Focus.*

Where would I hide a bloody artifact?

I crossed the room and went behind the desk to the filing cabinet. I pulled on the handle of the top drawer. Locked. Another job for my lockpick set. Pulling at the fingers of my gloves, I removed them. I slid the leather pouch out of my pocket and withdrew the tension wrench and got to work. The flimsy lock was no match for my wrench. It gave way immediately.

I opened the top drawer. Exhilarating. A filing cabinet. I was in my element.

Rifling through the file folders, I came upon one labeled G 1500. If I wasn't mistaken, that was the concession Jean-Baptiste Lorrain had taken over from the Germans. The tomb he'd died in.

My pulse quickened. I cracked open the file and took mental photographs of the pages as I flipped through them. Each page had a long list of artifacts found in G-1500. Some were followed by the notation "ENT," and some had two notations: "ENT" and

"TRANS." Others had no notations but were circled in red ink. One, *Isis statue*, was circled twice.

Interesting. But what the blazes did it mean?

I'd read somewhere that Isis, the goddess of nature and magic, was a precursor to the Virgin Mary. If memory served—which it usually did—Mr. Dilly Knox once told me that the name of the city of Paris was from *Par Isis*, meaning near the temple of Isis; and the church of St. Germain-des-Prés stood where the temple of Isis once was. Of course, Mr. Knox was known to flights of fancy. I doubted the German abbreviations had anything to do with Paris.

Presumably ENT and TRANS were abbreviations for German words. Hopefully Clifford could help. His German was much better than mine.

I opened the second drawer and found more files. I thumbed through them without finding anything of note. The third and lowest drawer was difficult to open. Whatever was inside was heavy. I had to squat down and yank on its handle.

After picking myself up off the floor, I peeked inside. *What have we here?* I tugged my gloves back on.

Astonished, I carefully lifted the stone bust of the young pharaoh out of the drawer. It was deuced heavy and tested the strength of my barely healed arm.

I plopped down on the floor, sat the statue next to

me, and fished out my torch. Using the torch, I examined every inch of the artifact.

Aha! Just as I suspected. A bloodstain. I'd found the blooming murder weapon. I repressed the urge to shout for Kitty. After all, I didn't know whether we were alone in the building.

The bust was so heavy, I heaved it from the floor with both hands. Carrying it like a stone baby, I strained to get it out of the office, down the hallway, and back to the lobby where Kitty was waiting. Whatever happened to using conventional weapons like knives, guns, or even candlesticks?

By the time I reached the lobby, my arms hurt, and I was more than a little winded. I had to unburden myself soon. I made my way through the display cases and marble pedestals to the empty place where this lad belonged. With one final heave, I lifted the stone head up to the corner of the base and slid it the rest of the way onto its stand.

I'd hide it in plain sight, a trick I'd learned from Edgar Allan Poe's *The Purloined Letter*. After all, Sherlock Holmes didn't have the corner on the literary detective genre.

Now to find Kitty.

I searched the institute high and low. No sign of Kitty.

Where had the girl got to now?

I didn't have time to loiter around the institute, especially with the murderer on the loose and Herr Gabler living in the back office. He could be back at any minute. I hoped to heaven that Kitty had left to follow some lead.

I hurried back to the hotel as fast as my legs would carry me. Although it was only a couple of streets away, I was winded when I arrived at the entrance. Hands on my knees, I stopped for a second to catch my breath.

Clifford was waiting for me inside. No sooner had I entered than he dashed across the lobby to my side. "Wait until you hear what I found out." His blue eyes danced with excitement. "Ali at Ali's Antiques told me that one of his suppliers trades with a local who trades with someone at the German Archeology Institute, which is not supposed to happen." He was talking a mile a minute. "State archeologists don't sell antiquities. But—"

"Let's sit down... and slow down." I took his arm and led him to a small sitting area off reception. Partially hidden by a fern, two overstuffed chairs with lacy antimacassars sat apart from the others. Perfect.

I was counting on Clifford to help me decipher the list—ENT, TRANS, and the circled entries. That could give us a clue as to motive. I wanted a crack case before going to the police, especially since they still suspected me of murdering Agent Relish.

Clifford waved his pipe in the air as he told me all about his exploits at the antiquities markets. He'd tracked down three different shop owners who had purchased artifacts from someone connected to the German Archeology Institute. Illegally purchased. Even Jean-Baptiste Lorrain was known to make a deal under the table from time to time.

Clifford was gleeful as he recounted how he'd got the tradesmen to tell all. His constant chitchat was disarming, if annoying. Maybe the tradesmen had just given in rather than listen to another of Clifford's stories.

"That's why Monsieur Lorrain had German money and his man Frigo lied to the police. As for Herr Gabler, he is underhanded, indeed."

As the winds of Clifford's adventures were subsiding, I ventured to change the subject. "Have you seen Kitty?"

He shook his head and then lit his pipe.

Blasted girl. Where was she?

Waving away the foul pipe smoke, I ventured to crack the case of the German code. I took out my notebook and pencil and recreated a few lines of the list I'd seen at the institute. "Any idea what ENT or TRANS might mean in German in the context of a list of artifacts?" I passed the notebook to Clifford.

He puffed on his pipe and studied the list. "Well, some items have both notations, and the circled items have no notation." His brow wrinkled. "ENT. TRANS." His mouth twisted as he thought. "TRANS could be *transportiert* or transported. Transported from the tomb? Transported back to Berlin?" He handed the notebook back to me. "ENT, that could be *entfernt*, removed. Removed from the tomb."

"If ENT means removed from the tomb, and TRANS means transported back to Berlin..." I stared down at the list I'd recreated. "Then the circled items could be ones still in the tomb." No wonder Herr Gabler didn't want Jean-Baptiste to excavate at G-1500. There were still treasures in there that he hadn't managed to get out of the country before the Germans were forced to leave. "That would give him a motive," I said under my breath.

"Give who a motive?" Clifford relit his pipe.

"Herr Gabler." I'd already taken too much time listening to Clifford's stories. "I found the murder weapon."

"Good lord." Holding his pipe in midair, Clifford sat there blinking at me. "Where?"

"A bloody stone bust at the German Archeology Institute."

"Did you notify the police?" He clamped his pipe between his teeth.

"Not yet." I turned my head to avoid inhaling a cloud of foul pipe smoke. "You call the police and I'll meet you at the institute."

"Shouldn't you wait for the police?" He puffed his pipe.

"Rubbish." I waved him off. "Good work at the antiquities market, by the way." Herr Gabler had been dealing in illegal antiquities. Getting caught was motive enough. Then there were the treasures still left in the tomb. Even more motive.

Blushing, Clifford beamed at me.

"Just meet me at the institute." I patted his sleeve. "I'm going to look for Kitty." I didn't want to worry him by telling him that the girl might be in danger. "And bring the police."

22

THE CONFESSION

Back in our hotel room, Poppy did circles around me, but Kitty was nowhere to be seen. Judging by the outfits laid out on her bed—outfits that had been there since morning—she hadn't been back. Kitty never came back to the room and went out again without changing her kit.

I was getting deuced worried about the girl. Foot-fighting or not, she was no match for a cold-blooded murderer or a nest of German spies.

"Come on, little beastie." I snagged Poppy's leash off the hook by the door and attached it to her collar, careful not to cut myself on that bloody sharp diamond. "Let's go and find your mummy."

At the door, I turned around and dashed back to

the dressing table to fetch my handbag and Mata Hari's gun, just in case. I wrapped the bag's drawstring around my wrist and made to leave.

Once outside the hotel, Poppy was eager to find a patch of green to do her business. After she'd completed the task, and given a few proud kicks of her hind feet, she trotted out in front of me like she knew where she was going.

Walking along the busy pavements with a dog was an adventure. As Poppy weaved in and out of passersby, her leash did too, which resulted in a few stumbles and quite a few more curses. Poppy jerked this way and that, alternating between a full-throttled dash followed by an abrupt stop to sniff a plant or a disgusting puddle alongside the road.

Her tongue lolled and her little feet moved as if she were on wheels.

By the time we reached the institute, I was bushed. I dragged the pup around to the side door, where she promptly peed in the stairwell. The door was still open from my last visit. As soon as we'd crossed the threshold, Poppy was off. I struggled to keep up.

She led me through the storage area, out into the hallway, and down to the lobby.

I scanned the lobby. Aside from the painted faces of ancient Egyptians, there were no others to be seen.

Trotting down a second hallway, Poppy and I peeked into every gallery and cubby hole as we went.

Poppy stopped in front of a door about halfway down the hall. I was about to turn the doorknob when I heard voices. My hand in midair, I froze.

Poppy yipped.

I scooped her up into my arms. "Shhhhh." Pricking up my ears, I listened at the door.

"*Meine Liebe, wir müssen etwas tun.*" The woman's heavily accented voice was familiar. She was obviously not a native German.

Neither was I. Far from it. I think she'd just said, "My love, we must do..." *Tun.* What was *tun*?

"She knows." When the woman spoke English, I recognized her voice immediately. Mori Al-Madie. La Sultana. "Fiona Figg knows."

Hearing my name made me jump back. Poppy let out a squeak. I held her tighter to my chest. Drat. I shouldn't have mentioned her mistakes or asked after the costume girl. How could I have been so stupid?

"Why did you let her out of the theater?" The man had a thick German accent.

"I tried to stop her, but I must have missed."

So, it was Mori Al-Madie who stabbed me.

"I should do for that nosy *Hündin* what I did for

your friend Monsieur Lorrain." The German's voice was harsh.

"I told you not to be jealous of him, *meine Liebe*." The way she said *meine Liebe* made my skin crawl.

"First the *Schweinehund* took my dig and then he tried to take you," he scoffed. "If your friends hadn't stuffed that British agent in *my* tomb, I wouldn't have had to kill the French *Schwein*."

My hand flew to my mouth. *Oh dear.* I nearly dropped Poppy. She struggled for traction against my blouse. I reeled her in. Herr Gabler killed Jean-Baptiste.

If your friends hadn't stuffed that British agent in my tomb. What friends? German spies?

He had killed Jean-Baptiste to stop the dig. To stop him finding Agent Dankworth's body in the tomb.

"If you'd been more careful, Dankworth wouldn't have discovered you were selling antiquities on the black market." She huffed. "My heritage to the highest bidder."

So, Agent Dankworth had learned about the illegal antiquities trade. That's why he was killed. This was the information Captain Hall needed. Herr Gabler was selling antiquities from the institute to fund the German spy ring operating out of the Isis Theater.

"You're lucky no one knows you went to the hospital to kill the other British agent." The tone of her voice soured. "That Relish creep."

And Agent Relish. Herr Gabler killed him too. When? How? So, it wasn't Fredricks after all, unless they were working together.

"We need to win this *verdammt* war so I can get back to my dig." The man's voice shook with rage.

"All you care about is your precious dig..." The sound of heels tapping on the floor indicated she was pacing. "Stealing our heritage. You're as bad as the British."

A light went on in my brain. This bloody war wasn't just over territory. It was also over culture. In addition to fighting on the Western Front and in the Sinai desert, my own countrymen were fighting the Germans over the rights to the spoils of Egypt. Major Lawrence was right. *Thieves are thieves no matter what color uniform they wear.*

"If I didn't know better, I'd think you were using me." He chuckled. "Whoring for your *precious* country."

Slap. The sound of a hand hitting a cheek.

"Why, you little *Hure*." His voice was a deep guttural growl.

La Sultana screamed.

I heard scuffling from the other side of the door.

What in heaven's name is he doing to her?

Poppy started barking.

"Shhhh." I tried to silence the little beast. But she jumped out of my arms and scratched on the door.

Whatever had been happening inside the room stopped. Silence.

We'd been found out. Blasted dog.

I pulled Mata Hari's gun from my handbag. I took a deep breath and turned the doorknob. Then I kicked the door open.

Holding the gun in both hands, I entered the room. "Unhand her!"

Poppy ran toward the closet. Yipping, she scratched at the door.

Kitty burst out of the closet and delivered a boot to Herr Gabler's chin. He fell back against a table. Several artifacts flew onto the floor and landed with a crash.

Her eyes full of tears, La Sultana rubbed her throat where the German had been trying to strangle her.

I pointed the gun at Herr Gabler, who had steadied himself against the table. I hoped Clifford had fetched the police and they were on the way.

Kitty slipped a pair of handcuffs out of her waistcoat pocket.

"Where did you get those?" I stared in disbelief. "Don't tell me, France."

She snapped the cuffs around Herr Gabler's wrists and cuffed him to the bars securing the window.

Foot-fighting, cat-burglar outfit, handcuffs. *Who is Kitty Lane, really?*

Her leash trailing behind her, Poppy stood guard next to the German.

La Sultana dashed past Kitty and tried to make her escape.

As the actress approached the door, I stuck out my foot. She tripped and fell to the floor.

"See." I smiled at Kitty. "I can foot-fight too."

"I heard their entire conversation." Kitty helped Mori Al-Madie up off the floor. "He killed Agent Dankworth after Dankworth discovered him holed up here at the institute. Isn't that right, Hermann?"

Herr Gabler glared at her.

"Yes. He killed two of the three."

"He killed Jean-Baptiste..." Kitty's grip on the actress's arm made a deep impression. "To keep him from finding the body—"

"Yes, dear." I held the gun steady.

"It's my concession," Herr Gabler shouted. "Everything there belongs to me and the German government."

"Is that why you killed Monsieur Lorrain?" I kept the gun pointed at him. "To keep him from finding the Isis statue?" The double-circled artifact on the list.

"Lorrain was an amateur. *Ein Kind*." The bars clanked as he tried to gesture with his hands. "He would have ruined my dig." His scarlet cheeks confirmed my theory.

"And what about Agent Relish?" I took another step closer. "Did you kill him too?" I needed to make him confess to clear my name.

"That was Mori." He jerked his head toward the actress.

"I didn't kill anyone." Mori Al-Madie put her nose in the air. "The only thing I'm guilty of is loving my country and respecting the dignity of my people."

"How touching," he scoffed. "I was trying to protect you and that's the thanks I get." He spat in her general direction.

"I don't need your protection." The actress spat back.

I didn't understand their relationship, but the actress was guilty of consorting with the enemy. And the archeologist was guilty of much more. He had killed at least two men.

"We caught him," Kitty said. "We caught the murderer."

"Yes, dear, we did." I had to admit, Kitty and I made a jolly good team. Now, if only the police would arrive.

Poppy growled at the German.

"Yes, Poppy, and you, too." With the gun still pointing at Herr Gabler, I reached down and patted the dog.

"You can't prove anything." When Herr Gabler pulled at the cuffs, the bars rattled again.

I'd always loved it in detective stories when the perpetrator said, *you can't prove it*. An admission of guilt, if ever there was one. "Actually, we can, and we will."

He narrowed his brows. "You don't have a murder weapon."

"But we do." I couldn't help but smile. "And I'm guessing your fingerprints are all over it."

"You found it, Aunt Fiona!" Kitty clapped her hands together. "Brilliant."

"Impossible!" Herr Gabler's cheeks darkened to a deep beet color. If he got any redder, he'd burst into flames.

"Not only possible, but actual." My damaged arm was getting tired, so I transferred the gun to my other hand. I wished the blasted coppers would hurry up. No doubt Clifford was talking their ears off.

"You're bluffing." His voice was indignant.

"The head in your filing cabinet." I was a file clerk, after all, and I never bluffed. Maybe a little fib now and then in the line of duty, but I didn't have high enough clearance for actual bluffing.

"Why, you nosy *alte Kuh*." He took a step forward. The handcuffs pulled him back.

Did he just call me an old cow? I'm only twenty-five, for heaven's sake.

Bang. Clang. Bang.

All heads turned toward the commotion coming from the front of the building. *Finally.* The police. They must be breaking down the doors.

"Fiona." It was Clifford. He'd brought the police. *Good man.* "Are you in here?"

"We're here," I shouted. "In the back office."

A minute later, Clifford arrived with two police-men. I recognized the plain-clothed man from my interrogation. Now maybe he would believe me that I didn't kill Agent Relish.

"You again." The wiry plain-clothed copper shook his head. "I should have known."

What did the man have against me?

"I've apprehended the murderer." I sniffed.

"Hand over your weapon." The copper looked at me.

Was he talking to me?

He nodded for his uniformed colleague to take my gun. "We don't want you *accidently* shooting someone." He flipped open his notepad.

I handed Mata Hari's gun to the officer. "I didn't kill Mr. Relish. I mean, I might have given him the fatal injection, but I didn't murder him. He did." I pointed at Herr Gabler. "This is the man who attacked Mr. Relish and tampered with the morphine bottle."

"I have no idea what you're talking about." Herr Gabler rolled his eyes.

"He's the man in the fedora." The man I'd seen in La Sultana's dressing room and then again at the hospital.

Wordlessly, the copper scribbled in his notepad.

"I never went to any hospital." Herr Gabler scowled at me. "I don't even know this Agent Relish." He spat out the words and then glanced over at the actress. "And I didn't put chloroform in any morphine bottle."

"Who said anything about chloroform?" I stabbed the air with my finger. "Only the murderer would know it wasn't morphine in that bottle."

Kitty and I exchanged looks.

"Ask Mori." Herr Gabler sighed. "She's the collaborator, not me."

Head down, the copper continued writing while his colleague stood watch with his hand on his club.

"You're a snake." The actress shot daggers from her dark eyes. "I'm a loyalist. I don't give a fig about the Germans. I just want to get those British boots off our necks."

"Why don't we all go down to the nick and sort this out?" The plain-clothed copper nodded to his associate. "Call for backup," he said under his breath.

"Not the ladies," Clifford said. "Surely they're innocent."

Good old Clifford. Always ready to come to a lady's defense, while underestimating a lady's abilities.

"Everyone." The copper snapped his notepad shut.

"Me too?" Clifford huffed.

"Everyone."

The coppers escorted us out of the institute and into two waiting motorcars. I squeezed in next to Kitty and Poppy, and Clifford squeezed in next to me. Sandwiched between my coworkers, pals even, I was grateful for their companionship, especially if I had to return to the nick.

Although Gabler had not exactly confessed to going to the hospital and tampering with the morphine bottle, Mori Al-Madie had accused him of doing so. And he knew about the chloroform in the bottle.

How else could he know unless he was the killer? But why? Why did Gabler kill Relish?

Did Herr Gabler kill Agent Relish to protect his lover, the actress? He'd said he wanted to protect her. Or was it to protect the codes? If Herr Gabler was the mastermind behind German operations at the theater, if he used money from illegal antiquities deals to fund those operations, then he had a double motive for killing both British agents. Agents who had discovered he was selling antiquities illegally and that the theater was being used to deliver coded messages to the Germans.

I only hoped the coppers got him to confess. Otherwise, I might be spending the rest of this bloody war in an Egyptian jail.

At the station, the police led us to separate rooms and questioned us. They took the actress and the archeologist to the lock-up. Eventually, they let me and my pals go. My plain-clothed friend advised me "not to leave town." Unfortunately, I was still under suspicion for killing Agent Relish. At least he didn't lock me up. If only I could prove Herr Gabler was at the hospital when Agent Relish died. If only I could prove he was the man in the gray fedora.

When we finally got back to Shepheard's, we were all completely exhausted.

It was all I could do to disrobe before bed. When I flopped into bed, I was out as soon as my head hit the pillow.

Tomorrow.

I would get everything sorted tomorrow.

23

CHRISTMAS EVE

The next morning, Kitty was bubbling with excitement. The girl whirled around our hotel room pulling dresses from the closet, holding them up to her petite frame, and then tossing them on her bed. Soon the pile was almost as tall as she was.

I sat on the edge of my bed and indulged Kitty's constant pestering about what to wear to the Christmas Eve party. She insisted on modeling every single dress—and she had a trunk full.

Even Poppy was in awe. The little beast sat on the floor, following Kitty with her big sad eyes.

Never mind that the party wasn't for another ten hours. Kitty could spend all day deciding which outfit to wear and still be flummoxed when the time came to

leave. Decisive to the point of obstinate about everything else in her life, when it came to evening kit, she
was as changeable as a monsoon wind.

"What do you think of this one?" Kitty held up a
frilly clementine number.

"Maybe if you want to be mistaken for a Christmas
tangerine." I hated to dash her hopes, but it was a truly
hideous frock. "Anyway, we're not here on holiday."

I liked balls as much as the next person, but Kitty's ob-
session with parties was ridiculous. We were here to stop
the sabotage of the Suez Canal—soon we would know
whether we had succeeded on that front—and to catch a
killer. Technically, we were not here to catch a killer, but
as it turned out, two of the victims were British agents, so
in my book, that was close enough. More to the point, I
suspected Fredricks was somehow involved. I just had to
prove it, especially as my own freedom depended upon it.

A knock at the door interrupted Kitty's fashion
show. She flitted across the room to answer it. She returned with a large rectangular pink box, which she
laid on the dressing table.

"What is it?" Curiosity piqued, I went to the
dressing table to find out.

She slid a tiny card out of its tiny envelope. "It's for
you."

"Me?" I didn't order anything.

Kitty giggled. "From your not-so-secret admirer."

Archie? Had Archie sent me a Christmas gift? My heart skipped a beat. I untied the red ribbon and carefully folded it.

"Open it!" Kitty clapped her hands together.

I glanced at her out of the corner of my eye. "What do you think I'm doing?"

Slowly, I lifted the lid. I was greeted by tissue paper sealed with a gold sticker embossed with the words *Les Grands Magasins Cicurel*.

"*Les Grands Magasins Cicurel*," Kitty squealed. "That's the chicest boutique in Cairo."

My stomach did a flipflop. I was neither chic nor boutique. My cheeks burned as I cautiously tore open the paper.

My hand flew to my mouth. *Oh, my word.* I gently removed a beautiful velvet gown from the box.

"Aunt Fiona, it's gorgeous!" Kitty held the hem of the evening gown up to her cheek. "So soft. So luxurious." She was practically cooing.

"I simply can't accept it." I admired the gown in the mirror... its elegant lines, sheer short sleeves, and silk roses on the bodice. "It's too extravagant." Tenderly, I folded the dress and put it back in the box. "He shouldn't have." How could he afford such a dress? A mere lieutenant.

"Why not?" Kitty fiddled with the tiny card.

I snatched it out of her hand and read it.

Horsefeathers. He didn't.

The dress wasn't from Archie. I should have known. It was from Fredricks.

Arrrrr. I could have screamed.

Fiona, my sweet blood peach, I can't wait to see you dressed in ruby red. Love, Fredrick

I tossed the card into the box, and then dropped into the chair.

Of course it was *that* blasted man. He expected me to wear it to the Christmas Eve party. What was it with Fredricks and women's clothing? Why did he always insist on dressing me? *Better than undressing me.*

I smiled at my reflection. Yes. I would wear his dress and turn it against him.

"You must wear it." Kitty's gaze was intense.

"Yes." I tented my finger. "I'll use it to set a trap for Fredricks."

She rubbed her little hands together. "The hunter hunted."

"And I'm the bait." I caressed the delicious fabric. I had to admit, the cad had good taste.

"Brilliant," she practically squealed.

"Just call me a *tethered goat*." I held the gown up and admired it in the looking glass.

Kitty made a bleating sound and then giggled.

As much as I resented wearing anything given to me by Fredricks, my duty to king and country came first. I would wear the blasted gown. I held the beauty to my torso. Gorgeous. My heart sang like a schoolgirl's.

And at least I knew Fredricks would be at the party. I could pump him for information about his propaganda campaign and plans to sway the Bedouins. Did he really think he could persuade the Muslims to unite against the British? More to the point, I could find out if he witnessed the man in the gray fedora tampering with the morphine bottle. Nurse Amelia said the man was visiting Fredricks. In any case, Fredricks was right there. He had to have seen the whole thing. He must know who put chloroform in the morphine bottle. I just had to get him to tell the police and clear my name.

He must testify or my stay in Egypt might be extended indefinitely. Instead of the lovely Shepheard's Hotel, I'd be languishing in jail.

I tightened my lips. I must be deuced careful not to mention the Suez Canal and give away the fact that the War Office—thanks to me—knew about the plans to blow it up on Christmas Day. Too bad. I would have loved to gloat. Fredricks always fancied himself the cleverest man in the room.

Ha! This time, I was one step ahead of the scoundrel.

* * *

Shepheard's ballroom was so festive with holiday decorations, you'd never know it felt more like summertime outside than Christmas. The Moorish arches were decorated with holly bows, and a giant Christmas tree with all the trimmings lit up the room.

A pang in my chest made me wince. At Christmas, more than any other time, I missed my grandparents and their farm in the country where I'd spent many a perfect holiday growing up. But the scene was so charming that I couldn't be melancholy.

I scanned the ballroom for familiar faces. Although I'd only been in Cairo for just over a week, I knew many of the guests. Gertrude Bell, Major Lawrence, and General Clayton and Lady Enid were huddled near the bar. Lord and Lady Carnarvon and their daughter Evelyn sat at a table with Howard Carter.

The women were beautiful in their silk and velvet evening gowns in various shades of red and green to mark the season. And the men were handsome in evening kit or dress uniforms. All except "Lawrence of Arabia," who still wore long, flowing ivory robes and headdress. With his brilliant blue eyes and fair hair poking out of his headdress, he looked as if he were at a fancy-dress ball and not a Christmas pageant.

Hair up in a chignon, Kitty looked pretty in pink. Clifford was sharp in his tails and slicked-back hair. And my new ruby dress fitted perfectly, as if Fredricks had had it tailored especially for me. I was loath to imagine how long he'd studied my figure to make such an accurate assessment of my size.

Clifford went to fetch champagne. Before I knew it, Kitty had cornered the most attractive young man at the ball. Given we'd solved the mystery of the murders of Jean-Baptiste and Agent Dankworth, unless she was somehow trying to prove me innocent of killing Agent Relish, she was definitely flirting this time. Although with Kitty, it was deuced difficult to tell the difference between investigating and flirting.

I headed for Lord Carnarvon's table to wish them a happy Christmas. When my eyes met Howard Carter's,

I stopped in my tracks. The man glared at me something awful. Then again, I had accused him of murder. Lady Evelyn smiled. No doubt grateful that I hadn't exposed their midnight rendezvous to her father.

I changed course and headed for the group from the Arab Bureau, secretly surveying the room in hopes of spotting Archie. He'd promised we'd meet again in Cairo. But if I could get Fredricks to testify to my innocence, I'd be leaving soon. If I couldn't, I'd be staying for a very long time... in an Egyptian jail.

I glanced around the room, looking for Fredricks. *Baaah. Bleat. Baaah.*

Gertrude Bell was an angel in ivory silk. Even Lady Enid was wearing a gown instead of her usual costume —although the frock hung off her like a flour sack. General Clayton was commanding in his dress uniform and waxed mustache.

Engaged in lively conversation, the group hardly noticed when I approached. I stood just outside their circle, troubling the string on my handbag, waiting to be acknowledged.

"Fine thing, archeologists killing each other." Major Lawrence waved his hands when he spoke, causing the whiskey in his glass to slosh. "What next? Brawls in the sand pits?" The sleeves of his robe danced a jig. "Tug-o-war with mummies?" One sleeve danced right into his drink. "Ludicrous." He shook the whiskey off his sleeve.

"*Men.*" Gertrude Bell sipped her Martini. "*Male* archeologists. You wouldn't catch a woman brawling or bludgeoning."

"No, they use more devious means." Major Lawrence chuckled. "Like poisoning your soup."

"And are too smart to get caught." Lady Enid winked.

"Women are just as capable of criminal activities as men." I stepped into the circle.

"Equal opportunity crime?" Major Lawrence smirked.

"Come now." General Clayton cleared his throat. "The fair sex is far too squeamish for bludgeons and battle."

Lady Enid elbowed him in the ribs.

"If women were in charge, we wouldn't need battles." My cheeks warmed. I really should learn to keep my mouth shut.

"They would find more subterranean ways to subdue their enemies." Major Lawrence raised his glass. "Take Gertie here. She can talk a serpent out of its skin."

"Speaking of snakes," Lady Enid said. "Is it true that Hermann Gabler killed Jean-Baptiste and a

British agent?"

"I found the murder weapon." Not to boast. But I was rather pleased with myself on that score. Too bad I couldn't tell them how I'd averted the bomb plot, too.

"The police confirmed the blood was Jean-Baptiste's." General Clayton shook his head. "And Gabler's fingerprints were all over the statue." He took a sip of his cocktail. "Rum do, that."

"Amazing police work," Lady Enid said, brushing a bit of lint off her husband's jacket.

Police work, my spying eye.

If Kitty were here, she would probably volunteer to give us all blood tests and explain the latest techniques in so-called forensic science.

I scanned the room for the girl. She was dancing with an officer—not the handsome man she'd been flirting with earlier, but another fine-looking fellow. My, the girl got around.

A tap on my shoulder made me swirl around.

The sight of Fredricks in full evening kit with black tails and starched white shirt took my breath away. I was used to seeing him in his ridiculous jodhpurs and slouch hat. With his thick unruly hair pulled back into a ponytail, I had to admit that he cleaned up rather nicely.

Every other woman in the place thought so too. For all eyes were on him.

"May I have this dance?" When he smiled, I saw why he was called the panther. His white teeth gleamed and the spark in his eyes was deuced unnerving.

I bleated, pulled at my tether, and took his outstretched hand.

Where was Clifford with the blasted champagne when I needed him? No doubt he'd found a beautiful woman who required his help.

Aha. There he was. On the dance floor, stepping on the toes of a pretty redhead.

Fredricks held me tight around the waist as we whirled around the dance floor. The scent of rosewood was going to my head. Feeling a bit faint, I pulled in a bit closer, just for support, mind you.

"You smell good enough to eat, ma chérie." He inhaled into my neck, which sent a very peculiar sensation rippling down my spine.

"I'm tougher than I smell." The rogue twirled me around until I felt like I was floating above the floor. Why did he have to be such a bloody good dancer?

A blur of pink ribbons and lace passed by me. It was Kitty, dancing with yet another chap. Was she leading the poor lad across the floor? She nearly bumped into me.

"Strong and sweet." Fredricks laughed. "My favorite."

"Just like chloroform," I said under my breath. The sickly-sweet smell came back to me. I should have known it wasn't morphine in that bottle.

"It wasn't your fault the bottle contained chloroform and not morphine." He pulled me closer. "I know you're innocent." The breathy way he said it made me flinch.

How did he know the morphine bottle contained chloroform? Had he heard it from the police? Or was he the one who put it there?

"You did it." I pulled out of his embrace. "You killed Agent Relish. Otherwise, you wouldn't know about the chloroform."

"Actually, if you recall, I tried to stop you." He pulled me in tight again... too tight. "I warned you not to administer that injection."

I twisted out of his embrace. "You knew it was sabotaged and yet you didn't stop me?"

"I tried." He shrugged. "But you're stubborn and don't listen." He took my hand, lifted it to his lips, and kissed it. "That's what I love about you. Strong and sweet."

"You must tell the police." I jerked my hand away. "Then again, you're such a faker, who would believe you, a known criminal?"

"Now, now, Fiona." He waved his hand. "Innocent until proved guilty and all that rot."

The other dancers were starting to stare.

"The police think I killed Agent Relish." I intentionally stepped on his toes. "Why didn't you come forward?"

"You said it, ma chérie." He tugged me closer again. "Why would they believe me? A known rascal." He twirled me around.

"I could go to prison." I squeezed my eyes shut. The thought of spending the rest of my days in an Egyptian prison was unappealing.

"Don't worry, ma chérie." He wrapped his arm around my waist. "Enjoy the moment."

"You mean my last moments of freedom?"

"What if a British officer were to testify?"

"Who?" My head was spinning from all the whirling. What officer? I didn't remember an officer in the hospital. Had I missed someone?

He winked and pointed to his chest. "Moi."

"You're no British officer," I scoffed.

He bowed. "Captain Claude Soughton, at your service."

Captain Claude Soughton. Poppycock.

Good heavens. I remembered the name from one of Fredricks's passports—fake passports. "You'll never pull it off."

"Spill it, Mr. Fredricks. Who tampered with the bottle?" Kitty appeared at my side. "I heard everything, including your amusing attempts at seduction."

Fredricks sniffed my hair—or should I say, my wig—the cad. "My sweet peach, we make quite a pear," he whispered into my ear, completely ignoring Kitty.

"Pit-i-ful." In a flash of insight, I realized Fredricks must have been following Agent Relish. "You hit yourself on the head, didn't you? You were never attacked." Fredricks was never working with Agent Relish. No. He was following him.

"Gabler left me holding the bag, so to speak." He sighed. "If I'd been found with the body of your fallen agent, I'd be suspect *numero ono*. So, yes. I did what any self-respecting fellow would have done."

Pitiful, indeed.

"We've got you now, Fredrick Fredricks!" Kitty lunged at him.

"That's my cue." Fredricks took a step back. He kissed me on the cheek. "Until we meet again." Like a snake, he slithered away through the crowd.

"I'll go after him." I kept my eyes glued on the path he'd taken. "You notify Captain Hall."

It was too late. Kitty had already bolted. She was halfway across the dance floor, hot on the heels of our nemesis.

I sprinted after them.

Thud. I ran smack into the plain-clothed copper who'd questioned me at the station.

"Have it your way," I huffed to myself. "*You* go after him." Truth be told, the girl could run a lot faster than I could... not to mention her foot-fighting. I only wished I could be there to see the girl take down the scoundrel.

"Miss Figg." The copper caught me by the shoulders. "Not so fast."

Why did the police always show up at the most incommodious moment?

"You were right." The copper looked me in the face. "It was Gabler. The man in the fedora at the hospital."

"I was?" I blinked up at him.

"This afternoon, a Captain Claude Soughton from the British army explained everything." He shrugged.

Oh, my sainted aunt. How was that possible? Unless... Fredricks had already gone to the police and cleared my name. *Cheeky cad.* I smiled to myself.

The copper proceeded to tell me how Captain Claude Soughton had reported everything—except his real name, of course. He'd told them Gabler was the man in the gray fedora who'd visited Relish at the hospital. That Gabler had tampered with the vial because Agent Relish discovered he was selling illegal antiquities. That Gabler was selling illegal antiquities to fund the German spy ring at the Isis Theater.

Chuffed. My chest expanded. I was right. I'd cracked the case.

But Fredricks had turned in his own people to save me from spending the rest of my life in an Egyptian prison. Why did he do it? Was it true he had feelings for me? I thought it was all an act.

Now, I almost wished I'd stopped Kitty from pursuing him.

Almost.

24

CHRISTMAS DAY

Like a child, on Christmas morning I awoke early in anticipation—not with good tidings of Father Christmas, presents wrapped up with bows, and sweet puddings, but rather with good tidings of sabotage averted, murderers arrested, and my fine name cleared.

Last night when I'd gone to bed, Kitty wasn't back yet. I had been too exhausted to go look for her. And, if this mission had taught me anything, it was that the girl could take care of herself.

I glanced across the room to her bed where she was sound asleep with Poppy draped across her neck. How in the world could the poor girl breathe with the furry beast suffocating her like that? And why hadn't I heard her come in? She was as stealthy as she was deadly.

Should I wake her? I was dying to know what had happened with Fredricks. Had she caught up to him? Did she kick him silly?

I swung my legs off the bed and inhaled the cool breeze coming through our open window. It actually felt cool. The curtains were flapping, so I climbed out of bed and tiptoed over to close the window, resisting the temptation to wake Kitty. The girl needed her rest.

"Aunt Fiona." Her sweet voice was full of sleep. "I got him. I got Fredricks."

"How?" How had petite Kitty overpowered the hulking hunter? Fredricks wasn't exactly a pushover.

"*Fouetté* to the back of the head." She kicked the bedcovers.

"You kicked him in the head?" *Fouetté* meant whip in French. A whip-kick. How clever. "Then what? The police? The army? Does Captain Hall know?" The questions poured out of me like an unquenchable thirst.

The infamous Fredrick Fredricks had been caught at last. We'd done it. Finally, we'd accomplished our mission.

I should be happy, but I felt as if I'd lost a limb.

"I delivered him into the capable hands of your Lieutenant Somersby." She flashed a coy smile.

"Archie?" Now I really wished I'd been the one to chase Fredricks. Then again, I couldn't have delivered a whip-kick to the back of his scheming head.

"You're lucky on that score." Kitty grinned. "He really does love you, Aunt Fiona."

"Yes, well." I cleared my throat. My cheeks hot, I changed the subject. "Where did you learn to foot-fight?" I already knew the answer.

"It's called *savate* and I learned it—"

"Don't tell me. In France." If I wasn't mistaken, *savate* meant old shoe.

She nodded and giggled. "It was developed by sailors who used their feet to fight so they could hold onto the ship's rigging for balance."

French boarding school. *Poppycock.*

"Not very sporting according to Queensberry rules." I shut the window with such force it made a loud bang. *Whoops.* "Still, I'm very proud of you, dear."

Kitty sat up in bed. "You know I'm not really your niece?" She cuddled Poppy to her chest. "Am I, little Poppy-poo?"

"Then why do you insist on calling me *aunt*?" Funny. It used to annoy me when she called me aunt. Now, I rather liked it.

"Out of respect." Kitty peeked up over the dog's furry topknot.

I couldn't tell if she was serious or being sarcastic. There was still so much I didn't know about her.

"Where did Archie take the bounder?" I slid my feet into my slippers. "To jail, I hope." Although judging from my experience with Fredricks, there wasn't a jail on earth that could hold him. A strange thought danced through my head. I almost hoped he would escape.

Almost.

* * *

Spirits were high as we dressed for Christmas breakfast. Kitty wore a candy-cane striped dress with an adorable matching hat. Even Poppy had a matching bow in her topknot.

For my part, I wore my best skirt—meaning the only one that hadn't been ruined during our adventures—and a fresh white blouse. Kitty insisted on adding one of her lace collars, a ruby red number with tassels. She also lent me a sweet little green silk hat adorned with holly. I felt rather like a Christmas tree.

We knocked on Clifford's door. He answered, looking dapper in a gray linen morning suit. Together, the three of us rode the lift down to breakfast. When we stepped out of the lift, we were greeted by a lovely choral rendition of "What Child is This." The music got louder as we approached the breakfast room.

Like the other common rooms at Shepheard's, the breakfast room had enormously high ceilings painted with ornate murals, along with grand Moorish arches, imposing columns, and colorful curtains and mosaics. Add the festive holiday decorations, and the scene was charming, if a bit frenetic.

At the front of the room, a boys' choir performed Christmas hymns, their angelic voices echoing through the chamber. Along the side of the room, a magnificent buffet was spread across long tables that extended the length of the wall. The centerpiece was an ice sculpture of a giant snowflake, something I didn't expect to see in Cairo.

The offerings included bubble and squeak, Irish potato cakes, Dutch baby pancakes with roasted plums, black pudding, and poached eggs with toasted soldiers. I could have broken out in song myself at the bounty of it all. I hadn't seen such delights since before the war. I felt like I'd been transported to another world.

If only Archie was here...

As I filled my plate, I glanced around the room. *A girl could hope, couldn't she?*

The room filled up with ex-pats, soldiers, and tourists. Except for the Egyptian tapestries and Moorish arches, we could have been having Christmas breakfast at Claridge's in Mayfair.

I tucked into my Dutch pancakes with gusto. The combination of sweet pancakes and strong milky tea was heavenly.

"May I join you?"

I'd been so enthralled with my breakfast I hadn't seen him approach.

"Archie!" I wiped my mouth with my napkin. "Please do."

In his freshly pressed dress uniform, he looked even more enticing than the buffet.

Archie pulled up a chair, ordered a cup of coffee, and then went to the buffet.

I watched him as he went. He cut a fine figure, especially from the back.

When he returned, smiling from ear to ear, he congratulated us for capturing Fredricks. He'd been chasing him around the world since the Boer Wars in Southern Africa. "Thanks to you, Fiona." His green eyes shone. "And you too, Miss Kitty."

"A toast!" Clifford raised his champagne glass.

"Wait," Archie said. "I'll fetch champagne for the ladies."

Once we all had champagne, Clifford proposed his toast. "To a successful mission and a most agreeable Christmas with beautiful women and food! So much good food."

With much laughter and cheer, we raised our glasses.

"Where is Fredricks now?" I sipped my champagne. "Rotting in an Egyptian jail?"

"*Waiting* in an Egyptian jail." Archie tapped his glass against mine. "Until we can transport him back to London to stand trial."

"We got him!" Kitty grinned.

To think that just a few months ago, I was a desperate divorcee, and soon after, a melancholy war widow—not to mention a mere file clerk—trudging around dreary old London. Now, here I was, a seasoned spy working for British Intelligence in Cairo, and part of the team that had finally caught the most notorious German spy in history.

Not in my wildest dreams did I ever imagine I could be sitting at Shepheard's in Cairo, sharing Christmas with a foot-fighting girl, an elegant if old-fashioned officer, and the most handsome man I'd ever met. If only this day could last forever.

Alas, the war had other ideas. Soon Archie would be back in the field doing heaven-knew-what, and Kitty, Clifford, and I would be back in dreary old London, waiting for another assignment.

Or would we?

Would I ever get another assignment now that Fredricks was locked up?

"We got him." Even as I said the words, my heart sank. With Fredricks out of the way, my career in espionage was over. The only reason Captain Hall had sent me on these assignments was because Fredricks had always invited me—taunted me—to follow him. With Fredricks locked up, I'd be demoted back to head filing clerk in Room 40.

Truth be told, I was going to miss the scoundrel. For a murderer and a German spy, he was remarkably charming. Perhaps I could visit him in jail and bring him the latest writings of Dr. Sigmund Freud or some French philosopher. After all, he'd saved me from a life in prison. The least I could do was bring him some light reading.

"He'll be tried in London within the month and most likely hanged." Archie's face lit up.

"On what charges?" *Oh dear.* I almost sounded like I was defending the bounder.

"Murder, espionage, impersonating an officer, you

name it." Archie smiled. "Thanks to you, Fiona, we got him."

As much as I wanted to, I couldn't return his smile. "Do we have proof?" After all, he hadn't killed any-one... at least not in Cairo. And, well, impersonating an officer, I did that all the time. Even the silk letter conspiracy was the brainchild of that Baron Max Von Oppenheim chap and had nothing to do with Fredricks—at least nothing we could prove.

"Who cares about proof!" Kitty snatched a butter biscuit off my plate. "The renowned spy is caught."

Archie raised his glass. "Calls for a celebration."

I hated to put a damper on the festive mood but sending a possibly innocent man to jail—or worse—without proof was nothing to celebrate.

"What's the matter, old bean?" Clifford tilted his head. "Aren't you feeling well?"

"Without evidence, we should not be rejoicing in sending Fredricks up the river—or across the ocean, as the case may be."

"We got him in the end." Archie raised his glass. "That's all that matters."

At the risk of sounding like a schoolmarm, I took up the cause. "The end doesn't justify the means."

"Where Fredricks is concerned, it does." Kitty clinked glasses with the men.

"If we use any means to reach our ends, then we are as bad as our enemies." I stood firm. "If we compromise our principles, then what are we fighting for?"

"Old Blighty." Clifford beamed. "What else?"

"Truth, justice, freedom." I stabbed the air with my finger. "To name a few."

"Just words." Kitty shook her head. "Abstract words disconnected from reality."

"She's right." Archie nodded toward the girl. "Catching Fredricks is all that matters."

I thought of Fredricks's words from the railway. *Nations are but ethics. If their morals are gone, thus are they.* Now I knew what he meant.

"Fiona," Archie's soft voice jolted me out of my musings, "can we talk?"

I stared into his eyes, wondering how well I really knew him. "Of course." I sat up straighter.

"In private?" He averted his gaze. "I want to ask you something important."

"Alright." My heart was racing. *Something important.*

He took my hand and led me to an alcove off the breakfast room. The cozy space was adorned with mistletoe and holly.

"Fiona, you know I think the world of you." His

cheeks turned pink. "You're a brick of a girl, the very best of the best."

The warmth of his hand radiated up my arm. "I like you too." As soon as I said it, I realized how silly it sounded. *I like you too.* Really? *Were we in primary school?*

He pulled me closer and wrapped his arms around me.

His words echoed in my head. *Catching Fredricks is all that matters.* What of truth and justice? Don't they matter? When I gazed up into his lovely face, it was as if I didn't recognize him.

"After the war is over, do you think..." His cheeks went from pink to flaming red. "After the war is over—"

"Go on..." My breath caught. What was he trying to say?

"After the war is over..." He nuzzled his face into my neck and whispered in my ear. "Do you think you would do me the honor of—"

"Aunt Fiona!" Kitty's voice interrupted us.

Couldn't she have waited just another minute?

"There you are." She came to my side. "Sorry to interrupt, but we're opening gifts." She pulled at my sleeve. "There's one for you from a secret admirer."

Archie pulled out of the embrace. "I should let you

go." A cloud had fallen over his face. "I have to catch a boat."

"Where are you going?" I tried to hide my disappointment. "When will I see you again?" So many questions tumbled out of my mouth. "What were you going to ask me?" Why did Kitty have to interrupt us?

"Classified. I don't know. It will wait." His tone was clipped. With sad eyes, he glanced over at Kitty, who was bouncing on her heels. He took my hand and patted it. "Stay safe, sweet Fiona."

I just stood there gaping, watching him leave me, not knowing if or when I'd see him again.

"Don't you want to know what it is?" Kitty pulled at my arm. "I'm dying to know."

Dying to know. I could have killed her myself.

Reluctantly, I followed Kitty back into the breakfast room. The ruckus from the crowd was unnerving. If it hadn't been for the girl's insistent tugging at me, I would have fled back to our room and thrown myself on my bed.

At the girl's insistence, I rejoined my pals at the table, which was filled with the remnants of our breakfast. Even surrounded by a room full of life and high spirits, the presence I felt most intensely was the *absence* of Archie.

Feeling numb, I drew open the strings of my handbag and withdrew a handkerchief. When I did, a photograph came out with it and fell onto the table. The photograph from Jean-Baptiste's wallet. I'd forgotten all about it.

I picked it up and took a closer look. Under her knit cap, the woman had the same soft dark eyes and fuzzy caterpillar brows as Jean-Baptiste. In fact, she had the same upturned mouth, *sans* mustache, of course.

Kitty stopped fiddling with my gift and snatched up the photograph. "Why do you have a picture of Marie Marvingt?" She stared at me with her mouth open.

"Who?"

"Marie Marvingt. The French aviator." Her tone was accusing.

"The photograph belonged to Jean-Baptiste." My pulse quickened. I felt as if I'd done something wrong. "Do you know her?"

"She was one of my instructors..." Her voice trailed off. She dropped the photograph back onto the table.

"In France?" Finally, maybe I'd get some details about this mysterious boarding school in France.

She nodded. Obviously this woman was special to her.

Clifford picked up the photo. "She'd be a darned attractive girl if she'd try a bit harder."

What did he mean by that? Just because she didn't wear make-up and instead sported an aviator's kit.

"What did she teach?" I dabbed my eyes with my handkerchief, trying to forget about my recent encounter with Archie.

"Fencing, boxing, swimming, flying." Kitty sighed. "You name it."

"Good lord." Clifford nearly choked on his pipe smoke. "A lady boxer? And pilot?" He shook his head. "Unnatural."

"Why is it any more unnatural for a woman to fly than a man?" I picked up a knife off the table and waved it for emphasis. "None of us are birds, after all."

Pouting, Clifford crossed his arms over his chest and returned to puffing his pipe.

"I wonder how Jean-Baptiste knew Marie." Kitty bit her lip.

The girl was entirely too pensive... not the Kitty I knew and... tolerated. Why did this photograph bother her so much? She was a mystery to me. One I was determined to solve, someday.

"Look." I held up the photograph. "Doesn't she resemble Jean-Baptiste? The eyes, the mouth."

Kitty leaned in to take a closer look. "No." She shook her head. "I don't see it."

"Maybe they're related." Could she be his sister? A cousin? His mother even? I brought the photograph closer for another inspection. "You know, she looks vaguely familiar."

"The lady version of Jean-Baptiste," Clifford scoffed.

I rifled in my handbag until I felt the stiff corner of another photograph. The one I'd purloined from the mysterious stranger in the tomb. The stranger who'd turned out to be Fredricks.

Although the woman in this photograph was on skis and thick with winter clothes, the smile was the same. I retrieved my miniature magnifying glass from my handbag and then sat the photographs next to each other on the table. *My word.* "They're the same woman!"

"Let me see." Clifford snagged the magnifying glass out of my hand and leaned over the photographs. "By Jove. You're right, old bean."

Of course I'm right.

"Why would Fredrick Fredricks have a photograph

of Marie Marvingt?" I stared at Kitty, waiting for an answer.

She just sat there, blinking.

"Well? Who is she?" I used my best maternal tone on the girl.

She tilted her head, grabbed the little box up off the table, and shook it. "So exciting." The clouds lifted from the girl's countenance, as if the photograph never existed. "Let's open your present."

"What about your teacher, Marie—"

Kitty cut me off. "It's Christmas." She glanced at me out of the corner of her eye. "Please don't ruin it, Aunt Fiona."

I was dying of curiosity about Marie Marvingt and her relationship to Fredrick Fredricks and Jean-Baptiste—and, even more so, her relationship with Kitty. But I held my tongue. Obviously, the girl didn't want to say more. I wasn't about to let it drop. I planned to investigate... all in good time.

For now, I sat patiently waiting while she unwrapped my gift. Her excitement made up for my lack of it. She clapped her hands and squealed like the winner of a beauty contest as she ripped off the red paper and ribbons to reveal a small black velvet box.

"Gosh." She looked at me with a gleam in her eyes. "Open it."

I knew better than to hope it was a gift from Archie. But after the question I suspected he might have been about to pop when little Miss Nuisance showed up... *could it be?* The box was the right size, *almost.* Alright, maybe just a tad too big.

I took a deep breath and snapped open the box. A heavy gold necklace sparkled up at me. Carefully, I lifted it from the box. "What is it?" A pendant with an angel and a woman hung from the thick intertwining gold chain.

"I say." Clifford took it from me and examined it. "It's the medal of the Supreme Order of the Most Holy Annunciation."

"What?" I'd never heard of it.

"Italian medal of honor." He held it up and admired it. "Catholic thing. Mostly kings and generals, that sort of chap." He handed it back to me. "Who is it from?"

"Good question." Who would give me an Italian medal of honor? And why? Was Archie being assigned to Italy next? I turned the piece over in my hand. It was incredibly heavy. How could anyone wear the thing?

As if reading my mind, Kitty plucked it out of my hand, ran behind me, and attached it around my neck.

It weighed a ton. "What does it mean?" I fingered the pendant.

"Looks like the annunciation of the Virgin," Kitty said. "See the tiny Virgin ascending into heaven?" She moved my finger to the small golden figure.

I gazed down at my chest. On either side, the medal had a lamb and a snake. It was at once beautiful and terrifying. I searched the box for a clue. Who had given me such a strange gift and why?

Of course, I had a sneaking suspicion. But I pushed those thoughts to the back of my mind. After all, the rascal was in jail.

Moving my finger around the inside of the velvet box, I managed to get a fingernail under the bottom cushion and wrench it out. Just as I'd dreaded. A small card embossed with a panther.

Fredricks! Not again. Even from jail, the man tormented me.

I lifted the card from the box and read it.

Captain Claude Soughton requests the pleasure of your company at his induction into the Knights of the Supreme Order. Basilica Minore dei Santi Filippo e Giacomo, Ampezzo. January 7, 1918, 15:00 hr.

"Where did you get this box?" I waved the box at Kitty.

"The waiter brought it to the table." She shrugged.

"Waiter!" I scanned the breakfast room looking for the waiter.

A young man in a white robe and red fez appeared at my side. "More tea, madam?"

"Who brought this box?" I held it out. "And no more tea, thank you." I softened my tone.

"A British officer asked me to give it to you." The waiter blushed. "Was I wrong?"

A British officer. I scowled. "What did he look like?"

"A big man, tall, muscular, with long black hair." The waiter made a whipping motion with his hand. "He wore a uniform and carried a riding stick."

A riding stick! "Fredricks." Good heavens. How could it be? Wasn't the rotter in jail?

"No, Miss. Not Fredricks." The waiter shook his head. "His name was Captain Claude Soughton."

"That irritating man!" I slammed the box down on the table. "Where's Ampezzo?" I looked over at Clifford. He was the world traveler, after all.

"The Italian Front, damnable high country, that." Clifford leaned back in his chair, puffing away on his pipe. "Dolomite mountains, formidable terrain." He sat up again. "You know, I was there once on a skiing trip with my good friend..." His voice trailed off.

"Don't tell me." I tossed the card onto the table. "Your best pal, Fredrick Fredricks."

He shrugged and gave me a sheepish grin.

"Does this mean Fredricks escaped?" Kitty clutched Poppy to her chest. "How is that possible?"

January 7. *That's two weeks from now.* Was it even possible to travel from Cairo to the Italian Front in two weeks?

"Fredricks has been known to do the impossible." I stuffed the box in my handbag and gathered up my gloves.

He was a sly devil. But how did he plan to get to this basilica in the Dolomite mountains in the next two weeks?

Good grief. Perhaps he'd already left Cairo. My pulse quickened.

More to the point, how would *I* get there?

My heart galloped as I planned my attack. First, I needed new disguises. *Do I have time to stop off in London at Angel's Fancy Dress?* What disguises would be best for the Italian Front? January in the mountains. *I'm guessing warm ones.* Next, I needed to find transportation. And, of course, get approval from the War Office. That went without saying.

"Why are you asking about Ampezzo?" Clifford narrowed his brows. "Freezing there this time of year." He got a startled look in his eyes. "Please tell me you're not thinking of going to the Italian Front."

Fredricks was on the move. The chase was on!

"That's exactly where I'm going." I threw my napkin onto the table. "And so are you." By now, I was resigned to the fact that Captain Hall would send Clifford along as a chaperone, no matter how many assignments I'd completed. Like most men, Captain Hall believed women couldn't do anything on their own... except maybe cook and tend babies. Neither of which were my fortes.

Clifford sat there, gaping at me. "You can't be serious, old thing."

"Deadly." I took a last bite of my pancakes and then drained my teacup and immediately regretted it. What was I thinking? Of course, it had gone cold.

"Oh, goodie. We can go skiing." Bouncing up and down in her chair, Kitty clapped her hands together. "I have an adorable pink ski outfit." The girl was as changeable as the desert wind. One minute, she was whip-kicking German spies and the next, she was flitting like a hummingbird.

"Of course you do." For a girl plucked off the London streets, she owned an extensive wardrobe.

"Except, my dear, we're not going for a holiday." I wagged my finger at the girl.

I wasn't buying the excited schoolgirl act for a minute. Anyway, skiing on the Italian Front. *How ridiculous.* Then again, I wouldn't put anything past Kitty.

There was no way I was getting on skis. Just thinking about it gave me a chill. Too bad my tea had gone cold. I could use some fortification. I wondered if I could get a good cuppa on the Italian Front. To hear Clifford tell it, in the trenches they drank tea out of fuel cans and ate tinned beef. *Hideous.*

"You're serious." Clifford's ruddy cheeks paled. "In that case, I'm switching to whiskey." He gestured for the waiter.

"There's no time to waste." I had to telephone Captain Hall and get his approval. "Kitty, Clifford." I stood up and brushed crumbs off my skirt. "We'd better get packed." I was half-tempted to tap my glass with my knife and make an announcement. "Ampezzo won't know what's hit them." I waved the blade in the air for emphasis. "Team, I'd say we have our next assignment."

My heart skipped a beat. Jolly exciting chasing Fredricks across the globe, and with two such good pals. I was a very lucky girl.

I glanced down at the fancy embossed card. *Why just do something when you can overdo it?* That was Fredricks's motto. *What cheek.* Using the tip of my knife, I pierced the heart of the panther insignia, pinning the blasted card to the table.

Sherlock Holmes had Moriarty, but I had Fredrick Fredricks.

ACKNOWLEDGMENTS

Thanks to the wonderful team at Boldwood books, especially my terrific editor, Tara Loder. They are a hardworking and delightful crew.

As always, thanks to Lisa Walsh, who has read the first rough draft of almost every novel I've written and still believes in me. She continues to make everything better.

Thanks to my writing group, Susan Edwards, Lorraine Lopez, and Benigno Trigo for helpful suggestions.

Finally, thanks to my family for their support and encouragement, especially my dad Glen Oliver, and my hubby Benigno Trigo... and of course, Mischief, Mayhem, and Mr. Flan.

A NOTE FROM THE AUTHOR
FUN FACTS

Although many events and characters in the novel are inspired by history, this book is not an accurate historical account. Rather, it is a work of fiction that plays fast and loose with history in a most disrespectful and cheeky way, all in the name of fun and entertainment. Hopefully, if you're reading this far into the book, you've found it amusing rather than disgraceful.

As readers of the series know, Fredrick Fredricks is based on a real-life spy, Fredrick Duquesne, infamous for clever disguises, disarming charm, and jailbreaks. Although this novel is entirely a work of fiction and more cozy than historical, you might have recognized a few other real-life characters.

T. E. Lawrence, aka Lawrence of Arabia, was a British archeologist and army officer famous for his role in the Arab Revolt. Another influential archeologist, Gertrude Margaret Lowthian Bell, played a crucial role in gathering information from tribal leaders for British Intelligence. Both Lawrence and Bell worked for the Arab Bureau, which was housed in the Savoy Hotel.

Archeologist Howard Carter is best known for the discovery of Tutankhamun. Like other archeologists, he had to suspend his work in Egypt when the war broke out in 1914. But by the end of 1917, when the novel takes place, he was excavating again on behalf of his patron, Lord Carnarvon. Although some have speculated that Carter had an affair with Carnarvon's daughter Lady Evelyn, she denied it as absurd.

Brigadier-General Sir Gilbert Falkingham Clayton was in charge of the Arab Bureau at this point. He was a British army intelligence officer. T. E. Lawrence called him a perfect leader for the wild men of the Arab Bureau, which was made up of archeologists and intellectuals rather than proper soldiers. His wife was Lady Enid. The rest is fiction.

Mori Al-Madie is *very loosely* based on a real-life actress, Munira al-Mahdiyya, known for playing male parts. She founded her own theater company and performed and recorded anti-colonialist songs. She was a committed nationalist who worked against the British occupation of Egypt. She was not, however, involved with German spies or murderers.

Hermann Gabler is *loosely* based on Hermann Grapow, a German archeologist who eventually went to work for the Nazis in World War II. Although he didn't work for the German army in World War I, he was known to be unscrupulous when it came to artifacts.

German archeologist Ludwig Borchardt is infamous for illegally removing the bust of Nefertiti from Egypt.

Recently (2022), the Metropolitan Museum in New York returned twenty-one precious artifacts illegally trafficked out of Egypt. Some of the greatest museums in the world, including the British Museum, display artifacts taken from Egypt. Stolen or not, the "repatriation" of antiquities continues.

My research for this novel included a lot of history books. Some of the most helpful were: *Spies in Arabia: The Great War and the Cultural Foundations of Britain's Covert Empire in the Middle East* by Priya Satia; *The Pyramids of Giza* by Annie Pirie; *Archeologists, Tourists,*

Interpreters by Rachel Mairs and Maya Muratov; *A World Beneath the Sands: The Golden Age of Egyptology* by Toby Wilkinson; and my personal favorite because it has lots of pictures, *Grand Hotels of Egypt in the Golden Age of Travel* by Andrew Humphreys.

NOW TURN THE PAGE FOR A SNEAK PEEK AT...

MAYHEM IN THE MOUNTAINS

A FIONA FIGG AND KITTY LANE MYSTERY

Kelly Oliver

Chapter One
The Cortina

Waiting was deuced distracting. Where was the scoundrel? He was supposed to be here yesterday. And he was never late.

Bloody war. It was trying my patience.

I gave up pacing and resigned myself to re-reading the latest version of *Detective Story Magazine*. I'd just settled into a chair in front of the fireplace when Kitty flounced into the lounge and flung herself onto an overstuffed chair. Her little dog trotted hot on her heels.

Kitty Lane was my new partner. We were thrown together by the War Office under direct orders from Captain Hall, the girl's guardian and my boss. Along with Clifford Douglas, our sometimes chauffeur and chaperon—as if we needed either, we were on a mission to follow known German spy and all-around cad, Fredrick Fredricks.

"I'm bored!" Kitty threw her head back and raised her hand to her brow like the doomed heroine of a tragic opera. "And so is Poppy. Right, Poppy-poo?" Poppy the Pekingese barked in agreement.

"Boredom is the result of a lack of imagination." I dropped my *Detective Story Magazine* into my lap. "Either that or indolence." I sniffed. "And you, my dear, suffer from neither."

Although I'd just met Kitty Lane two months ago —and under false pretenses, I might add—I knew the girl was as full of energy and mischief as Poppy, the furry beastie who'd jumped up into her lap and was licking her face.

Disgusting. Kitty giggled and kissed the creature's topknot, which was tied up with a pink bow. Obviously, mischief was not the only trait the girl shared with her dog. The girl's sense of hygiene was as questionable as the pup's.

"This place is so dreary." She sighed.

This place was the Ampezzo Valley of the Dolomite mountains in northern Italy, and anything but dreary. Rugged snow-covered peaks jutted out of the high plains like majestic overlords claiming the sky as their inheritance. The rock outcroppings, blood-red sunsets, and icicles that hung down from the roof like daggers were a far cry from the deserts of Egypt, or London for that matter with its crowded streets and thick fog.

No. Far from dreary, this place was a picture postcard.

Kitty bolted upright and pointed at the window. "We'll never get out of here if it doesn't quit snowing." She sighed and leaned back in the chair, sliding her legs over one of its arms. "Maybe that dreamy doctor will stop by again." Clapping her hands in front of her face, she let out a high-pitched squeal.

My hands flew to my ears. "Good heavens." The girl really did need to learn to stop behaving like such a ninny. "Don't screech and sit in that chair properly." I searched my memory for some dreamy doctor. From what I'd seen it was difficult to find any doctors on the Italian Front, dreamy or not.

"If only we could have a fancy-dress party." Ignoring me, she kicked her feet back and forth.

"A convalescent spa is hardly the place for a ball." I glanced around the cavernous lounge of The Cortina. Built into the side of a mountain, in the summer Italy's premier health spa served as a retreat for wealthy Europeans suffering from chest disease. In the winter, one wing housed hearty sorts seeking adventure, while another outbuilding sheltered wounded soldiers suffering chest disease and worse.

The war on the Italian Front was just as bad as anywhere else. In some ways, it was worse. The Italian Front ran along the rugged, rocky, mountains between northern Italy and Austria, which were better suited to rigorous sportsmanship than war.

"Why not?" Her rosebud lips blossomed into a pout. "Joy and beauty are as important to good health as bitter tasting medicines."

She had a point.

"Yes, but we have to take the bitter with the sweet." Speaking of bitter. A bitter, cold draft whooshed in from under the wooden door making the lounge bloody freezing. The Cortina's stone walls and high ceilings amplified the harsh winter temperatures. Hard to believe it was a health spa. More like a good place to catch pneumonia. Couldn't they light more fireplaces, for heaven's sake?

I knew the answer, of course. The war.

Every hardship or inconvenience was attributed to the Great War, which had been raging across Europe, and beyond, for three dismal years now. Up until the last few months, I'd spent the war stuck filing papers at the War Office.

"Bor-ring." Kitty kicked at her chair.

"Here." I thrust the magazine at her. "Why don't you read Arthur Conan Doyle's essay about Sherlock Holmes and the process of deduction?" *As Doctor Watson says, "A solution explained is a mystery spoiled."* I doubted Mr. Conan Doyle's readers would agree.

"Aunt Fiona." She groaned and waved the magazine away. "I'm too old for children's stories."

I wished she'd quit calling me *aunt*. A mere seven years her senior, I was hardly an old maid. The girl was barely eighteen but fancied herself a woman of the world.

"Horsefeathers." I scoffed. "You could learn a lot about detective—"

"Ha!" Kitty cut me off. "Orange monkeys don't commit murder, and criminals don't go around painting horse heads—"

"So, you *do* read." Now it was my turn to interrupt.

"And here I thought you just looked at the pictures in your high fashion rags." I grabbed my magazine and stood up. "You could help out next door at the hospital." The British army had commandeered an outbuilding next door for a makeshift hospital. Having volunteered at Charing Cross Hospital back in London, I knew firsthand the stomach and stamina it took to care for broken soldiers. "Unless you're too squeamish or afraid to walk in the snow."

Kitty guffawed. "You have no idea..."

It was true. I had no idea what the girl had seen or done. She was more of a mystery to me than our current assignment in Italy.

"Don't tell me." I tucked the magazine under my arm. "Boarding school in France."

"That's right." She raised her eyebrows and grinned. "Marie and I—"

"Miss Marvingt?" Rumor had it that Miss Marie Marvingt had once donned a mustache and dressed up as a boy and fought on the frontlines. A woman after my own heart. I would love to have tea with her and compare mustaches. I rubbed my hands together. Just thinking about my slender case filled with fake facial hair and spirit glue that I had hidden under my bed made me giddy.

"Marie was my ski instructor." Kitty pulled the

squirming puppy closer to her breast. "Wasn't she, Poppy-poo?" The girl used an especially annoying high-pitched voice when addressing her dog.

"Nurse Gabrielle told me she flew an air ambulance and may even visit us here." I moved closer to the fire and warmed my hands.

"She taught me to shoot and..." Her voice trailed off. Was the girl blushing?

"I bet she's a crack shot." I turned around to warm my backside.

A cloud passed over the girl's countenance. Yes. Her rosy cheeks had turned bright red. Her lips stretched into a thin line, but she didn't say a word. Apparently, I'd hit a nerve.

"What's wrong my dear?" What else had this Miss Marvingt taught the girl? Whatever it was, Kitty was unusually shy about it.

"He was supposed to be here by now." She picked at the pink ribbon tied around Poppy's topknot. "What if he doesn't show up?"

I bit my tongue, fighting the urge to feign ignorance. For I knew exactly who she meant. Fredrick Fredricks, of course. South African huntsman, American journalist, and German spy. The War Office had assigned us to trail the bounder and report back on his plans to sabotage the British war efforts. *Where the devil is he?*

It wasn't the first time he'd lured us to some far-flung corner of the globe. But it was the first time he hadn't shown up. It wasn't like him not to keep his word. Perhaps a jealous husband or ambitious spy had finally caught up with him. It would serve him right.

Posing as a British officer, the rotter was supposed to have been inducted into the Knights of the Supreme Order yesterday at the *Basilica Minore dei Santi Filippo e Giacomo* in the town square. Apparently, he did something to deserve a Catholic religious award. What I couldn't imagine. Truth be told, he was *supposed* to be in jail in Cairo for the part he *may or may not* have played in the murders of two British agents. But the sneaky cad had escaped almost two weeks ago. Why anyone would accept the scoundrel into a religious order was beyond me.

"I say." A familiar voice inserted itself into our womanly tête-a-tête. "I was wondering where you girls had got to." Pipe in hand, Clifford strode into the lounge. No doubt he'd just come from the hotel pub. Captain Clifford Douglas was tall and lanky with a long face, receding hairline, and prominent chin. In his late thirties, aside from his lively blue eyes, he resembled an aging racehorse. Still, he was a decent sort of chap. If only he could keep his mouth shut. He was a notorious blabbermouth, a quality deuced inconvenient in our line of work.

After five successful missions—*nearly* successful missions—I could hold my head up and say my line of work was espionage. Too bad Captain Blinker Hall, my boss at the War Office, wasn't as confident in my work. At least not yet.

Poppy jumped off the girl's lap and ran to Clifford. He scooped the pup into his arms. "What if *who* doesn't show up?" He cooed at the little beastie.

"If you must know, your best pal, Fredrick Fredricks." I scowled at him, thinking of his constant reminisces about hunting with Fredricks in Africa.

"Fredricks is a man of integrity." Clifford put the dog down and jammed his pipe between his teeth.

Ha! Fredricks, a man of integrity. That's a laugh.

"If he says he'll be here, he will." He struck a match. "Mark my words." After a couple of puffs, he blew out a cloud of foul smoke. "Once, when we were hunting in the Serengeti, the old boy was delayed by a charging rhinoceros—"

"Please." I waved my hand in front of my face. "Not another one of your gruesome hunting stories."

Red in tooth and claw. Tennyson had it wrong. *It's not animals, but men who are the true beasts.* I loved my king and country as much as the next girl but the horrors I'd witnessed at Charing Cross Hospital had quite put me off war. It wasn't exciting. It was bloody heart-breaking.

"Why do you think your pal the *great hunter* lured us to Italy? The only wildlife I've seen circling about The Cortina was a pair of bearded vultures. He's hardly coming to hunt." No doubt Fredricks had his sights on bigger prey. Double agents were his usual quarry.

"For the ceremony." Clifford warmed his hands in front of the fireplace. "That Catholic do."

"*That Catholic do* was yesterday. You know as well as I do that Fredricks is up to something."

"He always is," Kitty chimed in.

"That's why we're chasing him across the globe." The earthy smell of my wool skirt heating up encouraged me to step away from the fire.

"Why do you say that?" Clifford looked hurt. He still didn't believe that his old hunting pal could be a German spy. Why he always defended the rotter was beyond me.

"Let's see." I held up my hand and counted off on my fingers. "He killed an English countess at Ravenswick Abbey. And a Russian countess at a Parisian garden party—"

"I say, no one could prove he did for those two

ladies." Clifford tapped his pipe on the interior wall of the fireplace and tobacco ash fell to join the wood ashes below.

"Then there was that poor nanny in Vienna." I held up three fingers. "And in New York... well, he didn't kill anyone, but—"

"Enough!" Kitty stood up. "Fredrick Fredricks is guilty as sin and must be stopped."

Speechless, Clifford and I stood staring at the girl. Since we'd arrived in Italy, she'd been as changeable as a January sky. On the surface, Kitty was a sweet, bubbly teenager in love with frilly dresses and flirting. Underneath the high-pitched squeals and nervous hand clapping was an intelligence officer skilled in foot-fighting, forensic science, and heaven knew what else.

"He is an enemy of Britain." She yanked on Poppy's leash. "You two can stay here bickering like an old married couple but I intend to bring Fredricks to justice." She stomped off with Poppy in tow.

"Temper. Temper." I shook my head. There was no need to be insulting. *Old married couple, my eye.* Why I'd turned down at least one marriage proposal a month from Clifford.

Still, the truth sank in my stomach like a stone.

The reason Captain Hall had continued sending

me on assignments was because Fredrick Fredricks kept taunting me to follow him with personal invitations to operas, royal balls, or fancy induction ceremonies—that, and the fact all able-bodied men were off fighting the Germans. Otherwise, even now, I'd be back in Room 40 filing documents and delivering tea to codebreakers.

Roar. Clank. Roar. Whoosh.

A great commotion outside interrupted my lament. I glanced out of the window. The roaring of an engine was accompanied by a snow-devil whirling in the distance. What in heaven's name? Had the Germans lobbed a bomb?

I dashed to the window, used my palm to wipe off condensation, and stared out onto a wintery world. It was still snowing. The mountains were covered in a blanket of white. And a sudden burst of snow blew up from the valley below and enveloped The Cortina in a cloud. I shielded my eyes with my hand, but between the fog on the window and the whirling snow devil, I could barely see the icicles hanging from the roof let alone what was happening out in the meadow.

By the time I turned around, Clifford was already at the front door. *Where is he going?* As he went out, a frigid gust came in.

Shivering, I quickened my pace to fetch my coat,

which hung on a hook next to the door. I tugged on my coat and hat, slipped on my gloves, and bolted outside.

My wool velour trench coat was no match for the wind. And neither was my bare face. Icy snow pelted my skin. My eyes stung and watered, and half-frozen tears burned my cheeks. The air I sucked in clawed at my lungs and stabbed at my ribs. My nostrils crackled. No doubt my nose hairs were turning into tiny stalagmites. I smiled to myself. My mother would turn over in her grave if she knew I'd *even thought* of nose hairs.

I pulled my coat tighter.

The engine sputtered and then changed pitch from a deep roar to a metallic whine. I followed the sound. Eventually, I made out Clifford's silhouette up ahead. Reassured, I lowered my head and charged through the blowing snow toward the meadow. At least I hoped I was heading toward the meadow.

"Wait for me!" The last gasps of the dying engine drowned out my voice. *Blast it.* Snow had breached my lace-up leather boots. Not stopping, I reached down, hopped on one leg, and tried to fling the icy intruder away from my ankle. And I thought soggy London was hard on footwear. *Ruined.* My favorite boots would be ruined.

When I caught up to Clifford, he was standing arms akimbo watching the final rotations of an airplane's propellers. "Jolly exciting!" He smiled over at me.

"One of ours?" I raised my voice to be heard. I'd never seen an airplane up close before. It looked like a giant rickety wooden bird. How in the world did that contraption get airborne? Must be a crack pilot to land in this weather.

Wearing a plush fur coat and a hat that covered his entire head except for his ruddy face, the pilot sat high up in the cockpit. He snapped his goggles up onto his forehead. "Ahoy there." His voice was high and tinny. He waved and then jumped down from the cockpit and ran around to help his passenger out of the backseat.

Frozen in place, with my mouth hanging open, I watched what could have been a scene from an American war movie.

His handlebar mustache white with frost, the passenger was encased in brown fur and wore big goggles. He was nearly twice the size of the pilot. When he alighted from the airplane, a cloud of snow flew up in all directions.

The stuff was getting deep. Too deep for my paltry wardrobe. My teeth chattered. I hugged myself but couldn't take my eyes off the aviators.

Like a pair of brown bears, the pilot and his passenger trudged over to where we were standing.

The passenger ripped off his bomber hat and goggles and grinned at me. "Fiona, ma chérie." His long black curls fell around his broad shoulders. "How good of you to come." He took my gloved hand and kissed it.

Crikey. I should have known. Fredrick Fredricks. The cad always had to make a grand entrance. He stood there with a smug look on his face—a look I knew all too well. The cad.

"You're late." I tightened my lips.

"Apologies." He glanced over at the pilot. "Something came up."

"Fredricks, old man." Clifford extended his hand. "I told the girls you'd be here."

"Girls?" Fredricks pulled off his thick gloves and shook Clifford's hand. "Ah... the irrepressible Kitty Lane."

"Kitty's here?" The pilot smiled. "Delightful. I'd heard she might be here."

How did he know Kitty? I must say, the girl got around. When it came to young men, she was an irrepressible flirt.

The pilot removed his hat to reveal a long brown

fringe parted down the middle and... *wait a minute...* a messy chignon twisted up at the back. *What?*

His mischievous eyes betrayed an otherwise plain face. But it was the sly smile, thin eyebrows, and that voice—yes, the voice— that ultimately gave him away.

"Heavens." I repressed a gasp.

The pilot was not a man at all. *She* was a woman.

She winked and extended a gloved hand. "Marie Marvingt at your service."

I just stood there blinking like an idiot. Kitty's ski instructor from France. The famous woman aviator and inventor of the air ambulance.

"And you are?" She cocked her head and raised a thin eyebrow.

"Fiona." I finally managed to croak out my name. "Fiona Figg."

MORE FROM KELLY OLIVER

We hope you enjoyed reading *Covert in Cairo*. If you did, please leave a review.

If you'd like to gift a copy, this book is also available as an ebook, paperback, hardback, digital audio download and audiobook CD.

Sign up to Kelly Oliver's mailing list for news, competitions and updates on future books.

https://bit.ly/KellyOlivernews

ABOUT THE AUTHOR

Kelly Oliver is the award-winning, bestselling author of three mysteries series: The Jessica James Mysteries, the Pet Detective Mysteries, and the historical cozies The Fiona Figg Mysteries set in WWI. She is also the Distinguished Professor of Philosophy at Vanderbilt University and lives in Nashville Tennessee.

Visit Kelly's website: http://www.kellyoliverbooks.com/

Follow Kelly on social media:

- twitter.com/KellyOliverBook
- facebook.com/kellyoliverauthor
- instagram.com/kellyoliverbooks
- tiktok.com/@kellyoliverbooks
- bookbub.com/authors/kelly-oliver

Boldwood

Boldwood Books is an award-winning fiction publishing company seeking out the best stories from around the world.

Find out more at www.boldwoodbooks.com

Join our reader community for brilliant books, competitions and offers!

Follow us
@BoldwoodBooks
@BookandTonic

Sign up to our weekly deals newsletter

https://bit.ly/BoldwoodBNewsletter